BIRTHRIGHT

A novel by

RICHARD BLADE

BIRTHRIGHT

PRAY YOUR PAST STAYS HIDDEN

RICHARD BLADE

Also by Richard Blade

World In My Eyes

SPQR

and coming soon

Imposters

Acknowledgements

To my beloved wife, Krista, for letting me disappear into my world
of adventures

To Mum & Dad, always in my heart

To Mister Roxy, who kept me company as my story raced across
centuries, continents, and oceans

CHAPTERS

CHAPTER ONE

The Final Victim

November 8th, 1888

London disappeared under a deadly blanket rolling in from the river, obscuring the streets and famed landmarks. It was a toxic, foul-smelling fog, restricting the sight and breathing of the six million people living in the world's largest city. Heavy moist air, drifting upward over the Thames, formed a sulfuric soup when it mixed with the contaminated smoke spewing out of the blackened chimneys sprouting above the dozens of factories located within Britain's capital. Adding to the noxious poison, was the soot rising from the countless coal fires burning inside residential houses in a vain attempt to drive away the November night's damp chill.

For decades, parliament, mayors, and even the monarchy, had tried to clean up the putrid air that returned on these still, cold nights and killed thousands of Londoners every year, who perished from bronchitis, pneumonia, and black lung disease, but it was the people themselves who objected to any changes they were asked to make to save their lives. Wood was scarce and coal was cheap, and as winter drew in, they had to stay warm somehow, and if it gave them a bloody cough or made their eyes sting and run with dirty tears, then they would have to put up with it. They had more pressing things to worry about, like no jobs, food, or money.

The owner of the three-story mansion overlooking Regent's Park did not share the same concern about the scarcity of necessities the common folk stressed about, but he was very aware of the clinging fog surrounding him as he paced toward his waiting carriage. He paused and turned his gaze on the four gaslights in the corners of his expansive courtyard. He stared at the closest one and saw a faint flickering of flames behind the beveled glass but was unable to make out any details of the ornate lamp post, even though it was less than ten yards from where he stood. Good, he thought to himself, a night like this will be perfect for my business. He continued to the carriage, his long black cape hanging straight and barely moving, thanks to the lack of any breeze.

The coachman, standing with a servant next to the horses, saw his employer emerging from the heavy, green haze. Both men ceased their conversation and snapped to attention in a gesture of respect.

"Good evenin', sir. Your carriage is ready."

The dark figure stopped, "Good evening, Gregson. I won't be needing my footman."

"Yes, sir." Gregson turned to his waiting friend, "You're off. Go to your room and get warm." He looked back to his master, "Will he be wanted later?"

"Perhaps. I don't know yet."

"You heard the gentleman. Run along."

The young servant took off at a sprint across the courtyard and disappeared into the fog.

"It's a real pea-souper this evening. Where are we off to, sir?" asked the coachman.

The man delayed his answer until the footman was safely back inside the house and unable to hear before he replied, and when he did, it was just one word, "Whitechapel."

The coachman nodded in understanding and opened the carriage's door, lowering the steps to allow his employer to climb in. The man entered carefully, making sure he didn't dislodge his top hat.

"Would you like me to take that, sir?"

The dark figure involuntarily glanced at the brown leather utility bag he held, "No, it stays with me."

"As you will, sir."

He closed the carriage door and clambered into the familiar driver's seat, retrieving his whip from its stand. He called out a quick courtesy warning, "We're off, sir."

The coachman snapped his whip above the waiting horse team, and fearing the split leather cracking against their flanks, the two horses sprang forward, pulling the black carriage across the cobblestone courtyard and out onto the fog-shrouded streets of London on its mission of murder.

Dorset Street was well known as the worst area of London, and it had worked hard to earn the title. Vast areas of the massive city had become slums and were untenable to respectable people, as chronic unemployment, abject poverty, and alcoholism had run rampant for close to fifty years in much of those stricken neighborhoods, but Dorset Street remained in a league of its own. Crime was so commonplace here the London constabulary had stopped responding to lesser calls, and foot patrols had ceased in Whitechapel in the 1870s because of the number of policemen being attacked or stabbed. But still, Dorset Street was busy every night thanks to its reputation as a place for easy, cheap sex. Dockworkers, sailors, and migrants flocked here to find a woman to have their way with for less than a shilling. The real trick was to escape from the wretched area after the sex was done without being accosted and robbed of any money remaining in your wallet.

Three women gathered close together for warmth in a small, dead-end mews leading off of Dorset Street. Miller's Court was a claustrophobic alleyway framed by a cluster of crumbling buildings housing the poorest dwellers of London's neglected tenements. That night, the women huddling there, shivering from the cold and damp, hoped there would be sufficient business, with the weekend coming, that they could make enough money to pay their overdue rent and perhaps have a little left over to buy food in the morning.

It was several hours before the normal peak of their trade which happened when the pubs closed, but the three prostitutes had decided to come out from their dark, squalid rooms and be on the streets early in case there were any takers from the workers on their way home to their wives after a long day laboring in the factories and mills. The group of drunks at the end of the street, singing, pushing, and stumbling past, certainly wouldn't be wanting their services tonight, and after all the cheap beer they'd downed at the Britannia public house, probably couldn't function anyway.

One of the women, despite the overuse of powder and rouge smeared across her face, began to rapidly lose her color and started to gag.

"You all right, Mary?" asked her friend, Joyce, seeing something was amiss.

Mary shook her head, put her hand over her mouth and hurried to a corner, barely making it before she threw up against the moldy brick wall. She turned around, but a second tremor hit her and she tried to vomit again, but this time her retching was limited to a dry heave. Shaking, she shuffled back to her two friends.

"Take a swig of this," Joyce offered her a flask. "The whiskey will clean your breath a little."

"I'll swill, but I'm not gonna swallow. Nothing's staying down." She took the small bottle, gargling quickly and spitting out the sharp alcohol.

"You should go inside and rest. Try to get some kip." Sarah, her other friend, was concerned, "I keep sayin' to you, someone in your state shouldn't be out on these stinking streets."

"I 'ave to be, Sarah. With me baby on its way, I need all the money I can make."

"I thought his father-"

Mary cut off Joyce, "He can't right now. The family sent him away when they heard about the wedding. He's promised to help when he gets back, but you know what they can be like."

Joyce nodded in deep understanding, "It's quite a pickle you've gotten yourself in. Tell you what. Go to your room. If any regulars come for you, I'll take care of them and we'll split the money."

"You are such a love to do that, Joyce. I promise I'll try and pay you back when I'm feeling better."

"Don't you worry about that." She smiled, "Just name your little one after me."

"If it's a girl, I will. Joyce is a fine name." Mary coughed, a deep rattling coming from her lungs, and knowing she had to get out of the bitter night before her cold became the dreaded flu, turned toward the ramshackle terrace of Miller's Court, leaving the chilled, foggy mean streets behind her as she shuffled into her room to try and get warm and perhaps even sleep.

Sarah looked at Joyce with new respect, "You truly are a good friend to our Mary."

"She'd do the same for either of us." Joyce peered out of the foggy mews and down the deserted road, "It's not like I'm going to be killed in the rush."

The carriage pulled to a halt on Dorset Street, its wheels skidding on the damp cobblestones. The coachman jumped down and looked around cautiously before opening the door, "We're here, sir. I'll go and check for you."

The man inside replied softly, "Thank you, Gregson. And take care, many ne'er-do-wells and prowlers haunt this area."

The coachman grinned, "I'm prepared, sir. I wouldn't bring you here at night without one of these with me." He opened his heavy coat revealing a flintlock pistol tucked into his belt, "It'll keep us both safe."

The dark figure nodded in appreciation as he watched his well-armed servant enter the shadowy mews.

The coachman had only taken three steps when he saw two figures pressed hard together against a wall. Sarah Frost had her hoop skirt lifted while an inebriated dock worker took his money's worth. A little further down, toward the end of the alley, a second woman lingered, bored and fidgeting with her fingernails, paying no attention to the noisy sex happening only feet from her. She would be the one to ask, thought the driver.

"Is this 13 Miller's Court?" It was not a polite question. He addressed Joyce York as if it were beneath him to offer her even a pleasant tone.

Joyce pulled her gaze from her fingers and glared at the coachman, "You looking for directions, or are you man enough for something else?"

"Watch your lip, whore, and answer me."

"Yes, this is 13 Miller's Court. Home of the finest women in all of London." Her voice held mocking laughter in her reply.

"Good. I have someone who might be in need of your services." He spun on his heel and hurried back through the fog to the carriage.

"Well?" the figure inside asked.

"This is it, sir. But I can find you much better girls-"

"What I am looking for is here." The dark figure emerged from the carriage, adjusted his hat and cape, and reached for his leather bag. He started into the dimly lit mews.

His cautious coachman called after him, "How long, sir? So I'll know you're all right?"

"Thirty minutes. That's all I'll need."

Joyce saw the imposing silhouette appearing through the fog, and noted the expensive tailoring and top hat. Money was afoot and coming towards her. She smiled, maybe tonight would be worthwhile after all.

The figure stopped mere inches away and viewed her up and down.

She felt his examining gaze burning through her and spoke first, "You are a fine gentleman, aren't you."

He ignored her compliment and was all business, "I'm looking for Mary Kelly. I'm told this is her corner."

Joyce flashed her best smile back at him, revealing two missing teeth, "If you have silver, then you've found her."

The dark figure held up a single coin, "I have a gold guinea."

"Haven't seen one of those on these streets for years. A gold guinea will buy you a real good time. Come here, my love." She reached for his hand and pulled him toward the wall.

He wrenched away from her grasp as though her touch was offensive, "Not here, somewhere more private."

"For a guinea you can visit my room. Follow me." She led the way inside the dilapidated building.

Joyce's room was small, dingy, and damp. What had once been wallpaper peeled in long, tattered strips from the plaster, and stained floorboards peeked through the threadbare carpet. A narrow single bed, shoved in the corner, offered the promise of uncomfortable sex along with the souvenir of itching parasites, its worn, filthy mattress scarcely thicker than two blankets.

The working girl grinned at her client, "How would you like it, sir? In the dark or should I light some candles?"

"Light one. Enough to see what I'm doing," came his clipped answer.

"Naughty boy. Likes to see and feel the fun." The candle flickered into life, casting their silhouettes across the room.

"Mary Kelly, come here." He waved her towards him.

She stepped in close and embraced the well-dressed patron. Knowing her work was now underway, she changed her voice to give it a more inviting, flirtatious edge, "You know my name. What's yours?"

Joyce felt his hand sliding down between them as he replied, "You can call me Jack."

The poor girl had no time to react before the serrated blade plunged into her stomach and ripped viciously upwards, lifting her off her feet, as the vivisection started.

The killer thrust again with the knife, driving it in so hard and fast the impact violently pushed her backward, slamming her against the wall, painting the plaster red. As she opened her mouth to scream, he tore the blade out and sliced horizontally across her throat with such force that not only did he sever her windpipe but had the satisfaction of feeling the knife scrape across her vertebrae.

The unfortunate prostitute collapsed on her bed, her life slipping away; her voice, her arms, her legs, not responding to her mind's desperate commands to run, to flee. She was crippled, helpless, dying. The last thing her eyes were able to focus on was her murderer opening his leather bag and removing a surgical saw. She tried pleading for mercy but all that came from her mouth was blood, and thankfully, in seconds, what remained of her consciousness was gone – forever.

The temperature had dropped outside, and Sarah Frost rubbed her hands together, hoping to generate warmth, when the dark figure appeared from the doorway and stepped into the alley.

"Did you have a good time, sir?"

He didn't reply or catch her eye, and instead quickened his pace, hurrying to the carriage.

Sarah strained to see through the fog as he climbed in and the coachman whipped the horses away, the night swallowing up Joyce's rich client.

She turned from her view of Dorset Street and gazed at the window on the ground floor of 13 Miller's Court, "Joyce, how was your fine gentleman?"

Her words echoed down the empty mews, soaked up by the dense mist.

"Joyce?"

This was not like her. She was always the first to be laughing and sharing stories about the strange predilections of her men. She scurried to the building housing their rooms and stepped inside.

"Joyce?" she called again, before pushing her door open. That was when she stopped, unable to comprehend the horror of what she saw, as on the bed, the walls, and scattered across the floor, were the remains of her friend.

She repeated the name again, but this time the word was a drawn out, protracted, hysterical scream, "JOYCE!"

The carriage thundered through the darkness, leaving the dangers and dregs of Whitechapel behind as it returned to the more civilized locales of Britain's capital city. In minutes, St. James Park appeared and the coachman whipped the horses along The Mall toward one of the world's most imposing residences.

The guards saw the carriage approaching, but instead of snapping to attention and issuing a challenge, they moved respectfully to the side and opened the heavy wrought-iron gates, allowing it to roll through onto the courtyard of Buckingham Palace before pulling to a stop outside the main entrance.

The sinister figure stepped out into the light, and carrying his leather bag, strode confidently past the night watch and inside the iconic building. Had any of the sentries taken it upon themselves to inspect the carriage, they would have found a large canvas sack, tied tightly, concealing four towels the passenger had used to clean himself, soaked through with fresh, still-warm blood.

The long sweeping staircase and plush corridors were guarded by uniformed soldiers, and all had the same reaction as the man in the cape and top hat approached. They lowered their heads in acknowledgement and made no attempt to slow his approach to the upper chambers.

He paused as he reached two imposing mahogany doors, and tipped his hat to the red-uniformed officer of the household guard who manned his position. There was still no challenge to him, and he asked, merely out of courtesy, "Is she in?"

"Yes, sir. She is expecting you."

"Thank you. Carry on."

The soldier opened the door, his long, cavalry sword clinking in its scabbard as he moved, and the figure went inside. He stopped momentarily to remove his top hat and straighten his cape and bow tie in deference to the person he was meeting.

He could see her, standing on her balcony, wrapped in a heavy shawl to keep away the night's chill, gazing out over her city, the capital of her Empire. He walked towards her, across the spectacular floor constructed of white Thassos marble imported from Greece, and timed his steps as he paced. He made sure his footfalls were heavier than normal to alert her of his coming. He stepped through the hand-crafted blown-glass doors onto the terrace and came to a halt a respectful six feet from her.

"Ma'am," was his sole greeting.

"Sir William." Her voice was calm and measured; she had been waiting for his arrival, "Stand with me on my balcony."

He moved forward and took his place next to The Queen.

"London looks strangely beautiful when this fog rolls in, don't you think?" She kept her eyes locked on the ethereal, glowing cityscape laid out in front of her, "If only the wretched coal didn't mix with it and make the vapors so vile. No wonder so many have fallen sick."

It was not a question, and Sir William remained silent, at Her Majesty's Pleasure.

"Will we be reading about your exploits in tomorrow's newspapers and the Penny Dreadfuls?"

"Not mine, I hope," replied Sir William.

"I must agree. Even the Crown itself would be doomed if they found it was my Royal surgeon on the loose in Whitechapel. But will Jack receive another headline?"

"I think he will, ma'am."

"Good. And how was the operation?"

"A great success. The patient died."

"Then we are done and this is finally over," sighed Queen Victoria. "That woman, Mary Kelly, was always the one we were after."

"May I ask, ma'am, about the others before? It was not my place to inquire until now, only to carry out your bidding, but if it is truly finished, I would like to know why the other four whores first?"

"A mere distraction, to prevent the constabulary or Scotland Yard from becoming curious. Now, instead of looking for a reason why one unfortunate woman was murdered, your actions have created a panic that has swept all of London, and captured the imagination of the entire country. Because of the hysteria, the Yard is not searching for a why, but a who, a monster, a ripper, preying on prostitutes." The ruler of almost a billion subjects lowered her voice, "This one, Mary Kelly, was she dispatched as I instructed?"

"Indeed ma'am. Her face, limbs, and hands were cut away, and I removed her groin and stomach as you specified."

"When you pulled out her womb, could you see how far along she was with child?"

Sir William stiffened at this question and unconsciously took a half step back, "She was not with child, ma'am."

It was the Queen's turn to react in shock, "Impossible. She was expecting!"

"Ma'am I must assure you, as one who has delivered your own children and grandchildren, Mary Kelly was not pregnant."

"Then you have failed me and sliced apart the wrong whore!" Furious, Queen Victoria spun around, striking Sir William Gull in the face with her hand, using surprising strength for a sixty-nine-year-old woman. Her jeweled signet ring caught his skin and ripped open his cheek, knocking him backward.

As he staggered, he dropped his leather bag which snapped open on impact, sending the blood-covered implements of death, more suitable to a butcher than a doctor, spilling across the balcony's tiled floor.

Though morning had arrived, the heavy green smog still lingered as the warmth of autumn was long gone and with the early winter approaching, there was little strength left in the sun to burn the fog away.

Sarah Frost hurried with Mary Kelly down Miller's Court, helping with her bag.

"Get going before the police come again, and pray they never find out what really happened and it wasn't you he chopped up. And don't forget, you can never return. I heard the Ripper ask for you by name."

"And poor Joyce took his wrath, not me."

"Be relieved it 'appened that way. She is in a better place now and all our fretting won't bring her back. You have your baby to look out for. Where will you go?"

Mary had no doubt of her answer, "I'll make my way home to Ireland."

Sarah shook her head, "That's not the finest idea. If they discover their mistake, they'll follow you there. For a matter such as this, they will never stop hunting you, ever."

"If they come for me, I'll leave for the colonies and get lost in those strange lands. Australia or maybe the Americas."

A carriage clattered by on Dorset Street, and alarmed at the sound of its wheels and horses, the terrified women dove into an alcove and huddled together like frightened mice. Their fears were unfounded and the carriage continued on with its unknown journey.

As silence fell again over Miller's Court, the two women reappeared.

"Get as far from here as you can. Then you won't have to flee every noise." Sarah put her hand on Mary's arm and spoke tenderly, "But let me know your fate. I will miss you and worry about you each day. You and Joyce were my only friends."

"I promise I will write you when I know what I'm doing myself."

Sarah took out a small purse and handed it to Mary, "Take this. It's not much. Just what me and Joyce had saved. I can make more and God knows she has no use for it where she is now."

"Bless you both." Mary slipped the coin purse into a pocket. She hugged Sarah, and as she pulled away, showing the tears in her eyes, she added, "You will get a letter, I promise." With those final words, Mary hoisted her bag and hurried out of the cursed alley onto London's unforgiving streets to begin her fateful journey.

Sarah watched her go, and as she vanished into the fog, she heard the distant voice of a newspaper boy calling out today's terrible headline, "Read all about it. Jack the Ripper kills again. Mary Kelly cut up in Whitechapel."

CHAPTER TWO

The Grant

Today

The basement was dark, with no windows or doors leading directly to the outside, a deliberate choice made to stop sunlight from filtering in. Artificial lights wrapped with UV filters brightened certain areas, but they were positioned carefully to protect the delicate manuscripts and documents stored there, and the two dehumidifiers placed at either end of the long room announced their presence with a low hiss.

An old futon was jammed into a corner, the crumpled pillows and blankets showing its recent use, and three desks framed one wall of the basement, while floor to ceiling shelves, packed with thousands of books filled the opposing side.

Alex Turner sat hunched at one of the desks, surrounded by dozens of books on Family Trees, Lineage, Ancestry, and Genealogy. Five of the books were written by the same author, the very man who was working there, painfully punching the keys of an old typewriter as he referred constantly to his yellow pad of longhand notes to make certain he had all his facts correct. Missing was any hint of modern technology, and Alex's sole concession to anything outside of the world of academics was a single framed picture on his desk, a memory of him standing with his arms around a beautiful woman and a young child against a background of classic architecture.

A red light flashed its warning above the door at the end of the room, and Alex reluctantly paused his two-finger hunt-and-peck on his vintage 1936 Remington, and prepared for the visitor to appear.

He didn't have to wait long. The inner door opened and Dean David Hamlin, the head of the faculty, hurried inside, displaying a haste Alex had not seen previously demonstrated by this little man.

"Professor Turner, why don't you answer your phone?" the Dean demanded.

Alex folded his arms and sat back, sensing his day was about to be ruined, "Because I'm working."

"Well, excuse me, but there are times the University could use your presence above ground. After all, that is what you are paid for."

"If I can correct that statement, I believe a large portion of my salary stems from your enthusiasm with my writings, particularly the way you and the faculty like to take credit for their contents."

"I can't deny it's good to have our University connected with what have become textbooks and required reading at institutes of higher learning throughout the country, and it does reflect well on our academic standing and reputation." He smiled, "And it's that reputation which brings me down here today to get you. There's somebody you need to meet. Come with me." The Dean turned and headed back toward the door, his words and body language leaving no doubt in Alex's mind he was obligated to follow.

David Hamlin moved surprisingly fast for a person of his stature, and Alex found himself hustling to keep up as they raced through the corridors of the University of Wisconsin, past lockers and noticeboards decorated with signs reading *Go Badgers!*

Hamlin's overflowing excitement came through in his speech, as his torrent of words kept pace with his rushed walk, "This is the largest individual grant in the University's history, so please..."

Alex ended the sentence for him, "...be nice?"

"Professor Turner, Alex, in today's fiscal climate, money is hard to come by. The entire country is still recovering from the COVID-19 pandemic, and education is not a Government priority. Every dollar is important to the faculty. We can use it for computers, IT systems, servers, sports equipment, maintenance-"

"-books?" suggested Alex.

"Yes, books," answered the Dean. "But we need your expertise to get the money."

"So I gather. How big a grant are you talking about?"

"Ten million dollars." The amount echoed in the room, emphasized by the crisp British accent of the man offering the staggering sum.

Colin Brown, who had been waiting for their arrival in Dean Hamlin's office, was even more handsome than the dark blue tailor-made Brioni suit he wore, and had the confidence money brings, "That was the initial amount the Dean and I discussed."

Dean Hamlin shot a glance at Alex, betraying his anxious greed, "That will buy a lot of books."

Alex was not as thrilled by the huge offer and shot a questioning look back at the tall Englishman, "What do I have to do? You want me to write your son's term paper, or forge an application to get your daughter accepted into the faculty?"

Colin laughed, "Nothing like that, and I would not have you risk your pristine reputation on something so trivial. But it is your writing bringing me here. I have read your books both back in England and more recently while at our New York headquarters. The University is indeed fortunate to have a professor of your aptitude on campus."

The Dean nodded, eager to take the credit, "We met certain conditions Alex insisted upon."

"Like being left alone to do my research."

Colin picked up on Alex's irritation, "I'm sorry to be an interruption to your studies, but I too have a research project. I work for GPAD – Global Pharmaceuticals and Development. As our name suggests, we develop vaccines and medications which are used worldwide. I'm sure you can appreciate, with the current health crisis, we have been particularly busy over the past two years."

"That's very interesting, and possibly noble, but it's out of my field," stated Alex.

"Agreed. Where you come in is that our company's founder is dying." He sighed and shook his head, "It is ironic that with all our efforts to save others, we cannot save our own. I understand you have also lost those close to you."

Alex wasn't sure if that was a statement or a question, but either way he remained silent. It was not a subject he was willing to talk to anyone about, particularly a stranger.

Picking up on his reticence, Colin continued, "Our CEO wishes to leave the company to a family member and not let its ownership descend into a squabble between shareholders and financiers."

Alex still couldn't see what he would bring to the table on this issue, "That should be straightforward enough. Have your lawyers draw up a will stipulating the line of succession for the company and its assets." He raised his hands to signify how easy it would be.

"Sadly, there is no known living family. No obvious person to designate the inheritance to."

"Then what can I do?" Alex looked from Colin to the Dean, "I'm sorry, but if that's the case, why I was brought here?"

"We do see a role you can play." Colin was definite with his tone, "You are the foremost genealogist in the world. No one is even close to you, in reputation or in results. For years we have searched in vain for a relative of our dying founder. Now, in their final weeks on Earth, we have come to where we should have begun, and that's with you. Money is no object. Our corporation does exceedingly well. The ten million is merely a gesture of good faith to get you started. Find the relative and we will double the figure."

The Dean couldn't help himself and he blurted the number out loud, "Twenty million!"

"Twenty million for the University, and two hundred thousand dollars for you, Professor Turner, to demonstrate our gratitude for your time and efforts. Plus, any expenses, of course." Colin waited for the huge amounts to register.

Alex spoke first, "There is a problem."

"No, there's not!" The Dean was empathic, "He'll do it."

Colin ignored the Dean's greed and focused on Alex, "What is the problem?"

"The problem is, I can't conjure somebody up. There has to be an existing family tree that can be traced."

"There is." Colin smiled, "My employer's lineage shows a relative in England more than a century ago. She was pregnant when she disappeared."

"Disappeared?" This was not a common word among genealogists.

"Yes, disappeared. She sent a letter saying she was coming here with her son, to America. But we have been unable to determine exactly where the letter was sent from, and we couldn't locate a record of her arrival in the United States or find any of her descendants."

Dean Hamlin jumped in to bring a positive spin to the conversation, "But now we have Professor Alex Turner investigating the case."

Alex glared at the head of the faculty, "You make it sound like I'm hunting for a killer."

For a brief moment, Colin's expression changed, but then his smile returned.

Alex noticed the Englishman's hesitation, "I'm not, am I?"

"No, nothing of the sort. You're looking for an heir." He reached behind him where two thick packages of papers lay waiting on the Dean's desk, "Inside here you'll find my card and an accurate facsimile of the 1892 letter along with the actual envelope it was sent in, which sadly had no return address and the postage stamp is missing from it. Also, you will see the details of the extensive search we have already carried out and the leads which have been pursued. A backup of the contents has been scanned onto the included USB. One package is a reference copy for the Dean and the university; the other is for you, Professor. Make sure you take the correct one, because yours contains not only the original envelope, but also a cashier's check made out to Alex Turner for two hundred thousand dollars."

"You were pretty certain I'd do this, weren't you?"

Colin grinned, "I try to leave nothing to chance, Professor. If you need any assistance with your research, or have questions about what has already been done, I want you to know I am available to you twenty-four hours a day. You'll be able to reach me anytime at the number in the file. It's for our offices in New York. I'll be based there while you are carrying out your investigations. Do not hesitate to call if I can be of any help whatsoever."

Alex took a long, deep breath, "I see I am expected to do this. I'll start on it next week."

Colin threw an alarmed glance at the Dean.

"Alex, next week won't work. Because of Mr. Brown's employer's deteriorating health, time is of the essence. I'll find someone to assist you with your ongoing projects. You will start today."

"Thank you." The relief in Colin's voice was obvious.

Accepting he had no choice, Alex picked up the heavy package of papers, "Then I'll begin now." He started for the door and stopped as a thought hit him, "Mr. Brown, what was the woman's name? The relative who emigrated here?"

"Her name was Mary Kelly."

CHAPTER THREE

The Dungeon

The paperwork provided by Colin Brown covered two of the three desks in Alex Turner's basement study. To the untrained observer it might have seemed a random shuffling of the search so far, but at closer look, each paper could be seen to have a yellow sticky note attached featuring either a number or an annotation, handwritten by the professor.

Satisfied with his progress in arranging the chronology, Alex focused his attention on the one solid piece of evidence which had spawned this hunt, the original envelope and letter, mailed in 1892. He slid them gently from the package, knowing these items could be key to his investigation. The envelope felt old and unlike anything commercially available today, with a cotton feel to it as if elements of the fabric were interwoven with the paper. That's why it has survived so well all these years, thought Alex. But, as Mr. Brown had stated, there was no return address, and the postmark around where the stamp should have been was smudged, faded, and illegible. It would be of little help to determine where it had been sent from. He would get back to that later, for now, it was time to assess the letter itself, and Alex gingerly unfolded the full-color, high-resolution facsimile, the blue ink still standing out from the yellowed parchment. What could be learned from this, he wondered –

The red light flashed on, alerting him someone had opened the outer of the two doors. He looked up from the letter and was ready to ask who dared to disturb him, when the inner door flew open and a ball of energy exploded inside.

"Professor Turner? We haven't met." The voice belonged to a young firebrand of a girl whose very presence lit the dark basement with a glow as she hurried toward him, carrying a backpack and a laptop.

"We haven't met and you haven't learned to knock. What are you doing here?"

"I'm here to help. I'm Caitlin, but you can call me Cate. That's like Kate, but with a 'C'."

"I'm not sure why I would call you anything, with any letter," Alex responded, "apart from unwelcome. And that's with a 'U'."

Cate pretended she didn't hear his response and glanced around the dark, underground study, "So this is the dungeon."

"The what?"

She smiled, "It's a nickname some of the students who've been down here have given it. I haven't seen it before."

"Obviously. I'm not sure why you are seeing it today."

"It's because I'm here to help you work. That's why the Dean sent me. Or I kind of convinced him to send me."

She plopped down on the edge of Alex's desk, scattering his notes to the floor. She jumped back to her feet and dropped to her knees to scoop them up, "Sorry. My bad."

As she grabbed the papers willy-nilly, Alex raised his hands in warning and called out, "Stop! They were in a particular order. I will pick them up and arrange them after you go."

"But I'm staying. The whole University is buzzing about you getting an assistant for a big project."

Alex put his head back in frustration. This was going from bad to worse, and his sarcastic tone reflected his annoyance, "I'm glad the entire faculty is looking over my shoulder. Would you close the door on your way out?"

Again, Cate ignored his request, "When I heard how important this mystery assignment was, I went straight to the Dean and told him I'd be perfect for this. I'm good with computers, I'm quick on the uptake, and I get along great with people."

"And you'd like to work with animals and promote world peace. This is not Miss America-"

Cate cut off Alex's retort by picking up the single framed photograph on his desk. He reacted in shock at the affront as she gazed at the picture.

"Is this you with your family?" she asked.

Alex snatched the frame from her and carefully put it back in exactly the same spot. "It was."

"I'm sorry. I heard what happened." Her voice reflected a genuinely sympathetic edge. "But I can help with this, I promise. Plus, I need it. I've made it my goal to establish tenure here, maybe make professor by thirty, like you did. That gives me just under five years."

"It's a worthy ambition, but I am not willing to be your stepping stone to personal advancement. What is your field anyway?"

"Computer science," Cate was proud of her specialty.

Alex rolled his eyes, which did not go unnoticed so Cate added, "With a second in Genealogy. My papers and thesis were on your research methods. I've read all your books and studied your techniques."

"Good. In that case you know I work alone."

"Alex, can I call you that?"

"I prefer Professor Turner."

"Right, Professor Turner. Please let me help. I'm enthusiastic, I've got Irish roots and I've been there twice. I've even kissed the Blarney Stone. They say it gets rid of your shyness."

"Then it obviously works. But what does Ireland have to do with this?"

Cate smiled, she had his attention now, "It's where the letter was mailed from in 1892."

"How do you know about the letter?"

"The Dean gave me a copy to look over. Haven't you seen it yet?"

"You told me you were familiar with my methods. If so, you would be aware I take it one step at a time, and I was preparing to examine the letter. However, there was no return address and the stamp itself is long gone, and what remains of the postmark on the envelope is so worn it has become illegible, making the determination of the original point of mailing impossible. Why do you assume it was Ireland?"

Gotcha, thought Cate, "Because even though the legibility of the printing is too badly damaged to pick out individual words and determine its origin, the remaining edges which overlapped where the stamp would have been still show the franking from the postmark with its curving floral design and the green lead-based ink. That is our clue to its source, because the specific ink type is unique to Limerick in Southern Ireland and the time frame of the late eighteen-hundreds." She paused, before adding, "I've been to the place that made the ink. There is nowhere else in the world it could be from."

Alex said nothing. He held up the envelope and examined what was left of the faded postmark again with fresh eyes. He turned on one of the desk lights and studied it a second time. Finally, he looked from the envelope to Cate, his expression softening. "The quality of the ink is," he paused, looking for the right word, "distinctive. You're certain it's from Limerick?"

"I'm sure of it. I already double-checked with other samples still available from the time period." Cate grinned, "I told you I was good, professor. Can I stay?"

Alex lowered the envelope and placed it carefully on his desk before answering, "For today. Let's see what the letter itself can tell us. If you haven't deciphered it already."

Cate shook her head, and Alex took out the copy of the original, "It's addressed to Sarah Frost in London." He waved to Cate to come around the desk to join him, and laid it on the table for them both to read.

MARY'S LETTER

February 1st, 1892

Dearest Sarah,
 I write to tell you how I think back and treasure our time together. I am still haunted by what happened to Joy that night instead of me, and I intend to live my life in her memory. As vic Donovan told us, perhaps God has other plans for me.

My Bertie came to Dara's to see his boy washed but couldn't stay. Now he too has joined the list of the departed, and with his death I will save the money to travel to America. I shall sail there with my son later this year to start life anew. You will never hear from me this way again.

My love,
Mary Kelly

Alex sat back to digest the contents of the letter, thinking through the names, places and thoughts the writer had communicated almost one hundred and thirty years before. Cate watched him intently. She was like a racehorse at the gate, raring to get started. But she knew she had to wait and follow the lead of the world's greatest expert on lineage.

Finally, after an interminable time, he broke his silence, and his words were as much to himself as they were to Cate, "Normally I would start by piecing together the subject's background using their friends and family, but here we have a problem, there is only one full name to go on and that's Vic Donovan. And Mr. Brown's existing research shows there were more than one hundred and ten Victor Donovans in London in 1892 - all of whom are now lost to history."

"And the other names? Can you use them to start tracking any leads?"

"They are only partial; Joy, Dara, Bertie. No way to trace them. And Sarah Frost, the recipient of the letter, died a few years later of tuberculosis, with no children. It's all in Mr. Brown's package."

"Are you saying it's a dead-end already?" Cate was confused.

"Genealogy is about unravelling dead-ends. We know Mary's destination was here, America, so we start at Ellis Island and hunt for her entry record. Although Mr. Brown tried that route, perhaps he overlooked something. I have twelve volumes of archives we can begin with."

He gestured to one of the towering wooden bookcases, and a shelf holding a dozen intimidatingly large books, "I was presented them as a gift after I published my book, *'Immigration: The True Story of America'*." Even as he pointed, Cate opened her laptop.

"There's a faster way. They have an online site. We can check millions of names in minutes."

"That thing won't be of much use. There's nowhere to plug it in and go *'online'* down here."

Cate laughed as the laptop powered up, "*That thing* is wireless. The whole University is linked with a mesh Wi-Fi network. We're researching 1892, not living in it. Look, we're," she imitated Alex's contemptuous tone, "...*online!*"

Hours passed, and Alex stayed motionless in his chair, only occasionally reaching out to re-read a paper or compare one finding to another. A few feet from him, Cate relentlessly surfed the net.

Finally, she paused and stared at the unmoving professor, "Are you okay? What are you doing?"

Alex reluctantly turned to her, "It's called thinking. Try it sometime. Though it's hard to do when you're staring at that machine all day."

"Sorry. But *that machine* can't find Mary Kelly coming through Ellis Island in 1892. Maybe she changed her name?"

Alex shook his head, "If you'd taken the time to review Mr. Brown's files you would have seen he already made that assumption. Many immigrants changed their name to make a fresh beginning in America. And Mary writes - *to start life anew*."

"I did see that."

Sarcasm returned to Alex's voice, "Congratulations, you've read the printed word. Did you also notice she ended the letter with *you will never hear from me this way again*? A clear indication the next time she would make contact would be under another name."

"I didn't make that connection. I've been looking at the scan of the letter on the laptop, but I guess I missed it."

"I'm not surprised you did. But what name did she choose? That's the million-dollar question."

Cate grinned, "To be more precise, the twenty-million-dollar question."

Alex raised his eyebrows, "The Dean told you how much is at stake for the University?"

"Yes, everybody on campus knows. All the different departments are already planning what they will do with the money." Cate was open with her answer, "He didn't say who the person gifting the grant is."

"It's not a person; it's a large pharmaceutical company. GPAD."

Cate tried to cover her mouth to stop herself from laughing, "GPAD? That sounds like something you wear when Aunt Flo comes calling. But if their money is real…"

"It's real all right. Now if we can go back to work?" Alex concentrated on the letter, running his fingers across it as if the writing itself would communicate with him, "People often change their name to one that's familiar to them, or they'll use the same initials."

"So we're looking for names beginning with M.K.? Like Mary Kate? Oh my God, she became one of the Olsen twins!"

Alex stared at her, puzzled at the reference, "Your humor's lost on me. I have no idea who the Olsen twins are. Mr. Brown seems to have gone through every variation of M and K and come up with nothing."

"Then how do we figure out what name she chose? It's almost an infinite combination. Impossible."

Alex ran his fingers over the letter again and murmured to himself, "Who was it, Mary? Who did you become?"

The day slipped away from the two researchers as Alex paced back and forth holding the letter, urging it to speak to him. Cate closed her laptop and curled up in the basement's lone armchair, hoping to get a few minutes sleep. Restless, she pulled out her cell and sent a text.

She returned the phone to her backpack, opened her laptop and typed into the search bar *Global Pharmaceuticals*. The results appeared and she clicked on the home page. Her eyes opened wide as she scanned the pages. After a few seconds she turned her attention to Alex, "Professor, you should see this."

He paused his constant pacing, "What is it?"

"I'm on GPAD's website. They're huge. Massive. A real multi-national. They have branches everywhere, not only here in the States. They're in Japan, Australia, Hong Kong, Singapore, Sweden, Argentina-"

"What were you expecting, a local drugstore? Their name is *Global* Pharmaceuticals, after all. That should have been your first clue-"

It was Alex's turn to be interrupted as the red light flashed on, warning the outer door had been opened. He shot a puzzled glance at Cate who smiled back at him, "Delivery."

There was a polite knock on the inner door, and a student entered carrying two coffees.

"Someone texted for Starbucks?"

"That would be me," said Cate. "I thought it might help."

Reluctantly, Alex agreed, "Thank you." He pointed to the third, empty desk, away from the precious papers and notes "Put them there and get out."

The student did as instructed and fled the dungeon. Cate brought one of the drinks over to Alex, "This one's yours."

"How do you know which is which?" he asked.

"They put our names on the cups. You should like that. It's writing," she smiled.

"They have my name wrong. It says PAT."

"No, they got it right. PAT – Professor Alex Turner," she grinned.

As Alex reached for the cup, Cate noticed the bracelet around his left wrist, "Is that your Covid-19 vaccine band?"

Alex nodded.

"You do know the record of your vaccination and the date, can be automatically included on your driver's license and passport? That way you can cut the thing off your wrist. It always caught on my sheets and annoyed me when I tried to sleep."

"It doesn't bother me."

"Yes, but it's so much more convenient to have it listed with your IDs, particularly when you travel. It comes right up on the security scan and you are good to go."

"Another reason I haven't done it. I don't like to travel."

"That's a shame. It's a big world out there," Cate knew she was getting nowhere with this, and picked up her latte and sipped it. Her look of satisfaction said everything about the taste.

Alex returned to his studying and concentrated his attention on the letter. Distractedly, he took a drink from the cup.

"How is it?" wondered Cate.

Alex sat bolt upright, "My God! Joy!"

Cate stared at her coffee, surprised, "It's good, but not that good."

"No, no, no, not the coffee." Alex pointed to a passage in the letter, "Look at Mary's words. *I am still haunted by what happened to Joy that night instead of me and I intend to live my life in her memory.* Something happened to her friend Joy and she blamed herself. She wanted to keep her memory alive. To honor her, she became her. Try Mary Joy."

Cate quickly punched in Mary Joy to the online Ellis Island site. She looked up, disappointed, "No Mary Joy."

"Joy is short for Joyce. Try Mary Joyce. Or Joyce Kelly."

Cate typed and shook her head, "Still nothing."

"Then try looking for Joyce, wherever it appears, in any name."

They had drained their coffees before Cate tore her eyes from the laptop screen, "Two-thousand nine-hundred and three 'Joyces' came through Ellis Island."

"I thought that may be the case," admitted Alex. "Can you condense the search to 1892 and 1893. That should bring the numbers down."

"I can, but it'll take some time." Cate returned to her hunt.

Two more empty cups stood with the original lattes before Cate pushed her chair away from the desk and stretched to relieve her cramped body, "A total of sixty-one Joyces."

"A popular name."

Cate laughed, "At least she didn't choose Smith."

Alex joined her in the laugh, "You've done well. Show me the list."

"I'll print it out."

Alex raised his eyebrows, "I don't have a printer here."

"Yes, you do. You just don't use it." She clicked print, and in the corner a long-forgotten Epson buzzed into life.

"Wi-Fi?" asked Alex.

Cate's smile answered him, "See, I knew we'd get you into the twenty-first century."

She strolled across to the printer and grabbed the two sheets of paper. Alex took them from her and laid them side by side on his desk.

"How will we know which Joyce it is?" Cate asked.

"I'm looking for a mother and son," explained Alex. A red light appeared above the door. "What now?" he grumbled.

"Food," said Cate.

She jumped to her feet and met the delivery boy at the door with a crisp twenty-dollar bill in her hand.

He reached into his pocket for change, but Cate cut him off, "Keep it."

"Thank you," he replied. "Can I get you anything else?"

It was Alex who answered with a bark, "Yes, you can get out."

Cate snatched the pizza as the delivery boy bolted through the door. She grimaced at the grumpy professor, "Are you always so rude?"

"I don't like to be disturbed."

"Whatever. Do you like pizza?"

The pizza box stood empty next to the four coffee cups as Alex returned to pacing. Cate stared at him as he walked back and forth, "Thinking?"

"Trying to, when you don't interrupt me."

"Is this the norm for you?" she glanced at her watch, "Thirty-seven hours straight without a break?"

"You are welcome to leave anytime."

"And miss the fun?" She held up a single sheet of paper, "I have the list down to twenty-nine women with Joyce in their name, traveling with a young boy and sailing here from Britain during that specific time period."

Alex took the paper and poured over the list, the names representing a sea of immigrants coming to the promised land. The history of America in their dreams. He said nothing as he stared at the names and dates.

It was too much for Cate, "How will we ever know which one she was?"

Something stirred in Alex, a sense they might be close. He raised his hand to silence Cate and focused on the paper. He ran his fingers across it again, feeling the names, imploring them to talk to him. He blocked the surname, Joyce, with one hand, and used his fingertips to gently move over the first names. They seemed to dance off the paper at his touch, April, Daphne, Martha, Nelly, Ruth, Sarah. He stopped.

After a moment, he spun his attention to Cate, "I may have something. Who did she write to?"

"The letter is right there on your desk."

"I know the letter. I have it memorized, but my focus is here and I can't take my eyes from this list. You tell me. I need to hear you say out loud the name of the person she sent the letter to."

"Okay." Cate was surprised at the multiple layers this strange academic possessed, "Sarah Frost."

"Again. Say it again," demanded Alex.

Sensing he was close, Cate excitedly replied "Sarah-"

The red light above the door flashed on, blindingly bright as it interrupted them at such a crucial moment. Following the light, Dean Hamlin ambled into the basement study, "Hi there, I thought I'd stop by and-"

"GET OUT!" Alex and Cate's voices united in their command.

Stunned, the head of the faculty left as quickly as he had entered.

Alex lowered his voice and spoke again to Cate, "Put the two names together."

"Sarah Joyce," stated Cate.

Alex moved his hand. Beneath it were the words, Sarah Joyce.

Cate gasped, "How did you do that?"

"It was the only possible combination, based on her own words."

"You've found Mary! What's next?" Cate was stunned.

"Next? Now we follow her."

Two more coffees and three containers of Chinese food piled with the rest of the consumed refreshments, as Cate confirmed her latest find, "Sarah Joyce arrived at Ellis Island, Wednesday, September 14th, 1892, with her son, Edward Joyce, age three."

"We have them. They're here now in America. Let's stay on their trail and find out where they went to."

Cate emerged from her laptop, and compared her screen to a handwritten note from Alex, "You were right. They remained in New York. She worked there as a cleaner while Edward went to school and grew up."

"Have you found what he did after leaving school?"

"Yes," Cate was proud. "Edward became a cop. He got married in 1911. Had three children. But that's where I come to a dead end."

"Don't get discouraged," Alex consoled his young assistant, "There'll be more. Go into the New York Police Department records. Try researching his badge number or precinct."

Alex was still pacing when Cate called out with her latest discovery, "It's not good. Edward Joyce was killed in 1917 stopping a bank robbery. And it gets worse. His wife and two of his children died in hospital in 1919."

"Probably the Spanish Flu pandemic. How about Mary - Sarah, and the third child? Check the hospital's library. It should have records. The flu forced them to keep notes on everyone they saw."

It only took her a few minutes, and she confirmed Alex's prediction, "You're right. Sarah and her first-born grandson lived. The rest of the family died, along with millions of others."

"What did Sarah do after the pandemic was over?"

"She moved to Chicago. That's where I lose her again." Cate blew out a long, frustrated breath.

"Try something for me," Alex was encouraging, "Back then, families had patterns. Edward was a policeman. His son might have followed suit. Look in the Hall of Records. Check for public servants."

"What sort of public servant?"

"It could be any kind," answered Alex, "but if his father was in the NYPD, try someone who wears a uniform, a policeman, a firefighter, an ambulance driver. A similar job."

It was another thirty minutes before a smile returned to Cate's face, and she couldn't wait to share her find with Alex, "You were right. Victor Joyce became a fireman in Chicago in 1932. He married two years later. They had one child. A boy. Albert."

"Named after his great-grandfather, the person Mary mentions in the letter, her 'Bertie' - Albert." Alex was pleased, "That's our next task, finding out what happened to Albert Joyce."

For all Cate's skill on the computer, it was Alex, pouring over a reference book who came up with the subsequent lead, "We have to adjust the search pattern. I've come across a document filed in

Chicago in 1936. Sarah changed her family's name again. This time to York."

Cate stopped her typing, knowing she'd have to start afresh with this information, but she was puzzled, "Why would she change her name unless she was getting remarried?"

"No," said Alex, "She didn't remarry. This was a simple, legal name change registered with the city clerk's office in Chicago. But the puzzling thing is, it wasn't only for her. She went to the extra expense of having everyone in her family change their last names. That day, she ended the line of Joyce, and the entire family became York."

"I don't understand." Cate was confused, "She had already changed her name once, why do it again? And to have it take effect for all the family? Did she want them to disappear? It's like she was trying to throw people off their track, as if she was scared someone was following them."

Alex slipped a marker into a thick book, "I have another find. Albert's father, Victor, was killed at Iwo Jima. Then Sarah left for San Francisco with little Albert, her great-grandson. She died there in 1952, at eighty-nine. What a saga. What could have driven her for so long?"

"Maybe it's the thing they call Motherhood?" said Cate.

"I know how strong that can be, but this was something more. Let's find out what happened to Albert York. Did he have children?"

Cate had closed her eyes and dozed off when Alex interrupted her much-needed slumbers, "I have someone. Albert York's grandson. A teenager. Seventeen. Eddie York. He's in San Jose, California. I need you to double check the finding for me."

Cate was wide awake now, "Will do. What about his parents?"

"Both dead. No other relatives. This boy is the last of Mary Kelly's line. He's the successor Global Pharmaceuticals is looking for. We've found him."

CHAPTER FOUR

The Prison & The Penthouse

After seventy-four hours in the dungeon, Cate did the impossible, she convinced Alex Turner to take a break and leave his subterranean darkness to explore the outside world. It was an opportune time, as Alex was in a cooperative mood, knowing they'd reached the end of their search and successfully found the subject they had been looking for.

There were still a few final checks to make, to reconfirm his findings, but those would be easier; social security numbers, high school reports, and medical records including locating the boy's birth certificate. Those searches should only take a few hours, and because they were recent all the information was readily available and could be located by anyone he assigned to the task. The hard part was behind them now, their long walk back through the pages of history, so with that relief sweeping over him, he found himself sitting across from Cate in the faculty's deserted cafeteria.

Cate gazed around as she sipped her drink, "So this is what the outside world looks like. I'd forgotten." She smiled at Alex, "What do you think of computers now?"

He hesitated before answering, "They have a place in the right hands. I'll take books and the printed word over them any day. But for someone with your talents …" his words faded out.

"Professor Turner, that almost sounded like a compliment."

"That is how I meant it." Alex looked Cate squarely in the eyes, "Most so-called assistants they assigned me in the past did nothing but slow my research down. I found myself having to take more time explaining to them how to do things than if I had done it myself in the first place. You are different. You have the gift of being able to use your mind to visualize how events, times, and people somehow fit together. That's rare. I wouldn't be surprised if you do succeed in getting tenure before you're thirty."

"It's going to take me a while to absorb that." Cate was not being flippant. Alex's heartfelt statement meant so much to her, "I'll be thinking about your words on the flight."

"Flight? What flight?"

"To San Jose, of course. To meet with Eddie York."

Alex was totally taken aback, "Why in God's name would we do that? There's no reason we have to see the boy in person."

"I can think of twenty million reasons why we have to," explained Cate.

"No. We simply go over the final points we discussed, then send the results to GPAD in New York. Our job is done at that point."

"Really? You don't want to talk with him, ask him some questions to confirm beyond any reasonable doubt it is actually him?"

"We have the paperwork for that confirmation."

"There's an old saying my Irish grandma used to tell me, *ain't nothing better than the real thing*. Research is great, but sending a picture of you with Eddie to," she inadvertently grinned at the name, "GPAD, will clinch the deal. Come on, you told me they would pay for expenses, and a flight to San Jose is cheap, and it is the ultimate validation of all of your work."

Alex thought it through, "All right. I think Mr. Brown would appreciate the extra diligence. Should we call a travel agent to get the tickets?"

Cate laughed as she patted her laptop, "This is your travel agent. His first name is Mac."

The boarding announcement for the United flight to San Jose via Denver had the passengers lining up at the gate, waiting for their group to be called.

Cate could see Alex was anxious and reaching inside his jacket to recheck his wallet, then fidgeting with his briefcase. "Everything good?" she asked.

"I didn't know I'd have to show my ticket again. I put it in here somewhere," he looked through his open case before finding it.

"You'll need your ID one more time, as well," Cate reminded him.

"I will?" Alex started a second search.

Cate smiled, "Give them to me, I'll look after them for you."

"Thanks. I told you, I'm not the best traveler." He passed her his ticket and passport.

She gazed down at the official document, "We're flying domestically, you don't need a passport to do that. Just a driving license with a Real ID registration."

"I'm not sure if my license has that. I don't drive much these days. And I wasn't certain if I needed the passport or not. It's been a while since I was on a plane, so I brought it just in case."

"Better safe than sorry, I guess." She smiled, "I don't know why, but I didn't think you'd have a passport, particularly after what you said the other day about traveling."

"I've only used it once," answered Alex.

"For vacation? Where did you go? Somewhere nice and tropical? Like hanging out on the beach in Jamaica sipping on fruity drinks?"

"It was Prague, and it was winter. I was there for research." Alex's words were clipped and somber.

"Of course, I forgot. I'm sorry."

Ahead of them, the line began boarding, avoiding the awkward end to their conversation, and they commenced their shuffle to the gate.

After the seven-hour flight which included the long layover, Cate pulled their rental car into the courtyard of the Holiday Inn Express and checked into their separate rooms to relax, shower and sleep before their appointment to meet with Eddie York the next morning.

Cate was dressed for the warm California weather as she strolled through the hotel's reception area in her short summer dress, attracting admiring glances from the desk clerk and the bellboy. Alex was already waiting in the lobby, checking and rechecking his notes.

"Anything changed since you looked at them last?" grinned Cate as she plopped down next to him.

"No, why would it have?" Alex realized she was joking even as he replied. "I was running through the best questions to ask so we can confirm our findings. Because he's a juvenile, normally we wouldn't be allowed access to him, but the Dean reached out to one of our former students who is now on the bench in Wisconsin, and the court made an exception for us, and we've been given thirty minutes with him."

"I'm confident you'll come up with the right things to ask." She sprung to her feet, "I'll go get the rental car and honk when I'm out front."

"You should pick up a map from reception before we leave," suggested Alex.

"A map?" Cate laughed and held up her phone, "I've got a map."

Alex shook his head, "I should have known."

"And he talks to me. I have him set for a cute Australian accent. It's like having Hugh Jackman sitting in the passenger seat, telling me which way to turn."

"And it has where we are going?"

"It has everywhere, McDonald's, the airport, nearest Starbucks-"

"Does it have where Eddie York is?"

"Yes, it has where Eddie York is." Cate turned her phone to show him the Google maps display, "I already programmed it in, the San Jose Juvenile Detention Facility For Young Men."

The outside of the austere concrete building on Guadalupe Parkway reflected the harsh conditions waiting inside for the juvenile offenders serving their time. The three wide stairs leading to the entrance were monitored by multiple security cameras and two armed, uniformed guards who stood positioned by the twin tempered glass and steel doors. It was those officers who were first to address Alex and Cate.

"How can we help you?" It was not a warm greeting, more of a challenge.

"I'm Professor Alex Turner from the University of Wisconsin. This is my assistant, Caitlin Shannon. We have an appointment to see Edward York."

"Are you his parents or legal guardians? Only direct family has visitation privileges."

"We understand that, sir. When we made the appointment, we were granted a dispensation from Judge Reynolds in Wisconsin who liaised with your facility." Alex turned to Cate who produced the stamped and endorsed legal paper.

The guard scrutinized the form, passed it to his fellow officer to check, and received a nod in corroboration.

"Okay, sir, you can go on inside to the counter and the secondary security screening. But not you, miss," he stared at Cate.

"The court order states it is for both of us. You'll see my name and Caitlin Shannon's printed there," stressed Alex.

"I see the names, sir, but unfortunately we can't allow her in."

"I'm standing right here. I can hear you. What is your problem?" Cate was getting angry.

The guard refused to take the bait and kept his voice low, but officious, "I can't let you in dressed like that."

"Dressed like what?" Cate was shocked, "Are you guards or fashion police? What is this, Project Runway - Prison edition? You don't like my outfit?"

The guard waited patiently for her to finish and continued, "When the University was emailed the clearance, the dress code was attached. It clearly says females are not admitted to this facility with bare arms or legs, or sexually provocative outfits."

"Sexually provocative? You should see me on a Friday night."

"We are only following the rules. Any dress, above the knee, is considered too short. There's a shaded waiting area over there.

You can't enter our facility today." His voice reflected the finality of his statement.

Alex looked at Cate, "I'm sorry."

"It's not your fault, you go in. We came all this way. I'll let these guys have their hormone holiday and stay out here like a good little girl, my mouth shut and my legs crossed. What year is it anyway?" She whirled around and stomped over to a bench at the side of the stairs.

The stark concrete exterior of the Juvenile Hall was echoed throughout the inside of the building. Overhead lighting burned down and metal doors, spaced ten feet apart, stretched the length of the corridor. Alex couldn't help but think it wasn't set up to correct and inspire troubled kids, merely to keep them incarcerated for the duration of their sentence.

A much friendlier, and heavier, uniformed officer led the way to the meeting area arranged for Alex.

"I'm Sergeant Hernandez, but you can call me Oscar. I've been here fifteen years and seen them come and go. Eddie's a good kid, he tries to help out and works in my office two days a week, and does repairs for us in the metal shop. He's had some bad breaks."

"I appreciate your input, but this really isn't a social visit," said Alex. "Eddie is involved with something connected to my University."

Oscar gave him a double-take, "Did he steal a car from there?"

"No, nothing like that. It's a research assignment I'd been given, and his name came up."

"Good. The kid doesn't need any more problems." Oscar pointed though the heavy glass windows, "He's in there waiting for you."

Seated at a small table was Eddie York. Alex was surprised how normal he appeared. He had been prepared for a teen with tattoos, piercings and torn clothes, but instead Eddie was a good-looking boy whose only apparent nod to the rebellion of youth was the long hair falling past his shoulders. The boy sat quietly in the holding room, keeping himself occupied by beating out the rhythm to an unheard song with his fingertips on the metal tabletop. If it wasn't for the orange jumpsuit he wore with JUVENILE printed in block letters across the back, he could have been any kid in America, hanging out, killing time.

Oscar escorted Alex to Eddie's table.

Eddie glanced up and smiled, "Hey, Oscar."

"Hey, Eddie, here's your visitor." Job done, he turned and walked away.

Alex stepped forward, "I'm Alex Turner, nice to meet you."

"Welcome to my crib. What's up?"

"I'm here to talk to you. Someone has been trying to find you, and they asked me to see if I could locate you, so here I am."

"Dude, whatever it is, I didn't do it. I've been stuck in this shithole for seven months."

"This isn't any kind of legal problem. It's family business," explained Alex.

"Then you're wasting your time. My family's dead. Dad got blown up in Afghanistan, and Mom - she might as well have gone with him. She put so much crap in her body she left the planet within a year. Didn't care about me, just where she could get her next hit of meth."

"I'm sorry. Did you know your grandfather?"

"Not really. Heard about him. He was kind of a hero. Flew choppers in Vietnam. He died of cancer when I was a kid."

"Do you remember his name?"

"Yeah, Grandpa."

"How about his given name?"

"Same as my middle name. They called me after him, Albert."

"Thank you. That's all I needed to know. Someone will undoubtedly be in touch with you soon." Alex rose to his feet.

Eddie stood up as well, "That's it? That's all you're going to tell me?"

"It's all I'm at liberty to say at the moment. Again, thank you for your time."

"Glad I could fit you into my busy schedule," Eddie reached out his hand. Alex took it in his, and as they shook, Eddie's eyes rolled upward and he slipped forward, crashing into the professor. Alex caught him and helped steady the boy.

"Are you all right?" asked Alex.

Eddie pulled himself together and straightened up, "Sorry about that, I get shaky sometimes. The doc calls it vertigo. It doesn't last long." Eddie waved to the guard, "Hey, Oscar, we're done here."

Alex emerged through the twin doors and walked into the sunlight toward Cate who sat on the bench listening to music on her phone. She glanced up as Alex approached and pulled out her ear buds, "I've planned my revenge on these couture cops. I'm coming back tomorrow in my shortest mini and highest heels to make them suffer."

"That's not going to be happening. We'll hopefully be in New York tomorrow. If there's a flight available, we'll take the red-eye tonight."

"New York? What happened to Mr. I Don't Like To Travel?"

"We have to. I owe it to Mr. Brown to explain in person."

"Explain what?" Cate didn't understand.

"It's him. It's Edward York, for sure. But they are not going to be happy when they meet him or see his record book. Not CEO material. I need to prepare them for that, because I don't want them taking out their disappointment on us or on the faculty. I'm going to have the Dean call Global Pharmaceuticals and set up a meeting for tomorrow."

"Could be worse. New York's always fun. I have a girlfriend who lives in Manhattan we should look up. She knows all the happening bars in the Big Apple. We could even take in a show while we're there."

"My plan is to go directly to the company's headquarters, get this unfortunate situation out of the way as quickly as possible, and then leave. I think that is a lot more practical."

"Ever hear the expression *live a little*? You should try it sometime."

"Sometime, perhaps, but not now. We have this project to conclude first."

The line for Starbucks at San Jose airport was short at that late hour. Alex had only been waiting a few minutes before he stepped up and ordered the two lattes.

The young barista smiled from behind the register, "You can pick them up over there," she pointed to the end of the counter, "That will be nine-twenty please."

Alex reached into his jacket for his wallet and came up empty. Puzzled, he tried his other inside pocket, knowing it was never there, but he had to check. The same with his pants' pockets. But the wallet was nowhere to be found.

The barista smiled again, "Nine-twenty?"

Alex turned red and said one word as he left, "Sorry."

Cate watched him walking towards her empty-handed, "Did you drink mine as well?"

"The boy stole my wallet."

"Eddie? Maybe you lost it?"

"No. I never lose things. He picked my pocket."

"Talented kid. A regular David Copperfield. It's lucky I have your tickets and passport."

"I need some change for a phone call."

Cate handed Alex her cell, "Use this."

Eddie York stood in Oscar's office at the detention facility, pleading on his business phone, "Dude, it wasn't me, man."

Alex sat with Cate, concern written across his face, "Please don't lie to me. We both know it was. Look, I'm willing to make you a deal."

"What do you mean, a deal?"

"Inside the wallet you took, you'll find a photograph of my wife and child. Send it back to me. Keep the money. Keep the wallet. I only want the picture."

"Yeah, right. Then you report me and I get a year added to my time. You're already some kind of important dude that you can have a call put through to me this late."

"It's because I saw you under a court order, but that's not relevant. You have my word this will go no further if you send the photograph back. I know what you're going through, being an orphan, losing people you love. I only want the picture. The rest is yours."

"Let me think about it."

"Please. It's all I have left of my family. My address is in the wallet. If you will do it, no one else will know; this stays between us."

There was a moment's hesitation before the nervous teen replied, "Okay, I'll send it back to you. But you have to keep your promise."

"I will. You have my word," Alex clicked off Cate's cell.

Eddie held on to the receiver a second longer. He had expected to be yelled and screamed at, to be threatened and punished. Instead, the man's tone had been gentle, even understanding. He tried to remember the last time anyone had spoken to him as if they cared how he felt, but came up short. He took a pen from Oscar's desk and scribbled down the number from the business phone's display of the mobile phone Alex had called from and stuffed it into a pocket of his orange jumpsuit. Behind him, the door opened.

"You done here?"

"Yeah, thanks for letting me take the call. He was a cool guy. Hey, can I get an envelope?"

"What kind?" asked Oscar.

"Something big enough to fit this," Eddie held up a small brown wallet.

The weekday traffic in Manhattan was terrible as always, and drivers raced through the city with one hand on the wheel, the other on their horn.

The grey Prius pulled out of the madness and stopped in front of a towering skyscraper on the Avenue of the Americas. Cate and Alex piled from it, Cate leading the way to the huge building.

Alex shot a glance back at the car, "Don't we have to pay him?"

"It's Uber. It's all done through the app," answered Cate.

Alex raised his hands, not understanding, and the two of them shuffled through the revolving doors to clear security on their way to the 76th floor.

The express elevator took them directly to their destination, the North American headquarters of the multi-national company,

Global Pharmaceuticals and Development, GPAD. They walked from the polished elevator doors into the sumptuous lobby where a smiling receptionist presented them with laminated security badges and had them wait for their personal escort who guided them through the busy, luxurious office complex.

Cate leaned in to Alex as they took in the incredible workplace, "You should have hit them up for a lot more than twenty million."

Alex stayed silent as they approached the massive, glass-enclosed corner office.

"Through there," gestured the escort, as he swiped his encoded pass and the twin doors slid soundlessly apart. His job done, he turned and left. The meeting these two guests were going to was way above his pay grade.

Alex and Cate entered the room and were instantly overwhelmed by the breathtaking view of Manhattan, stretching on one side down past the Empire State to the financial district, and on the other to Central Park and beyond.

The three men inside allowed their visitors to take in the imposing sight before one of them stepped forward to greet them, "I never get tired of it myself. I think the only other building in our entire company more impressive is our office tower in Dubai. Thank you for coming, Professor Turner. It's good to see you again. We were excited to receive the call from your Dean yesterday and hear you were on your way. I apologize for making this a lunchtime meeting but I had some earlier appointments I couldn't move, and anyway, we wanted to get your passes and the offices ready for such an important person's arrival." He turned to Cate, "And you must be Caitlin Shannon, I presume. I've heard nothing but exceptional things about you. I'm Colin Brown."

Cate took in the fit, handsome Englishman's confident appearance and couldn't avoid noticing how the tailored jacket he wore hugged the muscled lines of his body, and wondered if she could come up with an excuse to stay on in New York for a few days and find a way they could have drinks together. She shook his hand as she caught his piercing eyes, "Very nice to meet you, Mr. Brown."

"Please, call me Colin. Mr. Brown's my father," he flashed a gleaming smile and gave her fingers a slight squeeze.

It's going to be hard to concentrate on this meeting, thought Cate.

Colin continued, "Can I get you a drink? I'm sure you must be tired after taking the red-eye."

Alex and Cate answered simultaneously, "No, thank you..", "Yes, please.."

Colin laughed again, "Water, Coffee, tea? Something stronger?"

"Coffee would be great,' said Cate.

One of the men hurried off to get the java.

Colin leaned back against his desk, his strong frame silhouetted by the famous skyline, "When the Dean called about today, he said you had made progress."

"We have," said Alex. He opened his briefcase and pulled out a thick folder and laid it on Colin's desk. "Inside are the details of Mary Kelly's journey to America, her name changes, and her lineage."

Colin hefted the findings, feeling their weight and the amount of paperwork and records it contained, "Very impressive. We've never gotten past her leaving England before. I've had an office set up for the two of you while you are here in New York; it's right down the hallway. And your security passes will give you full building access 24/7 for the next week. We can extend them, of course, for as long as necessary."

Alex raised his hand to interject, "I don't think any of that will be required."

"Why not?" Colin was puzzled. "I thought you were here to research Ellis Island and follow any leads to pinpoint the arrival date of Mary and her child?"

"We have already done it." Alex pointed to Cate, "My assistant was very thorough."

"That's terrific. If you have that information, then where does this put you in your search? How much more needs to be done?"

Colin's question surprised Alex, "Nothing, it's completed. We found an heir. A boy. He's in California."

Hearing those words, the men froze and the room fell silent. It was as if Alex had thrown a grenade in among them. Alex waited for the next question, but none came. The atmosphere became overpowering and a feeling of shock hung in the air. He felt obliged to explain.

"His name is Edward York. He's seventeen. I wanted to come here and tell you this in person because I'm afraid he's not the type you're looking for to run a company like this."

"Why not?"

"He's serving time at the Juvenile Detention facility in San Jose. He has a police record showing multiple arrests, and a very troubled past."

"Are you sure it's him?" Colin could hardly utter the words.

"I know you must be disappointed, Mr. Brown, but I wouldn't be here if I wasn't certain."

"Then it is true. After all these years of searching." Colin fought to pull himself together, "You have brought us wonderful news. Dean Hamlin is indeed lucky to have you." He reached into his desk and pulled out a small package, "This seems only fair. You gave me a gift so I should give you one in return. The envelope contains a little bonus, twenty-five thousand dollars. I hope you don't mind cash. It'll help you have an exciting evening in Manhattan."

Cate finally jumped into the conversation, "That sounds like fun."

"I don't think we'll have time for fun. We're flying back tonight," stated Alex.

"Then fly first class on us. I'll have one of my staff make the arrangements, and if you provide a number, we'll text you the details. Thank you, Professor Turner. I'm looking forward to reading this. Someone will escort you out. Goodbye, and leave knowing how important what you have done is to so many people."

His outstretched hand abruptly concluded their meeting, and a hastily summoned secretary led Cate and Alex from the palatial office.

Colin watched them go and waited until the soundproof doors closed behind them. It was then he exploded into action, barking orders at the other two men in the room, "Double check all the papers he brought. Have an official ID made for me, with the last name, York. Contact our attorney and get me guardian privileges to visit the boy. Prep the jet. I want to be in San Jose tomorrow. Call Langley, tell them he's been found and I'm going to need backup ready to roll. I'll text you after it's done. When you get the word, you'll have two hours to pull the plug on everything."

CHAPTER FIVE

The Coffin

The Capital Grill on West 51st Street bustled with its usual lunchtime crowd enjoying the massive steaks and overstuffed baked potatoes that were the staples of their extensive menu.

Alex sat with the two pretty girls in their mid-twenties, and failed to note the envious looks he received from many of the businessmen around him who wondered how he got so lucky while they dined alone or were forced to listen to an interminable financial pitch during their meal.

Cate was full of life and energy as she toasted her friend over their second dirty martini, "I'm so glad you could make it here and meet up with us before we have to leave. I can't believe it's been two years, Susan. Two years!"

"Closer to three," corrected Susan. "You'd just finished your Masters and broken up with Josh."

Cate sighed deeply, "Don't bring up Josh."

"Josh was a hottie," remembered Susan.

"Yeah, he might have looked like a Hemsworth, but he had nothing up here," she pointed to her head and laughed.

The girls' conversation was proving to be too much for Alex and he rose from the table, "I'm going to use the bathroom. Please excuse me." He quickly crossed the crowded room searching for both the restroom and the chance to escape for a moment.

The girls watched him go, and Susan leaned forward, "What's his story? He's handsome, but seems a little uptight."

"A little? Welcome to the understatement of the year club." Cate grinned, "But inside he's a good guy. I'm learning so much from him. His thinking process is unique. Most academics, like our old professors at Wellesley, are all logic and convergent thinking, which is what I expected from Alex, but then he will have a flash of inspiration from nowhere, similar to the way an artist does, and his brain switches to lateral or divergent thoughts. It's truly amazing."

"You're lucky to be paired with him." Susan took a deep breath, "I'm kind of stuck in my groove right now. I could use a change. But finding a good company to switch to, and even getting a meeting set up, ever since the shutdown and the quarantine, is hard these days."

"I have an idea," Susan reached into her little purse and held up the security pass from GPAD. "We were just at this huge corporation with loads of money, right across the street. They have branches all over the world. You can use this to access their office floor, then when you're inside see if you can set up something with their HR department. The worse they'd do is ask you to leave. It could be they'll admire your hutzpah and schedule an interview. With your degree and experience working in New York, who knows?"

Susan took the proffered pass, "Thanks. I guess I have nothing to lose, the worst is they'll say no. I'll see if I can work up the courage to use it."

Alex appeared through the busy restaurant and returned to the table but didn't sit down, "I think we should be leaving for the airport soon."

Cate checked the text from GPAD on her phone, "Hardly. The flight isn't until six-fifty. It's not even two yet. If we head out of the city at three, we'll have plenty of time to get to JFK. That gives us another hour to catch up with Susan. Have a drink, professor. Try to relax and have fun."

Alex looked around, searching for another reason to leave, but finding none, he sat down and resigned himself to enduring the mindless gossip before having to battle the inevitable crosstown traffic.

The Gulfstream made a perfect landing at Mineta International Airport in San Jose, taxiing across runway 12L toward the hangers of Pacific Aviation where a waiting Bentley Bentayga greeted them.

The luxury vehicle didn't cause a raised eyebrow for the staff of the private jet facility who were used to dealing with the expensive needs of the tech giants from nearby Silicon Valley, and assumed the well-dressed Englishman who descended the aluminum stairs from the G650 was on his way to enact a takeover deal. What they were unaware of was the intended hostile liquidation did not involve a company but a person.

A burly, ex-military type with a severe crewcut, stood beside the Bentley, and as Colin appeared from the twin-engine jet, he was greeted with a look of recognition and an offered hand, "Mr. Brown. Good to see you again. It's been a couple of years since you took care of the Jeffrey Epstein thing for us in New York. You did excellent work and left no traces of your presence there. I hope I can be as thorough for you here today. I received the instructions as to what you needed. I have everything with me, exactly as specified, and the other people and vehicles are already in place."

Colin took the man's hand and noted the strength in his grasp, "This will be our second terminal op together, Mr. Stevens; let's make sure this one goes as smoothly as the first. We should leave now and meet Eddie York."

They wasted no other words and climbed into the quarter of a million-dollar SUV and sped toward the exit gates of the private facility.

Eddie York was dressed in oily overalls, surrounded by machine parts, and expertly working on repairing a motorbike engine's carburetor in the metal shop of the Juvenile Detention Center when he felt a tap on his shoulder. He put down his spanner and turned to face Oscar.

"You're popular these days. Your guardian is waiting to see you in the holding area," said the friendly prison officer.

"My guardian?" questioned Eddie.

"Yeah. I think it's the first time your uncle has come to visit. I'm giving you thirty minutes. You have my permission to access the gardening facility and show him and his attorney the grounds."

"Cool, I'm on it."

"Good. Go get showered. Scrub some of the motor oil off you. Get cleaned up. You want to make the right impression with your family. And don't take too long, they're already outside, waiting."

"I'll be quick, I promise." Eddie got to his feet then paused, "Hey, Oscar. The envelope you gave me is in my room. How do I get it mailed?"

"I'll take care of it for you later."

"Thanks." Eddie grinned, "Did I ever tell you you're my favorite goon?"

The harsh gray concrete walls of the detention facility were only broken up in two areas, at the front entrance where visitors were greeted by a small grass strip and potted ferns, and inside the building's grounds, where a walled-in zone held a section designed for agricultural use. This featured a large lawn, tilled dirt for planting vegetables, thick bushes, and a dozen fully grown fruit trees, all of which were used for prisoners to practice and develop their gardening skills in the hope of providing for future rehabilitation, work experience and possible job placement after release. Four benches waited between the trees so inmates could reflect upon the problems that had put them there, and on their uncertain futures.

The guards opened the entrance to the outdoor complex, allowing prisoner number B-472, Edward York, outfitted in his orange detention center issued jumpsuit, to enter the restricted garden compound, accompanied by his legal guardian, Marcus York, and his lawyer, Jonathan Harris. Those were the names on the court papers submitted by the two visitors and accepted by the facility's officers without question that afternoon.

Eddie walked with the men into the Juvenile Hall's quiet wooded area.

"No way you're my uncle. I know, because I haven't got one. And what's with the weird Aussie accent?"

"It's English, actually. And why didn't you say something to the guard if you don't believe we're related?" asked Colin.

"Because it's a break for me. I'm not part of the gardening detail and they don't usually let me hang out here in the sun, so I wasn't going to call foul on you."

"They wouldn't have believed you anyway. Our paperwork is immaculate. Let's sit." Colin pointed to one of the benches and sat down. Eddie followed suit, while the third person, Mr. Stevens, hovered behind them.

"What's the real deal why you're here?" Eddie stared Colin in the eyes, fearless, "Did I rip off your ride or something?"

"Nothing so trivial. Let's just say you're important to my employer."

"That makes a change. I've never been important to anyone. Not even my mother."

Behind the two of them, unseen by Eddie, Mr. Stevens pulled out a small syringe concealed in the lining of his jacket's sleeve.

"I read about her. She died." Colin was matter-of-fact, not offering sympathy.

"Yeah, OD'd. My whole family's gone. I'm the only one still alive."

"Yes," said Colin. "But not for much longer."

Eddie changed his stare. He was confused now, "What?"

As he locked his questioning eyes on Colin, Mr. Stevens drove the syringe into the back of Eddie's neck.

Eddie felt the sharp pain of the needle and managed one word, "Fuck…" He tried to struggle but his arms and head became too heavy to lift.

Colin began to talk, his voice flat and cold, "You're feeling the first of two toxins. It causes paralysis and prevents you from moving or calling for help. The second is about to kick in. You'll know when it has, because you'll find it difficult to breathe and your chest will feel like an elephant is sitting on it. That's because your heart has stopped. I'm told the next few seconds are very painful."

Eddie's eyes opened wide with horror as his body started to convulse uncontrollably. Suddenly, with a tremendous spasm, he fell sideways on the bench, sprawling across Colin. As he lay there, Colin put two fingers against his neck and waited. Then he looked up at Mr. Stevens.

"No pulse. You know the plan. Explain the boy has had a seizure, and his uncle is staying with him as he's distraught. Make sure they call the hospital and the coroner."

Stevens turned and ran back towards the detention facility's doors. Colin watched him go, then stared down at Eddie and stroked the hair from his eyes, "A sad day. You were the last of your line."

The receiving office became a place of mayhem. The entire center went into lockdown, as they enacted the standard procedures set for an emergency, and officers herded the juveniles back into their cells. Two of the guards who had training in medical first response, rushed into the garden area to see what aid they could be to the stricken boy, while Oscar stood with Mr. Stevens listening to the account of the events. Even before he finished, Oscar grabbed the desk phone and dialed frantically.

A maintenance van, a few hundred yards from the detention center, was already on alert. It was parked next to a telephone pole and call junction box. Orange cones closed off the area, and cables stretched from the phone company's equipment to the vehicle.

Inside, a man and a woman wearing PacBell uniforms waited patiently for the LED indicator to light up, showing the anticipated call was being made. Suddenly it burst into life, signaling it was time to put everything into action.

The woman nodded to her partner and calmly clicked a switch on her headset. "County General. How may I direct your call?"

She paused as she listened, before replying, "What is the victim's condition?"

The man smiled; her rehearsed tone was perfect.

She spoke reassuringly, "I'll have an ambulance dispatched immediately to the Juvenile Detention facility. And yes, I'll notify the coroner for you, but hopefully they won't be needed. Please have your guards standing by to allow their vehicles access and avoid delay."

She clicked the switch to off and removed her headphones, "We're a go. I'm relaying the message now." She hit *SEND* on her cell and a pre-typed text went out. Job done, she slipped the phone into her pocket, "Okay, the plan is in motion. Remove the wiring, put everything back together and we'll get out of here."

The man opened the van's door and stepped onto the street to retrieve the orange cones. As he lifted the first, he heard urgent sirens splitting the air. He looked in the direction of the sound and smiled; they were responding even quicker than he had anticipated.

The two paramedics seemed in a state of distress at being unable to save the young boy, and placed him on a wheeled gurney, covering his lifeless body with a white sheet. The coroner recorded their actions and took a brief report from them, before having Oscar witness and initial his form. He tore off a copy and handed it to Oscar for his records.

The entire facility remained in lockdown as they rolled the seventeen-year-old boy's body out of the detention center. Oscar walked with them, his head hung low and his hand resting on the side of the gurney as he paid his last respects to his favorite inmate.

Eddie's corpse was loaded respectfully into the back of the coroner's van, where two men in scrubs waited for the tragic cargo. The double doors shut on the three of them and the large vehicle pulled slowly away.

Concealed from sight and feeling the motion, the men started with their assigned tasks. One removed a big sheet revealing a metallic silver coffin, while the other unclipped Eddie's unresponsive body from his restraints. They lifted the corpse from the gurney and lowered it carefully into the coffin, and reached inside, checking something, then shut and locked the heavy lid of the boy's final resting place.

Their job done, one of the men grabbed a wired microphone to relay a message to the driver up front. His words were simple, "All secured and ready. Go."

The lights on both the coroner's van and the trailing paramedics' ambulance blazed on, and the two ominous vehicles sped up and raced together through the busy San Jose streets, their sirens and urgent blue and red rooftop displays causing the cars in front to pull over out of their way.

A mile ahead was County General hospital. The speeding vehicles blew past it without slowing. They were heading for a different destination.

The gates of the private terminal at Mineta International airport were already open in anticipation of the somber procession. The medical vans slowed to a respectable pace, extinguished their lights and followed the waiting black Bentley to the gleaming Gulfstream prepared for their arrival.

A forklift was standing by next to the jet, and moved the heavy coffin up into the G650's large cargo hold where it became the only item in the eerily empty space. It was strapped down to stop it from shifting in flight, and the doors were closed and sealed.

Colin walked with Stevens to the base of the jet's stairs. He turned to the big American and offered his hand. The two men shook and said nothing as they parted company. Colin went up inside the plane, and Stevens returned to the Bentley, where he was driven off without even a backward glance.

Had he not left so quickly, he would have seen the plane taxi to the runway, its engines engage and the jet scream skyward to begin the five thousand three-hundred-mile journey to its ultimate destination.

Colin, the lone passenger onboard the sixty-five-million-dollar jet, reached into the liquor cabinet and removed the bottle of Macallan Scotch he knew was waiting there. It was a rare indulgence, but he had saved this particular bottle to mark the conclusion of his task and celebrate a job well done. As he poured the twenty-five-year-old single malt and savored the way its warm brown colors danced over the ice cubes, he realized he might not receive the acclaim he felt was deserved, but simply knowing what he had managed to achieve after all these years, when so many others before him had failed, was reward enough.

There was a slight shudder as the undercarriage retracted into the wings and he smiled to himself, recognizing the sound; wheels up, they were on their way. Time to send the message. He unlocked his cell phone, retrieved a 212 number from his contacts and texted two words in all caps, STRIKE EVERYTHING.

Colin Brown turned his phone off and relaxed back into the comfortable leather seat. This is how he liked things done, to have all goals accomplished and nothing left behind to attract the attention of the curious. After completing such an extended, stressful mission, he was finally leaving America, a country that had consumed much of the past three years of his life, and going home. He might even commemorate the occasion by having a second whisky before settling down to grab a few hours' sleep on the long flight ahead.

Below him, in the luggage hold, the silver coffin remained locked in place. Inside, an unmoving body lay there. Next to it, a green oxygen cylinder hissed very softly. And strangely, a hint of color returned to the corpse's lower lip.

CHAPTER SIX

HTTP error 404

Alex Turner was unaware of the beautiful morning in Wisconsin. He had not left his *dungeon* since returning from New York two days before. With his commissioned quest concluded, he'd thrown himself back into his interrupted work. He had a book to finish, a thesis to read and term papers to grade. He wasn't sure where he would find the time to do it all. And for some reason he was finding it hard to concentrate. It took him a while to realize why, and when he did rationalize it, he was taken by surprise. He missed Cate's company.

In the past, he'd always worked alone. Even before he lost his wife and child, he did his most effective work without anyone else around. He enjoyed the solitary, monk-like life of a driven academic. But now, he found himself missing Cate. Something about her had brought out the best in him. For all her foibles; her love of computers, her meeting up with her old University friend in New York, her spirited interruptions, she had many positive attributes. And it was their contrast of styles which made things flow together so well. Hopefully, he thought, there might be a project in the future we can once again collaborate on.

The ringing on his desk interrupted his reminiscence. He stared at the phone as it sounded a second, then a third time. He didn't get many calls put through by the University switchboard; they knew better than to disturb him. Finally, the insistence of the ring made him act, and he reluctantly picked up the receiver. "Yes?" he demanded.

He recognized the distinctive voice even before the man announced his name, "Professor Turner? I'm calling from the San Jose juvenile detention facility. It's Oscar Ramirez."

"What can I do for you, Oscar?"

"I hope you don't mind me bothering you. I got this number from your paperwork. This is about Eddie. He had asked me to send your wallet back to you and I need to confirm your mailing address is the same as listed on the forms we have here."

Alex risked a smile. The boy was living up to his word, "That's the correct address. I'd be grateful to get it back. I must have dropped it when I was visiting him. Eddie said he would look for it. How is he?"

There was silence on the line before Oscar spoke again, "He's dead, Professor."

"Dead? That's not possible. How?"

"He had a grand mal seizure yesterday. It turns out there is a history of those kinds of medical problems being common in his family. The blessing is Eddie wasn't alone when he passed. He died in the arms of his uncle."

"His what?" Alex had a hard time forming the question.

"His uncle. He was the one who explained how seizures ran in their family."

"You're sure it was his uncle?"

"Yes, sir. Marcus York. I saw his identification myself."

It was Alex's turn to fall silent. Finally, he said, "Thank you for letting me know," and hung up.

He sat motionless, transfixed, staring at the phone, before reaching for the thick file marked *Global Pharmaceuticals*. He flipped it open, and there, on the very first page bearing the heading *Edward York*, were the words, *NO LIVING RELATIVES*, circled in red ink.

The square box of a room wasn't large, only twelve by twelve feet, and felt even smaller because of the medical equipment jammed into it and the high, metal-framed bed wedged against the center of one of the walls.

Lying on the bed, dressed in an orange jumpsuit, torn open at the chest by paramedics gaining access for CPR, was a young boy with long hair. His left hand was wrapped in a bloody bandage, his neck tipped at a contorted angle to the side, as if from rigor mortis.

"Arrgh!" the noise from the corpse shattered any illusions of a peaceful afterlife, and Eddie jerked awake, his face a portrait of pain caused by the sudden movement. He collapsed back down and raised his hand to his head.

"Shit, that hurts," he said to himself, and sat up again, but much more slowly.

He gazed around the room, puzzled. Where was he? It didn't seem like a hospital, more a kind of converted office. But why all the medical equipment?

He contemplated the question but had no time to come up with an answer because of the heavy footsteps outside and the voices echoing toward him.

The door opened, and Colin Brown, accompanied by a man dressed in surgical white, entered. They saw Eddie lying there, unmoving.

"When will the drug wear off?"

"It should be soon, Mr. Brown. The dose you administered him was on the high end of my recommendation. It could easily have been fatal."

"It did its job and worked perfectly. It got him here. The sample was good?" He pointed to the bandage on Eddie's hand.

"It seems to be. We do need to reconfirm the match, and having the adequate tissue to run a series of tests is helpful to eliminate any possible doubts, but as of now, even with only the first provisional trial completed, it's more than ninety-nine percent certain."

"You're sure? We have to keep him alive until we know."

"I'd stake my reputation on it. Though it would be beneficial to have better facilities than this."

"Where did you think we'd take him? To your ward at St. Thomas' hospital? I had everything you said you needed brought here. Keep him unconscious until the final results are in, then we'll discuss options."

"Understood. I'll ready a sedative for when the nerve agent wears off."

"Do it." Colin's clipped utterance left no doubt his words were an order as he turned and marched out of the room.

The doctor let him leave and waited until the door closed to prepare the requested dosage. He retrieved a syringe from a drawer and filled it with a milky fluid. He pushed the plunger gently to expel excess air when…

BANG!

Eddie hit him hard from behind, across his head, with the edge of a metal tray. The doctor crumpled to the ground, out cold.

The boy grabbed the fallen syringe and plunged it in the doctor's exposed neck, emptying its contents into him. "I hope you got this dose right, doc."

The man shuddered as the serum took hold. Eddie recognized the shakes and knew what was happening, "Trust me, you'll have one hell of a headache when you wake up."

Eddie bent forward and stripped the white coat from the prone doctor, then pulled off his shoes and slipped them on. They were a little big, but with the choice being those or bare feet, they would have to do.

Eddie went for the door, listened, heard nothing, and slowly opened it.

Outside, the hallway was deserted; bland and faceless. No indication of what building it was or where it was located. But at one end he could see a way out – a fire exit.

Eddie sprinted down the corridor, gaining speed in case he was challenged, and careened hard into the metal door. It burst open and he dove through it into the heavy rain outside. His uncontrolled pace carried him stumbling across the narrow sidewalk and past the edge of the curb onto the street, and directly into the path of a monstrous red vehicle.

He desperately leaped backward and fell on his ass on the pavement as the huge double-decker bus sounded its horn in fury and hurtled by on the wrong side of the road. He looked around in amazement at the mass of flashing neon lights surrounding him, illuminating the night, and the people packing the circular street, umbrellas raised, in a futile attempt to protect themselves from the downpour.

Where was he? What was this strange place? He stared again, and there, across the busy road was an opening where crowds flocked in and out. Above it glowed a round, lighted red and white sign reading *UNDERGROUND*, and right below, the words, *PICCADILLY CIRCUS*.

Cate's room had the potential to be cute, if only she allotted herself the time to fix it up. Colorful throw pillows lay on the vintage chairs, but only their corners remained visible as they were concealed by the clothes she'd hurriedly dropped there and hadn't yet hung up. Her new flatscreen TV stood in pride of place on the dresser, however she'd been unable to hide the wires for the power and the soundbar, so they protruded out and dangled down in front of the drawers like limp, overcooked spaghetti. But Cate was not worrying about any of that right now. She had finally finished one of her required-reading course books and was asleep and intended to stay that way until the alarm on her cell woke her up at eight a.m. Unfortunately, she had not passed on that message to the long-distance operator who had other plans for her.

A Coldplay song sounded and after a few seconds of sharing the adventure of a lifetime with Chris Martin, her eyes fluttered open and she struggled with her hand to quiet the annoying cell phone.

"Yes?" she groaned.

A bright, female English voice came on the line, "I have a reverse charge call from London. Will you accept?"

She flashed a glance at her clock. It defied her with the numbers *3:25*. Still half-asleep she surprised herself by saying, "What? Yes, I suppose so."

"Putting you through now. Go ahead." The operator disappeared from the line as another voice replaced her. A boy's voice with an American accent, "Hello?"

"Do you know what time it is?"

"No, I don't have a watch. It's sometime in the morning," said Eddie.

"Yeah, sometime for sure. I'm going back to sleep." Cate pulled the cell from her ear.

"Wait, wait, wait. Is Professor Turner there?"

"In his dreams. Who do you think I am? And how did you get my number?"

"Professor Turner called me from it and I wrote it down and put it in my pocket. That was yesterday, or maybe a few days ago. I don't know for sure."

"Are you drunk?" asked Cate.

"I wish. Professor Turner's number is the only thing I've got. He was very cool."

"I'll tell him he has a fan. Good night."

"Lady, please, you have to get him to help me. Some shit's gone down and I think I'm in London." Eddie's tone was frantic.

"What do you mean, you *think* you're in London? You don't know?"

"It's just I was in California and now I'm here. I don't know how."

"I'm glad you're doing some traveling, but that's no reason to wake me. Send a text or an email next time. I'm going to sleep."

"Wait. Please. I've got to reach the professor; can you tell him Eddie York needs to talk to him?"

Cate sat bolt upright up in bed, knowing sleep was history for her now, "Eddie York? From San Jose?"

"Jesus, what's the deal? I don't hear shit from anyone for years and now everyone knows me?" It was Eddie's turn to be confused.

"Why are you in London, Eddie?"

"I don't know, honest I don't. One minute I'm in Juvie with some dude saying he's my long-lost uncle, the next I'm here with a mad scientist getting ready to operate on me and no money and no clothes. It sucks."

Cate thought through what she had to do, "Hey, can I call you back?"

"I don't think you can. I'm in an English phone booth. It doesn't have a number."

"Is there a building or a hotel around you can see? I could call you there."

Eddie stared across Hyde Park to the sea of hotels lining Park Lane.

"There's a bunch of hotels here."

"Choose one," instructed Cate.

"Okay. There's a big one. The Dorchester."

"Got it. The Dorchester. I'll try to reach Professor Turner today, but in case I can't, can you give me until tomorrow? Will you be able to hang on until then?"

"That shouldn't be a problem. I lived on the streets in Oakland forever, another night is nothing. But you have to call. I have to get out of here."

Cate didn't understand what was happening but could hear the panic in his voice, "I will, I promise. Be in the lobby of the Dorchester at six p.m. your time, tomorrow. We'll call and have you paged. Professor Turner will work things out and arrange to bring you home."

"Thank you."

The line went dead, and Cate stared at her phone, trying to understand the conversation she'd just had. She pulled up Alex's number from her contacts but looked again at the time. She couldn't call him this early. It would have to wait until the morning, even though she knew there would be no more sleep for her for the rest of the night.

The building situated on the banks of the Thames River was alive with activity, as a dozen men met in the main conference room on the third floor.

Colin Brown took the lead and addressed the group, "Thank you for allowing me to come here at such short notice. Simon, I especially appreciate you bringing in some of your key men and putting this together to run as a joint operation. Obviously, your experience in domestic threats will be invaluable. What do you have so far?"

Simon Foster stepped forward. His authority seemed a given, the way the room fell quiet as he spoke, "Based on the alert you brought me, I've made sure everyone from Scotland Yard through to this evening's news, and the late editions of the papers, have the boy's picture."

"That's good," asserted Colin, "But let's not wait for others. Have your men hit the streets. Whoever finds him will be well taken care of."

The men smiled back at him. That is what they had been hoping to hear.

"You heard the man. Those are your orders. Head on out, work your contacts, see what you can find. This is a level three op," ordered Simon.

The men wasted no time as they got to their feet and hurried out of the conference room.

Simon Foster remained with Colin Brown and stayed silent until the door hermetically sealed behind the exiting men. It was only then he spoke.

"I'm still trying to wrap my head around what you've told me about the boy. If you hadn't shown me the paperwork, I would have thought you mad."

"The paperwork was for your eyes only; it goes no further. What we are dealing with here is beyond NATSEN TOP SECRET," stated Colin.

The look on Simon's face questioned his words, "There is no higher category than NATSEN."

"There is, and it pre-dates the Official Secrets Act by quite a few years. This falls under its designation. The only person you are permitted to discuss this with is me. There is to be no written communication, paper or electronic, on this situation, and the only calls between us on this matter are to be on the number I have given you for my secure cell. Prior to today, this was an overseas operation, but as of now the risk has returned to the British Isles so I have brought you in."

"I understand, and I'll make our resources available to you," assured Simon.

"Good. Remember, the cover story for your teams and for your entire department is we are tracking a simple but deadly domestic threat. No one is to know the real extent of the danger that exists."

"I'll have a team standing by, ready to move on this at any time." Simon drew in a long breath as he considered what was facing them, "I can't even conceive how bad the repercussions will be if this turns into the worst-case scenario you're presenting."

"That's what you and I have to make sure doesn't happen." Colin Brown turned to leave, "I'm going back to my office. Keep me posted on what your men find. And for Christ's sake, let's bring this to an end quickly."

Alex labored with his typewriter as the outside red light flashed on, and almost immediately, the inner door flew open and Cate charged inside. She was surprised Alex spoke before she could apologize for disturbing him, and that his tone was so welcoming.

"Cate, it's so good to see you." He paused, and a touch of sadness drifted into his voice, "I was going to call you today about the boy we had been looking for. The one I saw in San Jose, Eddie York. I received some bad news about him."

"You did too?" Cate was startled he knew already, "That's why I came. I couldn't sleep after I heard."

"I know, it's terrible. But there's something very wrong with the story. Eddie doesn't have an uncle. He would have shown up during our search. We know he was all alone in the world."

Cate nodded in agreement, "That's why he called for you."

Her comment puzzled Alex, "No, I called him, from the airport. Remember, about my wallet? The one he stole?"

It was Cate's turn to be confused, "Eddie still has your wallet? He told me he didn't have any money."

"What? He doesn't have anything. Eddie's dead."

Cate took a step back, "My God. When did that happen?"

"Two days ago. He died at the detention facility. I found out yesterday when one of the guards contacted me to let me know."

"Wait. That can't be." She looked at Alex who appeared to be as lost as she was, "Eddie didn't die two days ago. I spoke to him this morning, really early. He called and woke me up."

"Eddie called you? How is that possible? He doesn't know you. You didn't meet him."

"I know, but you called him from my cell. He wrote the number down and called it back and got me."

"Cate, however he got your number, he couldn't have called you this morning. He's dead."

"We are going around in circles here. Look," she reached into her purse and pulled out her cell and hit *recents*, "That number. The one that starts 44. That's where he called from. He was very alive a few hours ago and in London."

"Eddie called you from London? Are you sure?"

"As sure as I can be. It was a collect call, put through by a British operator. I had to pay for it, he had no money."

"All right. Let's find out what is happening. Sit down." He pulled out the chair next to him for Cate, "I'm calling Mr. Brown. Maybe he knows what's going on."

Alex dialed the phone and waited. He looked at Cate, "It's just ringing."

"Put it on speaker."

"I'm not sure how."

Cate leaned forward and pushed the speaker icon. The ring tone sounded throughout the room. "You can put the phone down. It'll keep ringing until it's answered or we press this again," she pointed to the red button.

Alex cautiously replaced the handset. The unanswered rings mocked them.

"Did you get the number wrong?" offered Cate.

"No." Alex was certain, "I don't forget names, numbers, letters, ever."

The phone continued to ring.

Cate flipped open her ever-present laptop, "I'll see if they have another number."

She typed the company's name into the search bar and sat back in shock.

Alex saw the stunned expression on her face, "What is it?"

"I'm getting an error 404 message."

"I don't know what that means," Alex admitted.

"It means site not found. It's saying there is no Global Pharmaceuticals listed. Let me check if it's the server." She typed frantically, her face becoming more and more concerned as the seconds ticked by, "I'm not sure what's happening here. Google, Yahoo and MSN have no info on them. It's like they never existed."

"Is it a problem with your computer?" asked Alex.

"No. I'm in my laptop's search history and it shows I was on their website several times over the past week, but when I click on the links, no content comes up. That doesn't make sense. It's as if they've been erased from the internet."

Behind them, the phone kept ringing.

"Was the money real?" asked Cate.

"Yes. My cashier's check cleared and the twenty million dollars for the University went directly into their holding account, and you saw the twenty-five thousand in cash they handed me."

"Then who were they? And why pay so much just to find a kid?"

Alex shook his head,

"I'm going to call Susan. Have her go by and see what the problem is," said Cate.

"How will she get in? It's a security building."

Cate drew her breath in and looked guilty, "I gave her my laminate. It's meant to be valid for seven days. I thought she might want to apply for a job there. It'll get her in."

"Good," Alex's response was unexpected and without recrimination. "Have her see what the problem is in person." He pointed to the phone, "This button?"

"Yes," answered Cate.

Alex pushed it, and the unanswered ringing finally stopped.

CHAPTER SEVEN

999

Rush hour was in full force throughout London. Black cabs competed with Uber drivers for the two million workers fleeing their office jobs to escape to their homes in the suburbs. As the buildings emptied out onto the streets, everything reached an overflow point; the sidewalks, the tube stations, and the ubiquitous double-decker buses, all becoming jammed to capacity.

Eddie bolted from the pavement and jumped on the open back step of the number 390 bus to Victoria. He had no idea where that was, but if it was away from the crowded heart of the city, perhaps he could find an empty doorway in which to shelter and possibly even sleep tonight.

He scanned the overloaded bus. Every seat was taken and thirty people stood crammed in the aisle, balancing precariously as they clung to the provided leather straps hanging from the overhead rail running the entire length of the inside of the double-decker.

While the younger passengers studied their phones, Eddie noticed printed newspapers were still alive and well in Britain, and virtually every person over the age of thirty was buried in tonight's news. In horror, he saw they all carried the same banner headline, *ARMED JUVENILE DRUG SMUGGLER LOOSE IN LONDON - REWARD.* There, on the front page of the Evening Standard, The Independent, and even the late editions of The Mail and The Telegraph, was a large black-and-white photograph staring back at him. His picture!

He was not the only one to notice the marked resemblance. Two burly male passengers, jammed halfway down the packed bus, spotted the strangely dressed boy, wearing a white lab coat over a torn orange jumpsuit, and with a knowing nod to each other, elbowed their way among the standing crowd toward the wanted fugitive.

Eddie saw them coming and leaped from the slowly moving vehicle, dodging cars as he ran through the pouring rain between two lanes of traffic before disappearing into the night and the welcoming darkness of Hyde Park.

Alex and Cate paced back and forth across the basement study, tension and confusion showing on their faces. Finally, Alex stopped, "I don't see any other way. We have to follow your plan. We call the boy in London tomorrow and find out what's going on."

It was Cate's turn to hit the brakes, and the pacing had not helped her decision making, "But my plan's not great. I don't do my best thinking at three in the morning. Calling Eddie won't help, he doesn't know anything. He said he just woke up there."

"All right, I'll wire him money and he can fly back. We can work it out then."

"Professor Turner, he can't leave England without a passport and if he goes to the US Embassy, what's he going to say – '*hi, I just escaped from Juvie Hall in California and by the way, I'm dead!*'? He'll sound like he's lost his mind, and when he has nothing on him to show he's an American, with immigration as tight as it is these days, they'll think he's running some kind of scam and won't even let him in through their gates." She took a deep breath, knowing Alex wouldn't agree with what she was about to say, "I've got a new plan. We have to go there."

"Where? London?"

"Yes. It's the only way. Someone's got to help this kid."

"Cate, you haven't even met him."

"That's why the two of us have to go. We bring his birth certificate and the research showing his family line, and we present it at the Embassy. That should be enough to get him temporary papers so he can return to America with us. But it can't just be me, you have to come too. He's met you; he trusts you. We got him into this. If we don't try to help him, one day you'll regret sitting here doing nothing."

Alex heard her words and a shudder ran down his spine. They were eerily familiar to him. They were almost identical to what his wife had said when he told her he couldn't leave the hotel room and his research to join her exploring Prague with their little child. She had warned he might regret it, and he had. Those words had haunted him every day of his life since then. If he'd gone with them, if he had done something, maybe they would still be alive today.

Cate saw the change in him and the sadness clouding his face, "Are you okay, Professor?"

"Yes, I am. You're right. We should go. But how do we do this?"

"If we leave now, we can get our stuff together and be at the airport in Madison in an hour. We grab a flight from there to Chicago, which should get us in by six, seven at the latest. We take an overnight to Heathrow from O'Hare and meet him tomorrow evening at the hotel in person." She hesitated, adding, "It's last minute, so the plane tickets might be expensive."

"Do it. I still have all of Mr. Brown's cash. I'll bring it with me to pay for Eddie's ticket home."

Cate smiled, her first smile since hearing the news, and flipped open her laptop, "London, here we come."

The two travelers sat at the British Airways gate in Terminal 5 of O'Hare's massive airport waiting to board Flight 296 to Heathrow departing at eight fifty-five pm.

"Do you sleep on planes?" asked Cate.

"I have a tough time sleeping anywhere," answered Alex. "But I'll try."

"You'll have eight hours to see if you can. When I—" Her cell phone, and the Post Malone ringtone, cut her off. Cate glanced at the small screen, "It's Susan. Let me take this."

After a few seconds of listening, Cate interrupted, "Hold on, Susan. I want Professor Turner to hear."

She pulled out one of her earbuds and handed it to Alex, "Put this in your ear."

He looked at it strangely, but complied.

Cate gave him a nod of approval, and continued on the call with her friend in New York, "Go ahead."

Susan's voice sounded in the small earbud, "It's weird. I went by the building and had no problem with the pass you gave me, but when I got to their floor, there was no one there."

"Susan, this is Professor Turner," Alex spoke louder than necessary, "What do you mean, no one?"

"Exactly that. The entire floor was deserted. The furniture was all in place but it was as if I'd walked in during the middle of the night instead of four in the afternoon. And there were no signs anywhere saying the name of the company, and any paperwork and files were gone, there was nothing on desks, and not a single person was around. The whole thing was cleaned out and even the trash cans were empty. It felt like there'd been a zombie apocalypse and the survivors had fled the scene and taken everything with them. Really eerie. I went down to security and spoke to several different supervisors before one took a shine to me and told me no one from Global Pharmaceuticals had been in the building for two days."

"How could they be sure of that?" questioned Alex.

"When you access the elevators with your laminate badge it's recorded. Not one person had been to that floor in forty-eight hours apart from a janitorial crew. I thought I'd boarded a ghost ship drifting in the middle of Manhattan."

"Do you have any idea what happened?" asked Cate.

"As I said, one of the supervisors liked me, and he was kind of cute, so he gave me the lowdown of what he knew. The offices had been rented furnished for ninety days with an option for an extension of up to two years. They took it over only a week ago. The supervisor noticed the floor was empty yesterday and called the numbers for the office manager and the leasing company who had arranged everything-"

Cate jumped in, "Can I make a guess here?"

"Sure," said Susan.

"The numbers didn't work."

"How did you know? None of them. Not even the leasing agency. As if they never existed. But it wasn't a con game or anything. They paid their rental in full, in advance." She lowered her voice, "You won't believe how much. Seven hundred and eighty thousand dollars! That's a quarter of a million a month, plus a thirty-thousand-dollar lease fee for cards, parking and shit. And those numbers are right because Dave showed me the paperwork."

"Dave?" Cate raised her eyebrows.

"I told you he was cute, girl," giggled Susan. "What is this all about?"

"We don't know. That's why we're off to London to find out," replied Cate.

"London? We had fun in London," remembered Susan.

"Yes, we did," agreed Cate. "But this time it's not a pleasure trip." She looked at Alex, "Do you have any questions for Susan?"

Alex shook his head, "Too many, and I don't think Susan, or any of us know the answers yet. Thank you."

"Hey, yeah, thanks girl. I'll try to call you from England."

"Do that. Take care." Susan clicked off the line.

Cate slipped the phone back into her purse and stared at Alex, "Any idea what's happening?"

"No. None." The professor was baffled.

"The thing that gets me is the money. They are spending so much. Twenty million to the University. Nearly a million for what was only a week's rent. It's crazy."

"It's only crazy if you don't have it to spend. Maybe whoever is behind this has deep pockets," explained Alex.

"You think? I can't imagine anyone throwing those kinds of sums around."

"People do when they want something. Michael Bloomberg spent nine hundred million dollars of his own money in less than one hundred days on his failed presidential bid. He spent more in three days than whoever is behind this has spent in total."

Cate was still doubtful, "Bloomberg was after the White House, Global Pharmaceuticals was only looking for a seventeen-year-old kid with a record. How could he be worth that?"

"Let's hope the answer is in London."

Almost on cue, the announcement rang out from the overhead speakers, "Flight 295 to London is available for pre-boarding. Any travelers with small children or who need assistance, make your way to the gate. Please have your passports open and ready for inspection."

Cate flashed a glance at Alex, "They'll be calling us in about ten minutes. I should have time to grab a Starbucks to bring onboard. Want one, professor?"

He looked at the eager girl and smiled, "That would be very nice. And Cate, call me Alex."

The early morning sun chased the darkness away from Hyde Park, lighting the group of homeless people sheltering in the old wooden bandstand. One of them was young and wearing bright orange pants.

Eddie stretched to crack his back, sore from the hours spent on the unforgiving plank flooring. As he moved, he noticed some of his companions using bundles of newspapers for makeshift mattresses. On two of the papers, he saw his photograph.

Next to him, an old lady stirred, and as her eyes focused, she caught Eddie staring at the picture. She looked back and forth, from the photo to Eddie, "It's a good likeness, luv."

"Too damn good," agreed Eddie, getting quickly to his feet and heading off to lose himself in the vast park.

Fifteen admission booths were in operation at Heathrow Airport, and Alex was next in line. Cate had already cleared immigration and stood waiting for her travel companion.

The uniformed officer scanned the passport then looked up at the professor, "I'm not seeing a vaccine record?"

Alex raised his left arm and showed the official his Covid-19 wristband.

"Thank you, but I have to scan it. Could you place your wrist under the glass, please?"

Alex complied, and the hand-held reader displayed the results clearly on his monitor screen. The agent checked and noted the date of the vaccination, and wrote it on Alex's passport before stamping the entry and sliding it back under the thick Perspex, "Enjoy your stay in England, Mr. Turner."

The black cab wound its way through the inevitable late afternoon traffic circling Marble Arch and pulled onto Park Lane as it made for its destination, The Dorchester Hotel.

Alex checked his watch; it was a few minutes before six. "I thought we would have been here earlier."

"If we'd taken the Heathrow Express like I said, we would have. Instead, we lost two hours in the awful traffic on the *motorway*," she emphasized the word with a bad attempt at a British accent. "But we should make it right on time."

"I would always rather be early," stated Alex unnecessarily.

The cab swerved out of the flow of cars and onto the long sweeping driveway leading to one of the world's most acclaimed hotels. As it pulled to a stop, two bellboys hurried down the low flight of stairs to assist their newest guests.

The hotel's classic lobby buzzed with activity as visitors prepared for a night out in Europe's most exciting city. Cate led the way across the crowded floor to the registration where the desk clerk greeted them with a warm smile, "Good evening. Welcome to The Dorchester. How may I be of help to you?"

"We have a room reserved for Alex Turner," answered Cate.

"Let me check for you." He punched the name into his keyboard and looked back up, his smile now even bigger, these guests had booked a very expensive room, "Ah yes. A rooftop suite. Two bedrooms. I see we have a reservation with your credit card and passport details already on file. That's all we need here. Will two keys be enough?"

"It should be for now. We might want a third later, I'm not sure yet." Alex looked at the ornate wall clock hanging behind the desk. it was right at six, "Could you page someone for us?"

"Certainly. Is he staying at the hotel?"

"No. He said he would be in the lobby about now, but I can't see him."

"We do get very busy this time of night. What is his name?"

"Eddie York."

"Eddie York," repeated the desk clerk. "I'll do it right away."

He turned from Alex and Cate and raised a small wired microphone from the paging system under the counter. His voice boomed across the marble lobby, "Eddie York to the front desk. You have a party waiting. Eddie York."

As the clerk bent down to replace the microphone, he glimpsed a folded newspaper beneath his desk. The headline was hard to miss, *HUNT CONTINUES FOR ARMED AMERICAN TEEN – EDDIE YORK*

He tried to mask his concern as he turned back to them, "You are both from America, correct?" He already knew the answer but wanted to hear them say it.

"Yes, we are."

"Hopefully you'll have a wonderful holiday here with us in London." It was his usual wish to all the hotel's guests but somehow it felt false this time.

A young boy emerged from the crowd and worked his way through the people to the front desk. Cate saw him before he reached them; his disheveled appearance, a dirty white doctor's coat and bright orange pants, eminently conspicuous among the sea of Savile Row suits and sparkling cocktail dresses surrounding them.

Eddie stopped several feet short of the desk. He tried to understand what he was seeing. The kind professor was there, waiting. He had been expecting a trans-Atlantic phone call, not an in-person appearance. "Professor? What are you doing here? You were going to call. Who's she?" he pointed to Cate.

Cate spoke before Alex could answer, "*She* is Cate. You called me, remember? In the middle of the night? Woke me up?"

"We came to help you, Eddie," said Alex.

Eddie looked around the bustling lobby, all too aware of the unwanted attention his soiled clothes were attracting, "Can we talk somewhere else? Away from this crowd of stiffs."

Alex nodded, and turned back to the front desk, "Thanks for your help, we found him." He slipped the clerk a five-pound note.

"Shall we go to the room?" suggested Cate.

"Anywhere without so many people," pleaded Eddie.

"All right," said Alex, and the trio headed to the elevators.

The clerk watched them cross the lobby, and as they disappeared from view, picked up his phone and dialed. It was the same number, punched in three times, *9 – 9 – 9.*

It was answered almost immediately, "London Metropolitan Police. What is the nature of your emergency?"

Colin was still at his desk, gazing out at the river boats far below him, plying their way along the Thames. He had spent the past thirty hours there and not gone home, and the only time he had left his office was to head down to the building's fitness center for his daily workout, but even in that familiar environment, he had found himself unable to concentrate and develop the intensity he felt his body needed.

Normally, wherever he was in the world, when he hit the gym, his grueling dedication had others around him shooting envious glances at his extreme techniques, and the ease with which he manhandled the heavy weights and attacked the exhausting repetitions created doubts within them of their own commitment to exercise. But today, even his regular, comforting routines failed to distract him, and frustrated, he cut short his training session and returned, unsatisfied to his office.

Back inside those four walls, he couldn't see himself leaving again until this damn kid was taken care of. It was too important, not just for *Them,* but now, for him as well. If any of this nightmare got out-

His mobile phone ended his troubled thoughts. He recognized the specific ringtone and grabbed the cell, answering with one clipped word, "Yes?"

Simon's familiar voice came over the line, "Communications here at Five have intercepted a call to the Met from the Dorchester. They said Eddie York was in the lobby. The desk clerk confirmed his identity from the newspaper photograph and even heard his name used."

Colin was on his feet now, "Jesus. Is he still there?"

"Yes, but he's not alone. He's with two Americans."

"What Americans?"

"You know them. I checked the notes you gave me on this and you have them listed in your files. The Professor from Wisconsin and his assistant."

Colin's mouth fell open in disbelief, "Fuck! What are they doing here?" He thought for a brief second before barking orders, "Okay, have the Yard keep the cops back. Last thing we want is some flatfoot picking them up. Instead, assign them to run a cordon around the hotel. A two-hundred-yard radius. Nothing goes in, nothing comes out."

There was a momentary pause on the other end of the line as Simon tried to digest the instructions, "Colin, it's still rush hour! We can't shut down Marble Arch, Oxford Street and Bayswater at this time of night. It will tie up a million people!"

"Then I guess they'll be late home for tea. Shut it down! Get two tac squads ready and a Sea King equipped with a nightsun to follow us in. And tell them if they're not rolling in ten minutes, you'll have them up on charges. I'll meet you and your team from Five over there."

He clicked off the call and slammed his fist down on the desk to vent his anger as he tried to understand how the two other Americans could have become involved. Whatever it was that had brought them here had now made them a part of this, and he knew before he could proceed any further, there were people he had to consult about what was to happen.

He picked up his cell phone again and opened a drawer, taking out a mini-USB and slipping it into the power connector at the base of his mobile. A green activity light flashed on to indicate it was now active.

He scrolled through his contact list and located *Benny Hill*. He touched it and hit *dial*.

It was minutes before two in the afternoon in Langley, Virginia, and the CIA's incoming lines were manned by four operators. Colin's call was answered on the first ring, "Langley watch desk."

Colin spoke quickly but forcefully, "This is Signet, in London. I need the DNI."

"Sir, he's out on a business lunch. The director's meeting with a couple of lobbyists and does not want to be disturbed."

Colin had been expecting a similar response or brush off, "I don't care if he's at a Motel 6 humping his mistress. You can see what line I'm calling on. If you want to still have your job tomorrow, you'll patch me through to the DNI."

Her reply was short and fast, "Yes, sir." She punched a series of numbers and continued, "Connecting you now."

The Director of National Intelligence was into his third bourbon as he sought to ease his pain of listening to the fundraising agendas of the two political leeches sitting with him when the insistent and familiar distinctive ring pulled his attention away. "Excuse me a moment, I have to take this" he said as he answered his cell, "DNI, Langley."

"This is Signet, London. I'm calling on a secure line," replied Colin.

"Hold on." The DNI rose to his feet and gave the money grubbers at the table an overly large, exaggerated smile, "Company business. You know how it is. Have another round, I'll be right back."

The director hustled across the busy restaurant and outside onto the street. He moved a few steps from the entrance, and convinced the constant Washington traffic noise would stop him from being overheard by anyone of importance, he spoke into the phone. "Do you have him?" His tone was urgent, he had been anticipating this call for almost forty-eight hours.

"I just received his location and teams are moving in as we speak. It's now a joint op with Five. There is a complication. That's why I'm calling you."

"What is it?"

"Target is no longer alone. Two people are with him. US nationals."

"Fuck! How did that happen? Do they know anything?" demanded the DNI.

"They know he was in the detention center in San Jose and someone must have gotten him out and brought him to London.

It's the University professor and his assistant, the two people who found the boy. They flew in to meet him."

"Then they know too much. It leaves us no choice. Go ahead. Red card them, like the kid."

"Are you sure?" Colin sought the confirmation from his American ally, "They are your people."

"Don't get cold feet. When you brought this to me, we agreed it starts with us, it stops with us. We're our countries' gatekeepers. Right?"

"Right."

"Any leaks and we put together a cover story like teenage drug dealer killed when American professor sets up meth lab in a real life Breaking Bad in London. Joe Public will believe anything. Hell, if the press even gets an idea of what is happening and tries putting it out, we'll scream *Fake News,* and the people will eat it up."

Colin was still not sure, "And you think a story like that would work?"

"We'll make it work. They will have nothing to prove otherwise. If this thing goes south, we lose a lot more than a couple of bystanders, it would change the global balance of power. I'm not risking anything that could cost the US our strongest ally. We already lost France, Spain, and most of Europe. There's socialism everywhere, and a resurgence of communism barking up its ass behind it. And after all the protests in the streets this past summer the arrests in Portland, and the debacle at Lafayette Square, the US is not on anyone's favorite ally list. Without you Brits, we'd be on our own in a screwed-up world. Don't try pulling a Brexit on America, I won't let it happen. We need you more than ever, we need your bases, and we need your troops. Do whatever you have to do to end this as soon as possible. DNI rules red card on all three, American or not. Got it?"

"Got it," acknowledged Colin.

That was all America's Director of National Intelligence needed to hear, and he ended the call without another word.

Colin waited for the line to clear before removing the secure access USB from the phone's port.

He slipped the cell into his pants pocket and peeled off his suit jacket exposing his Kydex polymer shoulder holster. He crossed the room to a large steel panel inlaid into the concrete wall and pressed his right hand against a LASER scanner to recognize his palm print and open the digital lock. With a soft click, the heavy door released, revealing a mass of military hardware arranged inside.

He reached in and took out a Kevlar vest for body protection and an assault helmet with a tempered full-face visor. He swung his glance across the multiple firearms waiting in the armored enclosure and decided on a Heckler & Koch G36 automatic rifle. It already had a clip in place, but his years in the field made him grab a spare and drop it into his vest. He smiled to himself as he felt its welcome weight but knew it was almost definitely unnecessary as he was certain thirty rounds of the steel jacketed 5.56 x 45mm NATO issued cartridges would more than suffice to end the problem posed by an unarmed girl, a teenager, and a university professor.

CHAPTER EIGHT

Assault On Park Lane

The rooftop suite at The Dorchester was even more beautiful and elegant than they had been led to expect. The six-room apartment featured an ornate gas fireplace with intricate moldings, bay windows with a balcony, a long, exquisite dining room table, enough for a dozen guests, and canopied four-poster beds in each individual bedroom. A welcoming gift basket overflowing with strawberries, chocolates, and champagne sat waiting to be enjoyed, on a small, marble-topped table near the doors to the outside terrace.

Cate was in awe as she tried to absorb it, "This hotel is classic. I feel like we've stepped into a Cary Grant and Katharine Hepburn movie set."

Alex had to agree, "They may have stayed here. The Dorchester was designed specifically for Europe and America's elite back in 1931. They installed all the latest fixtures for the day, elevators, central heating, air conditioning..."

Eddie slid back a partially open wall panel revealing a big, deep area behind it, "Even a space for a built-in TV."

Alex smiled, "It's a dumbwaiter. They didn't have televisions in the thirties."

"No TVs?" Eddie was shocked, "What did they do at night?"

"They had conversations, played chess, read books, and listened to radio shows. Television didn't become widely available to the general public for another decade, until after the end of World War II," said Alex.

"How do you know all this stuff? Do you have degrees in it?" wondered Eddie.

"Sometimes I think I do," replied Alex.

The house phone rang, interrupting them. Alex crossed to the sandalwood desk and answered it, "Hello?"

A familiar voice sounded in the receiver, "Hello, Mr. Turner. It's the front desk calling. I wanted to make sure the room is to your satisfaction."

"Absolutely. It seems to have everything we need," assured Alex.

"Glad to hear it. And will the three of you be staying in your room for a while?"

"I think so. Why?" It seemed a strange question.

"I ask it of all our guests who are new to our town. If you plan to go out tonight, please don't hesitate to call us first before you leave, so we can help you with any arrangements or reservations you might need made for shows or transportation."

"We will certainly do that, thank you."

Alex hung up and turned his attention back to his companions, "What's going on, Eddie? What happened to you? We've been told so many different things."

"All I know is some English dude came to see me at Juvie Hall, stuck me with something, and I woke up in London. A doctor must have done this to my hand, because I heard one talking about samples and a match being positive. Then I got out of there. That's it."

"Can I see what they did?" asked Cate.

Eddie held it out, "Be careful, it's really sore."

Cate slowly unwrapped the gauze bandage and grimaced at the sight beneath it, "They surgically removed a square patch of skin. It looks nasty."

"It doesn't feel good. Why would they do that to me?"

Alex thought through the possible reasons, "Medicine is not my field, so I can't be certain. But for all its size, it's shallow and not too intrusive. Perhaps it was to get a DNA sample."

"Why would they take so much skin? I got a DNA test kit for Christmas last year and it used spit. Couldn't they have done a swab in Eddie's mouth?"

"It wouldn't have hurt as bad," grinned Eddie.

"From what I've heard, they use saliva for commercial purposes," said Alex. "For medical accuracy, if bone isn't available, blood or skin, or a combination of both, is preferred, and a simple swab obviously can't take that. But something like this, with so much skin removed is puzzling. All I can think of is they wanted to run multiple tests for confirmation and decided on a larger sample."

"I'm glad they think of my hand as a larger sample!" said Eddie, sarcastically. "But I don't understand why would anyone want to do tests on me? They could have asked and I would have told them who my mom and dad were."

"That's one of the things we have to figure out, Eddie. Anything else you remember?"

"Yeah. When I woke up here in London, the doctor was calling the other dude, the one who drugged me in Cali, *'Mr. Brown'*."

Cate and Alex shot surprised glances at each other. Eddie picked up on their look, "Do you know him?"

"I think we do. It must be Colin Brown, the man who paid us to find you. You had no knowledge of him before, right? No meetings, calls, letters, anything?"

"No. He just showed up saying he was my uncle. I played along to get a break from working in the metal shop. I didn't know he was psycho."

"I'm more confused now than I was back in the States," Cate shook her head to gather her thoughts, "I'm going out on the terrace."

"Good idea. Let's all get some air."

They stood together on the wide stone balcony overlooking London's famed Hyde Park more than a hundred feet below, and gazed out at the spectacular view of the lights and the city at night.

"If we have time, maybe we could explore the park tomorrow. Susan and I saw The Cure play there a couple of years ago. Awesome experience," recalled Cate.

"Who are The Cure?" asked Eddie.

"The Cure are only one of the all-time great bands."

Eddie's look remained blank.

"Come on. You must have heard *Just Like Heaven* or *Friday I'm In Love* or *Fascination Street*?"

"Nope. Not on my playlist. Let me know if Billie Eilish comes in concert. I'd score tickets for that."

"I don't think we'll be seeing any shows while we're here. We need to figure out what's going on then get you back..." Alex almost said *home* and realized his error, "back to America."

"We should enjoy tonight. It's a beautiful evening. There's no traffic now."

They stared down at Park Lane. Cate was right. There was not a single car on the wide, multi-lane road.

"That's weird," said Eddie. "It's never once been like this since I got here. Usually it's a racetrack. There's always cars, and trucks, and buses, and bikes, all going around the park, twenty-four seven."

Cate pointed into the distance, "That could be the reason. See the flashing lights? It looks like an accident at the far end of the road. And there are more lights in that direction as well. Could be a couple of crashes holding up the traffic."

Alex stared at the red and blue lights and wasn't so sure, "But then it would be backed up here as well because nothing would be getting through or getting out. There'd be cars stuck below us, and they wouldn't be moving. Instead, the roads right here are completely empty. It's as if this hotel is the epicenter of something and they've cleared the area around it and are not letting traffic in. Almost like it's been sealed off." He sensed a serious problem and swung to Eddie, "Have you told us everything? Is there anything you've holding back?"

Eddie hesitated before he opened up, "There is one thing, but it's not true. I didn't want to tell you in case you thought it was."

"What is it?"

"They have my photograph in all the newspapers. They say I'm wanted for drug smuggling. But it's a lie, I've never done drugs, I never will, not after what happened to my mom. Worst I've done is steal things and hotwire cars. But the papers say it's drugs...and guns."

"Was your name in the paper with your picture?"

"Yeah. Huge letters. *EDDIE YORK*. Like I was an ad for something."

Alex's eyes opened wide, "My God! We told the clerk downstairs we were looking for you."

"And he saw you with us at the desk," added Cate, picking up on his urgency.

"And then he called to check we were all still in the room-"

A blinding light cut off his words, as a thirty-million candlepower nightsun spotlight burned across the three of them and the thundering of a Sea King helicopter's twin rotor blades drowned out their voices as the massive craft roared into view, hovering yards from the balcony.

Alex screamed to be heard, "Inside!"

They turned and high-tailed it into the suite that blazed white from the chopper's intense floodlight.

"What do we do?" Cate was frantic.

"We have to get Eddie out of the hotel," urged Alex.

Knowing when not to argue, Cate grabbed her backpack, and the fugitives sprinted for the door.

The Dorchester's busy lobby had been cleared of guests, and in their place, twenty heavily armed men in assault gear were assembled, waiting for their orders. Colin, equally equipped, marched forward with the desk clerk scurrying after him, and spread open a blueprint schematic of the hotel across one of the lobby's antique mahogany tables.

"Are they still in their room on the top floor?" demanded Colin.

"Yes, sir. They were when I called to check, as you told me to do. I haven't seen them come down." The clerk tried to conceal his nerves, confronted by these fearsome para-military troops.

"You have three elevators, correct?" Colin barked at the clerk.

"Three guest elevators. There's also a service elevator in the kitchen," the clerk quivered as he replied.

"I want them all shut down – but not the service elevator. My team will take it up. Can you do that?"

"Yes, sir, I can."

"Then don't stand here, get to it. Throw the switch or pull the plug. Whatever it takes. Shut them down now."

"Yes, sir." The clerk raced off to do as ordered.

Simon, also dressed in full tactical gear, joined Colin. "All my teams are in place. The entryway is sealed. This entire downstairs area is clear of civilians."

Colin nodded in approval, "Good. Our targets are on the top floor. The only way down now will be the two sets of stairs used for emergencies. Split your men into two groups of seven. Take both sets of the side stairs, leaving a man on each floor as you go up. No one is to pass them. That will seal off those exits. And remember, these people are armed and extremely dangerous. Take no chances. All measures can and should be used. I will not have any of your men hurt or injured. Understood?"

"I appreciate that. I'll have my teams on the stairs now. I will stay here and monitor the lobby. You can coordinate with me by radio."

"Roger that." Colin waved to the remaining five men waiting for their orders, "With me. We are going up."

The six trained killers pounded across the marble floors to the only elevator that remained functioning in the hotel.

In the hallway of the penthouse level, Alex, Eddie and Cate waited anxiously for an elevator to arrive. Cate reached forward and stabbed the already lit button.

"That won't make it come any quicker," Alex's tone was disparaging.

Cate shrugged, "Always works for me."

To spite him, she pushed the call button again. Alex glanced up at the antiquated display above the golden elevator doors. The three stationary arrows showed they were all still on the ground floor, not moving.

"It's no use, they're not coming. They've shut them down. We have to take the stairs." He turned and saw the lighted sign at the end of the long, carpeted hallway showing *Fire Exit.* "This way," called Alex, and the three of them took off at a run.

They reached the stairs in seconds and Eddie pushed open the fire door, but even as he hit the stark concrete landing of the hotel's emergency staircase, he paused. Below him, shaking the narrow passageway, was the unmistakable sound of men racing toward them.

"Shit. They're coming up," warned Eddie.

"We can't go this way either," said Alex, and they hustled back into the corridor.

"What now?" asked Cate.

Cate and Eddie stared at Alex, hoping this man who had uncomfortably assumed the mantle of leadership, could find a solution. He dropped his head forward into his hand. He was not used to this role, this responsibility. What should he do? A light went off in his brain.

"Back to the room," he cried.

"The room?" questioned Cate.

"Follow me." Alex was already running to their rooftop suite.

The door flew open and the hunted trio barreled back inside the luxury apartment.

"What are we doing?" Cate demanded.

"Getting out," yelled Alex.

"Are you nuts? There's no way out of here unless we jump off the balcony and die." Eddie frantically looked around what had become their palatial prison.

Alex was still moving. He reached the far wall by the dining room table, and slid open the panel concealing the ancient dumbwaiter, "We can go down this way."

Cate joined him, and even as Alex heaved on the heavy rope to bring up the big wooden box, she stared into the dark shaft plunging straight down eight floors through the hotel.

"We can't go in there," the fear in her voice was obvious.

"We have to. The stairs and the elevators have been closed off to us. There's no other way out." Alex did a last heave and the dumbwaiter clicked into place. "Okay, get in."

Cate looked at the big, open box dangling over the one-hundred-foot drop. It was four feet square, designed for bringing up huge, heavy trays loaded with dinners and drinks for the fortunate guests of the opulent penthouse suite, and secured only by an antiquated rope and pulley system. She shook her head violently, "In there? All of us?"

"Yes. It'll be tight, but we can make it work."

"Look, professor, I've got an idea. We've done nothing. We'll be okay. Eddie should go by himself. We can meet up with him later." Cate was desperate.

"Cate, something's happening here we don't understand. They have already faked Eddie's death, stolen him from a secure detention facility, transported him against his will between two countries, and carried out an unsanctioned operation on him. Those are all huge international violations of human rights and would not have been done lightly. You yourself said how much they have been willing to spend. Whoever these people are, whatever their motives, we can't let them take the boy. We have to get him out of here and go to the embassy on our terms, otherwise who knows what could happen to Eddie, or even to us."

Eddie pushed between the two of them and seized Cate's attention, "The professor is right. We all have to go. You saw what they did to me. If you stay, they'll do the same to you, or worse! They sent a helicopter after us, for fuck's sake. You don't do that if you're here to talk."

As Eddie finished his plea, the sound of thundering feet echoed down the corridor.

Cate flung her hand to her face, "Shit. I hate it when a kid's smarter than me." Not wanting to give herself the opportunity to change her mind, Cate scrambled into the dumbwaiter with her small backpack.

"Now you, Eddie," instructed Alex.

Eddie squeezed past, into the hanging box, as Alex gripped the rope.

"I'm getting in. Eddie, you and Cate hold the rope. It'll be the only thing keeping the dumbwaiter up after I release the brake and shut the door. Let go and we all drop straight down eight floors."

Cate grabbed the rope so hard her knuckles turned white.

Alex wedged his way into the open box, forcing himself to fit between Cate and Eddie. He reached back and closed the wall covering and then the door. "I'm releasing the brake lock now. Hold on so we don't fall." He hit the lever removing the metal rod acting as the braking mechanism.

CRASH!

The noise scared the dumbwaiter's passengers, but it was not made by them, it was the door of their suite being broken down and smashing onto the polished marble floor.

Knowing time was running out, they carefully lowered themselves through the darkness. Above them, they heard a voice they recognized calling out urgent orders as Colin Brown instructed his assault team to search the room.

Alex whispered, "That's him." He hesitated as a thought hit him, "I left my papers there, along with Eddie's records and birth certificate. And my notes."

"I don't have a copy of the birth certificate, but the research is in my laptop. I scanned it in, remember? I've got our passports and all your money, too."

"Thank God," replied Alex.

"Yes, because it's too late to get them now. Plus, I don't know what this is my hand is on, and I don't want to find out."

Slowly, quietly, they continued to lower the dumbwaiter inside the black shaft as they listened to Colin Brown's angry voice echoing down to them as he shouted in the room.

Colin paced the suite, watching as his men tore it apart room by room, searching for the fugitives. His radio crackled to life and he clicked it on, "Speak."

"The lobby's locked down. The stairwells are secure. No movement in any of the corridors. They must still be in their room," informed the voice on the radio.

Colin was furious, "Listen, Simon, I'm in the room, goddamn it, and they're not here! Find them. You have the girl's cell number in your files. Get Five to run a satellite tracker on her phone and pull up their location. I want it now!" He snapped the radio off and yelled to the team scouring the suite, "What do you have? Report."

The officer closest to him stopped and raised the visor of his assault helmet so he could be heard, "We've got nothing, sir. We swept the entire suite and found a couple of small bags containing clothes and toiletries, and a few papers. The room and the balconies are clear."

"How could they be clear?" Colin spun from the officer and scanned the room for the hundredth time, "Where did you go? You couldn't just vanish."

He stormed across to the long dining table and kicked over a chair in frustration, "Damn it, damn it, damn it." He whirled around and punched the wall violently with his gloved hand. The strength of his blow moved the wall slightly. But not inwards from the impact of his fist, instead, it slid sideways.

Colin stared in surprise and realized the intricately patterned design was not simply a part of the room's décor, it was a moveable board. He jumped forward, grabbed its edge and wrenched hard, and the panel rolled across revealing a door behind. He pulled it open and saw the vertical shaft dropping into a black hole. He ripped the LED flashlight from its Velcro holster on his chest and shone it into the darkness, illuminating the cables running up and down.

He jerked back out of the concrete shaft and shouted to summon his men, "On me now. They've got a way out."

In seconds, the tactical squad assembled, waiting for their orders.

"They've gone down this shaft. Sergeant, find out where it goes and have a team from the lobby get there yesterday. Two men will stay in this room in case it's a diversion. The other three, head to the ground floor now, double time. I'm going in there after them myself."

Colin stretched into the shaft, grabbed the first of the two heavy cables and swung himself into the tight, vertical chute. Instantly, he was climbing down the rope, hand over hand, with the speed only years of field experience can give.

It took him less than thirty seconds to make the one-hundred-foot descent, and his steel-toed boots thudded onto the roof of the dumbwaiter now locked in place on the ground floor, blocking his way. He stabilized himself by keeping a grasp on the rope and kicked. The ninety-year-old wooden frame was no match for his ferocity and his reinforced military issue footwear, and crumbled before his violent onslaught, turning the antique fixture into worthless kindling.

As it fell apart, Colin let himself drop into the shattered box and crawled quickly through the dumbwaiter's opening.

He sprung to his feet and found himself alone in the original kitchen of the Dorchester, now an unused storage area since the 1989 renovation. He spun the beam of his flashlight around the dark room, piled with boxes, tables, and chairs, and saw on the far side, an open door and outside light filtering in. Damn it, he thought, a way out.

Ignoring the automatic rifle strung across his back, he pulled his polymer-framed Glock 17 pistol from its holster and sprinted to the exit. He ran through it, into a long, dark alley stretching behind the Dorchester and the multiple hotels lining Park Lane, an alley with a hundred possible exits leading on one side to a myriad of narrow streets, mews, and even international embassies, and on the other to Hyde Park, big enough to hold festivals and gatherings for a million people, and full of trees, lodges, lakes, and rivers. An easy place for three scared Americans to disappear at night.

Colin pulled off his headgear and flung the carbon-fiber tactical helmet to the ground. As it clattered and rolled across the paved passageway, he glanced down and saw a smashed cell phone lying there. He screamed a single word that echoed in both directions between the high walls of the almost endless alley, "FUCK!"

CHAPTER NINE

Whitechapel

The derelict bandstand in Hyde Park had once again been Eddie's shelter for the night, but along with the half-dozen homeless people curled up there, keeping him company, were Alex and Cate.

As the early morning light swept across the massive grounds, Alex stirred, forcing himself awake. He willed his eyes to open and saw Cate sitting up against the wooden rail, staring around.

"How did you sleep?" asked Alex.

"Don't ask. I kept dreaming about those four-poster beds at the hotel. I got two hours, maybe a little longer."

"It was the same with me. I'm going to wake Eddie. We should get moving."

The sun was higher now, and the three of them ate an unhealthy breakfast of powdered doughnuts and instant coffee as they sat in front of a small café overlooking the sparkling, centuries-old man-made lake, the Serpentine, snaking its way through London's largest Royal park.

Eddie looked up from his third doughnut, "Do I have to wear this?" He tugged at the cheap, white T-shirt he had on with the enormous logo, *I Love London,* exploding across his chest.

"It's better than the filthy doctor's jacket. Having that over your jumpsuit was a beacon to alert everyone looking for us," said Alex.

"Now you look like a regular goofy tourist enjoying their European vacation," grinned Cate.

"With orange pants!" He raised a leg to show his jumpsuit below the T-shirt.

"I'm sorry, but the café only had a few things like souvenir T-shirts and baseball caps for sale, no jeans. Hardly haute couture. We're lucky the doughnuts are edible," said Cate.

"Keep it on, and the sunglasses and hat, otherwise you're too recognizable." Alex brought his companions back to earth, "We must decide on what to do next and put together a plan of action. Obviously, we have to go to the American Embassy, but without a copy of Eddie's birth certificate, we need to know how to explain to them what has happened, otherwise they may just take Eddie away and turn him over to whoever was after us at the hotel. Let's go through this, what do we know?"

"Apart from the fact last night was the most miserable and scary of my life, you smashed my beloved cell phone, and Global Pharmaceuticals has an army at their disposal? Nothing," said Cate.

"If you buy another phone, get one of those cheap pay-as-you-go ones. It won't have a listed number they can track us with. My friends and me used to get those so the cops couldn't listen in and bust us. We called them *burners*," offered Eddie.

Alex raised his eyebrows as he learned more than he wanted to know about the teen's troubled past.

Cate was more upset about losing her phone than bothered by Eddie's dubious tips, "At least I had my contacts and photos backed up to the cloud so I can download them from there."

"I hope it won't come to that and we can take care of everything today and put all of this behind us," Alex was trying to keep them focused on the task ahead.

Eddie kicked in a thought, "One thing I can't stop thinking about is, how did you know where I was when the Colin dude wanted you to find me?"

"He didn't say 'find Eddie York'; he was looking for any surviving descendants of one particular person. We began back in 1892 with your great-great-great-grandmother, Mary Kelly. Did you know your family's roots are here in London?"

Eddie shook his head, "I barely knew my own folks, never mind some great-great from the stone age."

"Right," agreed Alex. "I think we should start over and check if we missed anything that could give us a clue to what is going on and gather as much information as we can. Let's go to where Mary lived and see if we are able to find something there which could help."

The taxi rank at Marble Arch was packed with cabs waiting for a fare. As the trio approached, the driver at the head of the orderly line called out, "Where are you off to today?"

Alex answered the cheerful, ruddy-faced cabbie, "I'm not sure what part of London we're going to. All I have is a street address, 13 Miller's Court."

"I can tell you where that is, it's Whitechapel. And this is a cab, not a TARDIS, mate."

"A TARDIS? I don't know what that is?"

"It's a bleedin' time machine. You'd need one to get to where you want to go."

"I'm sorry, I'm not following?"

The cabbie slowed down his cockney delivery to make himself understood, "Miller's Court ain't been there for more than a century. And everyone's safer with it gone."

"Why would that be?" Alex still didn't understand.

"Now that's a story. They called it the wickedest street in all of London. In the end people got so scared they bulldozed the whole bloody thing to get rid of it. Tore down more than two hundred houses. Miller's Court, Dorset Street, all of it, gone and reduced to rubble. Did a better job with their bulldozers than Jerry did with the Blitz."

"Some pretty awful things must have happened there," Cate found it hard to comprehend how bad it would have to be to merit the destruction of so many homes.

"The worst. The city had never seen the likes of it. The devil himself walked those streets and they never caught him. Some say even now, Jack's out there, waiting, watching."

"Jack?" Alex had not come across a Jack in his lineage research.

"Jack the Ripper. I thought you knew that? I get a lot of Yank tourists like you asking about old Jack. I could make a bloody fortune and do me own private tours if 13 Miller's Court was still standing."

"Why there?" asked Alex.

"It's where he did in his final victim. Chopped her up a treat, he did. There were bits of her all over the room. They found what was left of her body on the morning of the ninth of November. And it was the last time he killed. No one heard from Jack again after he turned the place into a slaughterhouse back in 1888. It's like poor Mary was his masterpiece." The driver was proud of his knowledge of London's dark history.

"Mary?" The name gave Alex pause.

"Mary Kelly. The whore who lived at 13 Miller's Court. She was the Ripper's final victim."

The massive road split apart and slowly lifted in two sections into the air. A thousand tourists captured the moment on their cell phone cameras and then took videos of the sailing barge passing beneath the iconic structure of Tower Bridge.

Cate, Eddie and Alex had a clear view of the occurrence that only happened on average twice a day, but they were not concerned with recording the spectacular event and texting the pictures to jealous relatives on the other side of the world. They were at the river because they knew they had to keep moving and stay invisible, and this was the perfect place. The fortress-like structure over the Thames, with its magnificent hanging blue cables, gave them a chance to disappear unnoticed into a crowd because all the attention was focused away from them and onto the monument and the majesty of the bridge opening, a sight which always attracted vast numbers of tourists.

Alex was still running through what the cabbie had told him and trying to find a meaning to it, "I didn't think to put Mary's name together with Jack the Ripper's killings, because the letter was sent four years after the last murder was committed. How could our Mary Kelly have been killed in 1888 when she wrote the letter in 1892?"

"Maybe the cops got it wrong. Maybe it wasn't her," suggested Eddie.

"The driver said Jack the Ripper did terrible things to his victims, that she was cut up and bits of her were all over the room," Cate shuddered at the thought. "What if she couldn't be recognized?"

"And the cops made the wrong ID?" added Eddie.

"That's possible. They didn't have forensics in the nineteenth century like we do today, and usually relied upon witness statements and word-of-mouth identification. And the name and address definitely matches, along with the letter Mary wrote which says she was haunted by what happened to Joy that night, so we know she was there. Could Jack have killed Joy instead of Mary, and for some reason he thought, or the police thought, the victim was Mary Kelly? Though why that mistake would happen, I don't know," Alex racked his brain to make sense of it.

"But it was more than a hundred years ago. None of it's got anything to do with me. I want to go back to the States."

"And back to Juvie Hall?" asked Cate.

"Yeah, better than this shit."

"I understand," Alex was sympathetic to the young boy's plight. "But before we go to the Embassy, we have to be able to give them an explanation. You've got no passport, no birth certificate and you escaped from a detention center in California. They'll ask how you got here and what your point of entry into the UK was. Without that, even with our word," he glanced at Cate, "it will all mean nothing. They'll hand you over to the British authorities for charges and deportation. And they want you for more than illegal entry, after last night we can be certain of it. I feel responsible for what is happening to you. Why are you so important to them, Eddie? That's what we have to find out. We must learn more, and fortunately it all seems to lead right here, to London. And there's one place close by that will have the answers we need."

The taxi dropped them on Great Russell Street, and as they climbed out of the cab, they gazed up in awe at the building sprawling in front of them.

"It's like a Greek temple," said Cate.

"It was built to look that way, but as much as I would enjoy standing here, appreciating the design, we need to go inside and find the library," suggested Alex.

"The library?" Eddie was not excited at the prospect.

"It's called the Round Reading Room. I'm told it is quite something."

The three of them joined the crowds pushing through the wrought-iron gates into the long, paved courtyard leading to the dozen steps marking the entrance to the British Museum, a treasure trove containing the history of the world.

The museum was always packed, as visitors from across the globe were drawn there to not only admire the magnificent architecture but also to explore the labyrinth of unique exhibits on display within. Alex led the way past the sculptures, marbles, paintings, and exhibitions as he followed the signs to the venerable British Library.

They entered the immense circular room featuring three levels for the two million-plus books housed there, and stared up at the enormous dome arching one hundred and forty feet across, lined with curved windows allowing the natural light to filter in on them.

"This is unbelievable," Cate was stunned by the room's beauty.

"It's always been a place I wanted to visit," said Alex. "Definitely one of the world's great libraries. I have read so much about it." He reluctantly forced himself to look away from the intricacies of the construction design, "If only we had more time. But we don't, we have to get to work and find the section dealing with London in the late eighteen hundreds and Jack the Ripper."

They started toward the librarian's circular desk in the dead center of the gigantic room, when Eddie began to drag his feet. Alex looked at him curiously.

"Hey, guys. I'm not into libraries and stuff. Books kind of give me the creeps. I saw a sign for a race car exhibit upstairs. Can I check it out while you do this?"

"If you must," said Alex. "But meet us back here in thirty minutes."

"Will do!" Eddie was all smiles as he ran off through the crowd.

Alex turned to Cate, "Books give him the creeps? There's something very wrong with that boy!"

He started toward the shelves containing the reference files on The Ripper's case and related murders in Whitechapel.

Cate grabbed his shoulder, "I'll be here at this table. I need to charge my laptop and they've got power outlets. I'm going to do an online search."

"That makes sense. I'll find the books we want and come back with them. We'll go through them together." Alex continued to the shelves.

Cate sat and pulled the laptop from her backpack, plugging it in. She flipped open the screen and clicked on *view available networks*.

The British Museum home page filled the screen with a prompt asking for a charge card number for internet access. Cate found her credit card and keyed in the details. After a few seconds *charge accepted* appeared and Cate began her search by typing in Jack the Ripper.

Less than a mile away, in the stone and glass building at Vauxhall Bridge overlooking the Thames, ten operatives monitored individual screens and giant floor-to-ceiling displays showing watch lists and locations from around the world.

An alarm sounded at one of the desks and the staffer immediately focused on the information coming across her screen. She hit a series of keys to confirm what she was seeing, then picked up her internal phone. When it was answered, she spoke quickly and succinctly, "It's them, sir."

The staffer was overwhelmed to be in Colin Brown's office. Access to this area of the building was highly restricted, and employees with her lowly clearance designation never had the chance to see it, but she had been summoned, so she seized the opportunity to find out what actually happened on this hallowed floor. She tried to conceal her excitement as the man, a section chief and top-ranking agent with the Overseas Operatives, far above her almost entry-level position, faced her.

"Sir, the charge card matches a name on the watch list, Caitlin Shannon. The IP address is linked to the British Museum on Great Russell Street."

"They're there?" It was a demand, not a question.

She quivered slightly at his aggressive tone, knowing his reputation, "I don't know if all of them are, sir, but it was Caitlin Shannon's card being used, for sure."

Colin picked up his phone to convey the information to the person waiting patiently on hold, "Simon, after yesterday's debacle, my people have done Five's job for them. We've traced one of their computers to a location at the British Museum. I want your ready teams from Five to roll now. Details will be sent on route. You'll be there before me. Don't wait, and don't screw this up. You know the drill; I'll meet you there."

The staffer raised her ears at what she heard; Five were working with them on this? A joint op? This was big.

Colin hung up the phone and saw the surveillance operator hovering in front of him. "Why are you still here?" he snapped.

"After I recognized her charge card, I hacked into her computer to see what she was doing. I thought it might be helpful for you to know what files the girl was accessing in the museum," she explained.

"And?"

"They were on Jack the Ripper, sir." She didn't understand why it happened, but as she spoke those words, the blood drained from the hardened officer's face.

Alex was lost in the books chronicling The Ripper's killings. He diligently jotted down notes as additional information presented itself. While he worked, Cate took a moment to lean back and stretch after being hunched forward over her computer.

She flexed and glanced longingly at the inviting sunshine through the old windows. It was a beautiful late summer day in London and here she was, stuck indoors. But better this famed library than *the dungeon* in Wisconsin. Cate swung her gaze further down the long street and stiffened in horror.

Three armored vehicles roared onto Great Russell Street and slammed to a halt outside of the museum. The double doors at the rear of each transport flew open and armed assault teams leaped out, checking their heavy weaponry as they assembled in squads, awaiting their orders.

Stunned, Cate snapped her laptop shut and talked quickly as she stuffed it into her backpack, "Alex, we got to go. They're outside. The same men as last night. They've found us here!"

It took one look out of the windows to confirm Cate's words, "We have to get Eddie," he said.

They jumped to their feet and hurried through the silent library.

The arrival of the armed tactical teams threw the huge lobby of the British Museum into confusion. Already two black-uniformed men with automatic weapons had taken their place on either side of the long staircase blocking access to the upper floors. Seeing their presence, and a dozen more armed men assembling in front of the main doors, caused a wave of panic to sweep through the throngs of tourists, many of whom pushed toward the exit, trying to leave.

Cate stared at the men guarding the stairs, "They've got the way up closed off. We can't get to Eddie to warn him."

As she spoke, a series of low thuds rang out, as bolts pushed down into the marble and locked the gigantic glass entry doors in place. Only the center two remained open, with the armed guards stretched in line in front of them to monitor everybody leaving.

"We're trapped too," said Cate.

Alex spun his gaze around the lobby, searching for a way out as the flood of worried visitors heading for the exit continued to increase. He saw four colorful flags moving through the air, marking the whereabouts of a large group of Japanese students who hurried to leave the museum.

"This is our chance," Alex said to Cate, "Stick close to me." He pushed across the tide of people in the lobby and forced his way into the middle of the students. As they matched their pace and flow toward the door, Alex raised his voice and commenced a lecture at the top of his lungs, "As we leave the building please look up at the columns at the front of the museum. They were built in the classic style of Ionic construction, and designed by the acclaimed architect Sir Robert Smirke, who had them installed in 1823.”

The group was now past the doors and crossing to the steps where another squad of military-outfitted personnel waited to do a secondary screening if needed. Alex continued in his most bombastic voice, “The initial origins of the British Museum lie in the will of Sir Hans Sloane.”

The children around him didn't understand a word this strange man was saying and kept moving forward hoping to be rid of him soon. To the waiting guards it was yet another school group with their teachers, one of the hundreds coming every day to visit this national landmark. Definitely nothing for them to be concerned with.

Alex's unrelenting lecture echoed across the smooth stone steps, “Sloane wanted his collection of 71,000 objects preserved. He bequeathed it to King George II. If refused, the collection, in its entirety, was to be offered abroad.”

Armed men raced by the large cluster of children and their boring professor, ignoring them as they headed inside.

Now they had reached the massive gates leading to Great Russell Street and past the cordon of guards. The waiting teacher heard Alex's ongoing dissertation and marched angrily into the packed gathering of young students, “What do you think you are doing?” was her challenge.

Alex faked a smile, “Teaching the class about the museum.”

“You know they don't speak English? Please leave now.”

“With pleasure.”

Alex and Cate ran across the wide street to safety, hunkering down behind the rows of parked cars to stay out of sight and wait for Eddie.

Cate stared over the road to the museum's portico where a string of armed men now fully blocked the exits and only let the people through a few at a time, so each could be individually checked and vetted, “We just made it out.”

“But what will Eddie do? He's trapped inside,” Alex's tone reflected the boy's hopeless position.

Two floors up, in the main exhibition hall, Eddie stood transfixed and drooled over a 1957 Vanwall race car painted British Green. A large walk-through display celebrating the career of the famed driver, Stirling Moss, surrounded the classic vehicle.

He pulled his eyes from the racer as he sensed a buzz going through the crowded room. The cause of the anxiety soon appeared, two uniformed assault officers, brandishing automatic rifles, were beginning to sweep the area.

"Shit," Eddie whispered to himself, as he started away from the imminent threat. He pushed through the people and found himself at the back of the exhibit, his way blocked by a wall.

He stayed against the wall and followed it until he saw a narrow blue door marked *Staff Only*. He tried the handle and the door opened. Relieved, he slipped inside.

He clicked the light on and saw he was in an electrical room and cleaning closet. It was small and tight, with a bank of fuses and heavy-duty throw switches on one wall, and on the other side, mops, buckets, supplies, and uniforms packed the shelves.

Eddie took one of the dark blue, full-length janitor's outfits and zipped it on, gladly discarding his torn and filthy prison jumpsuit, I Love London T-shirt and baseball cap. He grabbed a cloth hat which was more of a hairnet, and pulled it on, tucking his long hair up inside. He'd worn a similar head-covering once before, to keep his hair from the frying oil, when he needed money and worked the cooking line at a hamburger joint in Oakland. He'd hated the hairnet then, and he hated it now, but it was his only option.

He stepped back out from the closet, carrying with him a mop and bucket to complete his working appearance, and carefully maneuvered towards the exit. It was slow going through the mass of people, and soon he saw why. Only one of the four doors was open, and it was blocked by the guards who let the visitors leave one by one only after checking their identity against a photograph they held. He was convinced he knew whose picture they held, and that this little disguise wouldn't be enough.

Eddie pulled out of the line once again and this time headed to the windows. They gave him no hope. His was on the third floor and the old building had leaded glass designed to filter the direct sunlight and protect the irreplaceable exhibits. He might be able to break through one, but it would take too long and attract unwelcome attention. Everything this museum had in place to guard the precious displays; the heavy doors, the thick windows, the stone walls, acted as a prison to keep him in.

It was then he saw something they had installed to shield the building that actually might work to help him. Every seven yards along the wall, mounted at five feet above the floor, running in a perfectly straight line, were a series of small, glass enclosed fire alarms. He looked at the packed crowd of at least a thousand people already unnerved and pushing to get out of the hall and smiled. He knew what was about to happen.

Eddie edged his way to the nearest alarm, hit the glass hard with his elbow, and in seconds was rewarded with the sound of piercing sirens.

Instantly the mass of people froze, trying to understand this new threat. Did it affect them or was it someplace else in the vast museum? Eddie cleared up any doubt they had in their minds by yelling at the top of his lungs, "Fire! Fire! There's flames!"

A group of women spun to his voice and in their eyes saw a uniformed employee calling out a terrifying warning for help. That was all it took. Eddie's yells were picked up by hundreds of others who turned them into panicked screams and cries of fire.

Eddie hurried back into the janitor's closet and threw the switches on the fuse panels. Immediately the overhead strips went off and small emergency lights powered on, the sudden lighting change unleashing more shrieks of terror from the trapped people.

Eddie jumped out and yelled again, letting panic rip through his words, "Run! Everything's burning back here."

Mob mentality seized control and the people rushed forward for the single exit, surging past the two armed guards who were helpless to stop this racing army of frightened souls.

Eddie allowed the momentum of the pack to carry him on, and in seconds he was through the doors and on the landing above the first flight of steps.

Two floors below him, the patient crowd waiting to be released through the museum's doors saw the horde tumbling out onto the upper stairs and heard the piercing sound of the fire alarm. They looked back and forth in horror and shock, and as the fearful throng from the exhibition hall battled down the stairs, their screams of *FIRE!* filled the air.

The entire museum became a madhouse, with people running, sprinting, sobbing, and pushing their way to the main exit. Men elbowed past women and children to save themselves, and the sheer weight of their numbers bowled over the thin line of guards who vainly attempted to block the doors as the first of the tidal wave of panic-stricken people burst from the museum onto the huge portico outside.

From across the street, Alex and Cate watched the explosion of bodies pouring down the steps toward the road, and behind them heard the multiple sirens of approaching firetrucks ringing out, adding to the mayhem.

Alex pulled his eyes from the chaos and looked at Cate, "Eddie?"

She grinned, "Eddie."

The culprit had now reached the massive lobby and the doors to safety were only yards from him when he saw an elderly lady knocked roughly to the ground. Boots and shoes pummeled her as people ran past, ignoring the helpless woman and her struggles to get up, but Eddie rushed over, used his body as a shield to block her from the terrified, pounding crowd and helped her back to her feet.

"I don't want to die in the fire," she sobbed. It was hard for her to catch enough breath to talk.

"You won't die, I promise. I'll get you out," reassured Eddie.

"Bless you."

Eddie looped his arm under the old woman's shoulders and continued toward the enormous doors, but much slower now.

Outside, among the police cars and firetrucks continuing to arrive at the scene, a blue 850i BMW screeched to a halt by the main gates and Colin jumped from it. He was in his civilian suit, but wore an identifying laminate badge around his neck. Whatever was printed on the ID worked, and the police waved him through their security barrier without a challenge.

Colin took only a few paces onto the grounds before he realized the extent of the uncontrolled chaos. A sea of distressed tourists pushed past him in their desperate flight from the building and the blaze they thought was waiting to consume them. Knowing this pandemonium had probably ended any chance of his operation being a success, he threw his hands to his head in frustration, then pulled himself together and sprinted to the museum's steps in a last-minute attempt to try and restore order.

Eddie was on the enclosed portico and moving toward the supporting colonnade when he saw Colin Brown approaching at a run. He turned slightly so the old lady he half carried was on his far side and protected, and lurched violently into Colin. He hit him hard with his shoulder, and threw him off balance. The running man reeled from the unexpected impact, and staggered backward, but Eddie reached out and caught him with his free arm, steadying him, and brushing him down.

"Sorry about that, mate. Me and me Granny didn't see you," Eddie used his best Dick Van Dyke English accent.

"Fucking idiot," barked Colin, who pushed himself away and ignoring the clumsy janitor, blew past him and the old lady, disappearing inside the crazed museum.

At the bottom of the steps, Eddie gently let go of the pensioner. "Will you be all right now?" he checked.

"I will. You're an angel." She gave him a peck on the cheek and hobbled off.

Eddie started out of the gate and saw Alex and Cate waving to him from across the street. With a huge grin he raced over to them.

"Did you see their big-ass guns? So cool!" riffed the excited teen.

"Except they wanted to shoot us with their big-ass bullets," answered Cate.

"We'll talk later. Let's get out of here before we're spotted," said Alex, taking over.

"Okay. But we're driving." Eddie dangled a set of car keys.

"Where did those come from?"

"A gift from my uncle. Along with this," he waved a crocodile skin wallet at them.

"Did you get them from him the same way you got mine?" asked Alex.

"Pretty much. Now where's his car?" Eddie saw the BMW logo on the key fob, "We're looking for *The Ultimate Driving Machine*." He hit the alarm and right across from them, the lights on a blue Beemer blinked twice.

"Good job. Let's go." Alex led them to the car and their ticket to freedom.

The immense museum and courtyard stood empty of tourists, and was occupied now by a hundred confused firefighters called out to answer the thankfully false alarm, along with thirty armed police, and Simon's assault teams. Simon led Colin away from the others to a quiet alcove at the edge of the portico.

"I set it up exactly as you had instructed, closing down the exits and running a tight perimeter. It would have been easier if I didn't have to rely solely on Five's resources. If I could have called on the police department right at the beginning-"

"No." Colin cut him off, "You know we can't risk this getting out and that's why we have to keep our dealings with the regular cops to a minimum. They're not bound by any secrecy oath. The fewer people aware of this the better. Let them think they're after armed criminals and terrorists. It has to remain that only you and I, and our American equivalents, have a grasp on the truth."

Simon's face showed his reluctant agreement with the rationale.

Colin continued, "We need to pull the museum's security tapes and hard drives before anyone else gets to them. I'll have them reworked, then release them along with a story to the press. I should be able to have it out within the next two hours."

He walked with Simon down the steps towards the street, furious at his failure to end this, here and now, "How can it be so tough to find three Americans? They don't even know the city for Christ's sake!"

The entire block was in chaos. The thirty firetrucks that had raced across London from four different stations, summoned to save the treasured building, re-spooled their heavy hoses and locked back down their ladders. Police cars, which had responded after picking up on the news of the disturbance, were now needed elsewhere and pulled away, leaving behind only six vehicles and their officers positioned to safely disperse the remaining stragglers fleeing the three-centuries-old museum.

Adding to the tumultuous scene were hundreds of curious onlookers, along with camera crews from the BBC, ITV, Sky News and CNN who had arrived to film the fire.

Colin stopped to take in the mess stretching up and down Great Russell Street, and saw his hopes of keeping this a limited and quick operation, dashed, "This is a damn circus!" It was then a thought hit him, and he looked hard at the road right in front of the main gates, searching for something that should have been there. He turned to Simon, even though he knew he wouldn't be able to answer his shouted question, "Where the fuck is my car?"

CHAPTER TEN

Legoland

The BMV drove fast through central London, too fast. But its excessive speed was not the reason so many people turned to stare at the racing vehicle. It was the fact the high-powered car was hurtling in the wrong direction down a one-way street.

Eddie wrenched the wheel hard to the left, fishtailing the sports sedan and barely avoiding yet another collision as a delivery truck swerved by, angrily sounding its horn.

"These Brits are crazy. They're all on the wrong side," stated Eddie.

"You're on the wrong side. They drive on the left. You're going to get us killed," warned Cate.

"Slow down and pull over. We're far enough away now. We have to decide our next move," Alex was all business, knowing the huge problems facing them still had to be solved.

Eddie saw his opportunity ahead and pulled into a small cul-de-sac and stopped.

"Hot car," said Eddie as he admired the precision German vehicle.

"Right." Alex didn't care what they were driving in, he was looking for solutions, "What do you think happened back there, Cate? How did they find us?"

"I don't know. Is there a way we could have been followed?"

"While you guys are working things out, check out the dude's stuff. But I claim dibs on any money." He tossed Colin's wallet to Alex who was next to him in the front passenger seat.

Alex flipped through it, "About four hundred pounds in here, a driving license, and some business cards, including his. Not much to go on."

Cate leaned forward from the back seat, "Anything in the glove compartment?"

Alex tried to open it but failed, "It's locked."

Eddie grabbed the keys and handed them to Alex, "Try one of the smaller ones."

The glove box opened on his second attempt. Alex reached inside and snatched his hand back almost as quickly, "He's got a gun in there!"

"And you're surprised after what we've been through?" Cate rolled her eyes.

"This is England, not Texas. Nobody has handguns here," answered Alex.

"Any other cool things?" wondered Eddie.

"If you consider a gun *cool*," said Alex. "Let me see."

He pulled out some paperwork and a manual for the vehicle, along with a manila envelope. "So what is in here?" Alex unclipped the envelope's flap and shook the contents onto his lap. Six passports tumbled out, and a tightly wrapped, bank-labelled set of one-hundred-pound notes.

"Is that-" asked Eddie.

"Yes," confirmed Alex. He read the amount printed on the label, "Ten thousand pounds."

"Wow, Colin Brown is nothing but money," said Cate. "How about the passports?"

"That's what I'm checking now." Alex opened them, one after another. They all featured Colin Brown's photograph, but only two used that name. The other four not only had different names, but also different birth dates and countries of origin.

"Our man is very intriguing. He has six passports. Two are from the UK, but they're not the same, only one has him as Colin

Brown, and the other four are from all over the world, Australia, Canada, South Africa, and even the US."

"I've made a bunch of fake IDs. I used them to buy beer," offered Eddie.

"I think Mr. Brown's motives may vary considerably from yours. And it's worth noting all the countries the passports are from are English speaking."

"Is that a big deal?" asked Eddie.

"It would be if you wanted people to believe you are from there. If he had a Swedish passport but didn't speak the language fluently, it could arouse suspicions," explained Alex.

"But why would anyone have six passports, and how would he get them?" Cate was not following Alex's train of thought.

"I'm not sure. I don't know why a businessman would want so many aliases unless it was for tax fraud. He might have them for setting up multiple bank accounts in different countries which could be used for transferring and laundering money. That would explain all his cash." He looked again at the wallet, "He has a blank business card with just his name and a central London address, 85 Vauxhall Cross, Albert Embankment. Let's find out where that is and see what company he really works for."

"The car's got navigation. If it's his workplace, it's probably in there already." Eddie pressed the ignition button and fired up the car. He reached out to the touchscreen and opened the navigation, "There you go, under previous destinations, 85 Vauxhall Cross. We'll do a drive by."

"On the left side," reminded Cate.

Eddie pulled the car carefully out of the alleyway and turned so he was finally heading with the flow of traffic along the one-way street.

He glanced at the screen, "It says we'll be there in eleven minutes. We follow the river and turn left on the third bridge."

The blue BMW cruised down Victoria Embankment, paralleling the water, past the gigantic London Eye on the far side of the Thames then inland as they passed The Houses of Parliament and Big Ben.

They stayed silent as they drove, each lost in their own thoughts about the crazy world they had been thrust into, and it wasn't until they crossed Vauxhall Bridge that Eddie spoke, "There it is. The white and green building. It's the first new thing I've seen today. I thought all of London was ancient and rundown."

Alex had a thousand things he wanted to explain to the young boy to contradict his *ancient and rundown* statement, starting with the words, *living history*, but knew it would take too long, and they were almost at their destination.

Eddie stopped the car on Albert Embankment, across from the enormous complex, "That's it, whatever it is,' said Eddie.

"I'm not sure what to make of it. I don't know if I like it or not." pondered Cate. "It's kind of a cross between a Mayan Temple and an art deco hotel in Miami."

"It's weird," said Eddie. "But it looks sort of familiar, like I saw it online or in a movie."

"There are no signs anywhere on the building. Certainly nothing saying Global Pharmaceuticals, and there are people outside taking pictures, as if it's a tourist attraction," Alex was stumped. "Can you pull up, Eddie? There's a bus stop ahead. Let's see if someone there knows."

Eddie put the car into gear and rolled forward to the Vauxhall Cross stop. Alex leaned out of the window and called to a waiting passenger, "Excuse me. Do you know what the big building across the street is?"

The man shrugged as if it were a stupid question, "Of course I do. That's Legoland."

"Legoland? It's an amusement park?"

"Hardly. It's what we call it 'round here on account of the way it looks. You know, like they built it out of blocks of Lego. It's the MI6 headquarters."

Eddie heard the comment and butted in, "MI6? What's MI6?"

"Are all you Americans daft or something? MI6 is the British Secret Service. It's where James Bond works."

"Thank you," said Alex. He rolled his window back up, and Eddie saw the professor's face had changed. Concern was written across it, "I think we had better go right now."

"Where to?"

"Anywhere but here. Go!"

"Done." Eddie slipped the car into drive and squealed away.

"Slow down!" Alex yelled. "We can't attract attention."

Surprised by his aggressive tone, Eddie reluctantly eased his heavy foot off the accelerator and dropped the car to the speed limit.

As they headed along Albert Embankment, Alex saw a sign and continued his orders to Eddie, "Take a left up ahead, and go down toward Covent Garden."

Eddie did as asked, and after a few hundred yards Alex barked out another set of instructions, "Right, at the next corner. Where it says Miles Street. Turn and park."

The blue Beemer pulled off the busy street and stopped on the quiet road.

"What's here?" asked Cate.

"I don't know," replied Alex. "But we're away from the main streets and there doesn't seem to be anyone around. We need to dump the car and this seems to be a good place."

"Dump the car?" Eddie was shocked, "Why? She's beautiful. Can't we take her to a freeway so I can open her up?"

"Eddie, everything has changed. We're not being sought by a pharmaceutical company; we are being hunted by MI6. Do you understand we have stolen a British secret agent's car and are driving around in it less than a mile from his headquarters?" He paused to let that sink in, "Don't you think he could have a tracking device in here?"

"Like a LoJack from Hell? Fuck. He might even have a self-destruct and blow us up!" His teenage fantasies took over and in seconds Eddie was out of the car, and right behind him, Alex and Cate followed suit.

Alex hesitated before closing the car's door and reached in for the money and passports, and stuffed them back into the envelope. "We should bring them with us," he said, and handed them to Cate.

She was unsure about taking them, "Isn't this theft?"

"No, it's evidence. We can show the fake passports and all the cash as proof of our story when we go to the American Embassy, otherwise they'll never believe us and it will be our word against theirs."

"Should we bring his gun, too?" asked Eddie.

"No. It stays in the car. The last thing we need is to be caught with a firearm in a country that has strict gun control like Britain. They would lock us up and throw away the key."

As they hurried down Miles Street, Eddie shot a glance over his shoulder, "Still there. It hasn't blown up yet. Nicest car I've ever-"

"Stolen?" Cate offered.

"I was going to say driven," grinned Eddie. "But whatever." He stopped for a second and gazed wistfully at the Beemer.

"Don't even think about going back, Eddie. We'll keep walking, put some distance between us and Mr. Brown's vehicle, and see if there is anywhere around here where we can eat. We have to make plans and get our story straight for the embassy."

Cate checked out the buildings on the big street they were crossing, "There are hotels there. Could we...?"

Alex shook his head in denial and pointed across the road to a sign reading Victoria Park, "No hotels, we can't risk it. They'll want to see our passports and run a credit card. We'll come back and find a place to sleep in there tonight. Hopefully, we can put all this behind us tomorrow when we have figured things out, but until then..." It was Alex's turn to let his words fade away.

Grease dripped from the walls of the little back street fish'n'chip shop, but it was out of the way and the beer-battered cod was hot, and that's all Alex cared about.

Eddie paused between bites and became wistful, "I would have loved to have cranked the car just once."

"And how far do you think we would have gotten?" Alex burst his bubble.

"Yeah, it probably would have turned into me leading the secret service on a high-speed chase down the freeway and ended with a shootout and a couple of cars flipping over and blowing up like in the Fast and Furious." Eddie stuffed a handful of chips into his mouth and sprayed some of them on the table as a thought hit him, "I wonder if it had a passenger ejector seat?"

"Screw the movies. Will you promise this is our last night of sleeping rough? Can we please go to the American Embassy tomorrow?" complained Cate.

"We will, first thing in the morning. We'll take our chances. We've done nothing really wrong. We'll show them what we found in the car and explain-"

Eddie cut them both off, "Hey guys, we're on TV!"

Cate and Alex swiveled in their seats to see the little television above the counter where the six o'clock news had started and was running their big story of the day.

The concerned newsreader continued, "...an unprecedented attack on the British Museum was foiled today by the Metropolitan Police and MI5 before the trio of bombers could detonate their explosives."

The presenter was replaced by security camera footage showing the three of them entering through the museum's main doors together.

The announcer continued to talk beneath the video, "More than eight thousand people were evacuated and six pounds of military grade C4 explosives were removed from the heritage building which the female suspect is believed to have carried into the museum in her backpack."

A close-up zoomed onto the screen of Cate and her bag.

"The suspects are three Americans."

Individual photographs and names flashed on the television to match the commentary, "Alex Turner, 45. Caitlin Shannon, 25. Eddie York, 17. York was previously wanted on firearms and drug charges. He has been joined by two other Americans who have a record of radical political activism back in the United States. The bombers are heavily armed and considered extremely dangerous. If seen, do not approach them. Call 999 and give the police your location. Do not attempt to approach…"

The three fugitives didn't hear the rest of the broadcast. They had disappeared from the chippie into the fading light, their remaining food left uneaten on the table.

Cate couldn't remember the last time she had been this cold, miserable, and uncomfortable. "I don't know if I can make it through the night."

"It's only a few more hours. Tomorrow we'll find out why all this is happening."

"That's what you said yesterday, Alex. We're no closer and it's gotten worse."

"And I feel responsible. At least we have shelter tonight."

Eddie chimed in, "What is this crazy thing? It looks Japanese."

"It's a Chinese pagoda given to Queen Victoria in the eighteen-hundreds. The London council thought it was appropriate to put it in the park named after her."

"Is there any shit you don't know?" asked Eddie.

"He doesn't know why they are after us," grumbled Cate.

"You're right. Let's go over the facts we are sure of," Alex was dead serious. "Someone wanted to find Eddie and was willing to pay handsomely for him. And that someone is linked with the British Secret Service and somehow Jack the Ripper's murders are connected to it. All we have to do is put the pieces together."

"All?" Cate shook her head, "I love doing research but not if it means we are hunted by spies, chased by helicopters, accused of being bombers, and left to freeze our asses off out here in some damn pagoda!" She spat out the last word.

Eddie moved cautiously to the side, "What is this? A lovers' spat?"

"NO!" Alex and Cate both yelled the answer at the same time.

The pagoda fell quiet and Alex felt compelled to speak, "I know you don't want to hear this, but after what we saw reported on the television, we must find out why they're after us before we go to the embassy. If we turn ourselves in, they'll arrest us on the spot and put us away. They have already trumped up enough charges for three life sentences. We have no other choice."

"Are you sure they won't listen to us?"

"Cate, you saw the news story. They are claiming we are radicals and terrorists. They'll say we stole the car, and even though we'll return the passports and money, with the video footage of us at the museum, it wouldn't take a Perry Mason to convict us. If they detain us as armed fugitives, we wouldn't even be allowed to post bail. We have to keep going."

"I know what it's like to have people after you," Eddie understood what Alex was saying. "You both know I was locked up inside and it's definitely not cool. But we're stuck and we have no options. We can't clear our names sitting here, and we can't go anywhere without being recognized. Not after they had our pictures on the TV. Now it's not just me out there but you guys too. They would find us in minutes."

"Then there's no other way; tomorrow we must change the way we look before we can be seen together again," stated Alex.

"You're right. I guess we have to. I can cut my hair and color it." Cate put her hand on Eddie's head and ruffled his long hair, "You too, Dave Grohl."

It was a little before eight when Alex returned to the pagoda with three hot coffees and a pair of scissors. Eddie was happy to take the drink but leery of the scissors.

"Why can't I go to a hairdresser's?" he asked.

"Because a certain long-haired American teen's picture is all over London," answered Cate. "If I cut it short first, then a barber can clean it up and might not know it's you." She grinned, "I'll be gentle, I promise."

"You better be. Took me seventeen years to grow it." Eddie turned around as Cate advanced toward him with the scissors.

The men's barbershop on Golborne Road was hardly high fashion but it was exactly the mom and pop operation they had been looking for, a small business pleased to take cash from an early customer. Eddie emerged, obviously unsure about his new buzz cut. Alex stood waiting for him; his hair slicked back with a pomade he'd picked up when he had bought the scissors that morning.

"Where's Cate?" asked Eddie.

"Getting her hair done, same as you did."

"I didn't see her in there," wondered Eddie.

"She's not. We couldn't all use the same place. They're looking for the three of us. She found a little salon two streets over. We're going to meet her back at the park when she's done."
"Then what?"
It was Alex's turn to be unenthusiastic, "Clothes shopping."
"Seriously?"
"Yes, seriously."

Portobello Road's famed flea market was in full swing with a dozen streets closed down to traffic and packed with people looking for a bargain.

A thousand stalls crammed each street, alleyway, and mews, selling food, fruit, antiques, bric-a-brac, signs, fake Rolexes, classic vinyl, books, furniture, and clothes, new and used, of every type and decade.

Noise filled the air, not only from the stands' proprietors yelling to lure in customers, but from the street performers on every corner playing original songs and cover tunes in the hope their busking would earn them money.

The hordes of eager shoppers concentrated on finding bargains, and paid no attention to the three people sifting through the vintage clothes on display. Perhaps one or two heard the excited laughter from the cute girl who held up a psychedelic sixties kaftan and giggled "How about this? It's hippie chic and it'll match my do," but if they did, they probably didn't realize her red hair and short bob was less than an hour old, and still new to her.

Alex discouraged the bright paisley outfit Cate liked, "The idea is to blend in, not draw attention to yourself."

Reluctantly, Cate returned the flower-power flashback to its hanger.

Eddie saw something and grabbed it for Cate. It was a matching pink T-shirt and hoodie, "This'll look good on you, and everyone will think you're a local."

Cate held it up and took one look at the two crossed hammers and the red lettering and grimaced in disgust, "I am not walking around wearing an ad for meat!"

"West Ham is a soccer team."

"Really?" Cate took a second look, "I like soccer players. It is kind of cute."

They paid the vendor at the stall and turned back to the crowded streets.

"Next up, some clothes for you boys."

"I'll be easy, as long as it's not another *I heart London* T-shirt," said Eddie. "What about him?" He pointed at Alex.

Cate grinned, "I'll find him something less…professorly."

Costa Coffee was always busy at lunchtime, and with their transient in and out crowd, it was the perfect place for the three fugitives to disappear in plain sight. And had anyone been looking for the long-haired teen, the pretty blond and the wavy-haired professor whose picture had been splashed on every television news channel and in the papers the night before, they wouldn't have recognized them as the hip-hop kid in the baseball cap, Clash T-shirt, baggy jeans and Nike knock-offs, or the hot red head in her tight soccer top, yoga pants and matching hoodie.

Alex came back from the counter carrying a tray of drinks and sandwiches. As he slid the refreshments on the table, Eddie laughed, "At least we look good."

Alex was taken aback for a moment and reassessed the leather jacket he wore over his plain white T-shirt and dark pants. "I thought you said I looked cool?"

"You do," reassured Cate, "and when all this is over you should keep your hair like that. Slicked back looks good on you."

"I don't know about that," said Alex. "And this leather jacket might be a bit too *Village People* for me."

Cate and Eddie stared back at him with blank looks.

"Come on. You know the Village People."

Their faces said the opposite.

"YMCA?"

Still nothing.

"Okay, so disco is dead. Down to business. Are the new cell phones working?"

This was more Cate's speed, "Yes, all three are up and running. They have twenty hours of pre-paid calling in them, so if we get separated, we can let each other know where we are. But they're really basic; cheap camera, no maps, limited internet search capability, and a small flashlight."

"Spotify?" asked Eddie.

Cate shook her head.

"Let's assume the pay-as-you-go phones are good enough and we know for certain they are not linked to us, so right now we can't be tracked. It's *why* they are tracking us we need to find out," said Alex.

"There's so many questions," said Cate. "Like why did the British Secret Service come to the States to kidnap Eddie? What has Mary Kelly got to do with MI6? And whose DNA did they test Eddie's against?"

"Could it have been Jack the Ripper's?" asked Eddie.

"Definitely not. We can be certain of that," stated Alex. "He was never caught so they had no DNA from him, and we already proved you are descended from Mary so that DNA test would be pointless even if they somehow had a sample from her. The only person who makes sense would be the father of Mary's child, to cement both sides of the bloodline. If only I hadn't left the letter in the hotel when we ran."

"I have a copy. I scanned everything in, remember?" She flipped open her laptop and logged in. Alex stared at the screen as the image faded up.

"That isn't the same letter I had. There's something different about it."

"You are good! This is a file of it I copied and pasted into Word. I'll pull up the original." Cate found it in a desktop folder.

"Can you bring up both? Side by side? I'd like to see the difference," asked Alex.

Cate opened a second window and slid the two letters, the original scan and the Word version, next to each other.

"There, that's where they vary." Alex pointed to the screen.

"Oh yeah," Cate saw it too, "Spell check picked up a mistake. Mary didn't capitalize a name. *Vic*. Word red lined the error for her, or at least, for us."

"Hold on." Alex studied both letters then looked away from the screen, "How did your computer know it was a mistake?"

"Because it happens all the time, you screw up a word or forget to capitalize something. That's why spellcheck is so useful. It catches your mistakes and points out your errors. Helped me with my term papers," admitted Cate.

"Yes, but back then, people were more careful. There were no phones and no internet, and using the mail was the only way of keeping in touch. Letter writing was an art and considered very important. That's why families saved and treasured correspondence, and Mary didn't make any other mistakes and her handwriting is clear, it doesn't look rushed."

"If it wasn't a mistake, what was it?" Eddie hadn't seen the letter before and was puzzled.

"Maybe it was part of her message and she knew Sarah would understand. The letter says '*vic* Donovan told us, perhaps God has other plans for my son and me' and everyone has always assumed Mary was talking about a Victor Donovan. But if she meant to write *vic* Donovan, and it wasn't an error, it would be entirely different."

"But aren't Vic and Victor the same? Like my name, Eddie and Edward, or Cate and Caitlin?"

"If it was a name. But it's not capitalized and all the other names are. What if it's an abbreviation?" Alex's mind was racing.

"What kind of abbreviation?" Cate picked up on his train of thought, feeling his excitement.

"Like doc for doctor, or cop for copper, as the British call them. If it is, then in this case, vic could be short for vicar. That changes the letter's meaning and it becomes vicar Donovan, a man of the church, who tells Mary that God has other plans for them."

"If you're correct, it would be huge for us. We couldn't locate a Victor Donovan back then, but there couldn't have been many vicar Donovans in 1892." Cate was getting excited too.

"But even if that's right, how would we find him when it's so long ago?" Eddie was confused.

"We track down vicar Donovan's parish from the late eighteen-hundreds and see if there is evidence remaining of any interaction he had with Mary Kelly."

"How would you do that?"

Alex finally smiled, this was his area of expertise, "Fortunately the Church is very precise at keeping records over the years. And here in London, there's one place where we can certainly find them."

Throngs of tourists packed the outside of the massive former cathedral, photographing the building that had been the site of every monarch's coronation since 1066 and then immortalized across the globe when it held the funeral of Princess Diana in 1997. Situated close to Big Ben and the Houses of Parliament, Westminster Abbey remained a towering example of classic architecture and British history.

Two people waited impatiently on Sanctuary Road for their companion to appear from the legendary church. When he did, his walk was brisk and confident, reflecting he had found what he had been looking for inside. He quickly reached Cate and Eddie.

"Well?" asked Cate.

"Sorry if I kept you waiting, it took me awhile, but I have the location of his parish."

"You do?"

"Yes. We have to make our way across town and get to Liverpool Street Station. We're leaving London."

CHAPTER ELEVEN

Thaxted

The trio sat huddled in a first-class compartment of the Stansted Express as it hurtled northwards to meet the connecting bus which would take them on to their final destination. With the reserved cabin to themselves, Alex went over his discoveries with them.

"Vicar Donovan's parish was St. John The Baptist's church in Thaxted. It's ninety minutes by train and bus for us, so it would have taken Mary many hours, even a full day, to get there by carriage."

"Why would she go so far to a church? My Sunday school was ten minutes away and I used to bitch about that," wondered Cate.

"I don't know. None of her friends would have been there, we can be certain of that," answered Alex.

"Perhaps that's why. Maybe she didn't want anyone she knew to see her," suggested Eddie.

"You could be right," Alex hadn't considered that. "But why didn't she want to be recognized? And what was she doing at a church, of all places, that she needed to keep a secret so badly?"

His friends had no answer, and Alex fell deep into thought as the speeding train left the sprawling metropolis of London behind and the crowded buildings were replaced by green fields and lush countryside.

Colin Brown riffled through the notes piling up on his desk. How could there be no leads on these three, he kept asking himself. If only his agency were in charge of domestic surveillance, things would be different. It was at that moment his cell rang.

He knew the number as he grabbed the phone, "What?"

Simon heard the anger and anxiety in his counterpart's voice, "Hopefully, good news. The Met picked them up on CCTV at Liverpool Street Station. They've changed their look and their clothes, but we have confirmed facial recognition."

"About time those bloody cameras found something. How long ago?"

"The video is a little more than two hours old. An agent was monitoring the platforms for pickpockets and came across them. They left by train for Thaxted."

"Thaxted?" This was not a town Colin knew, "Where the hell is Thaxted?"

"It's in Essex. About ninety minutes from here by train."

"Shit." Colin did the math in his head, "That means they're there by now. Contact the local constabulary. Send pictures and tell them who to look for but if they are located, they are only to follow them. We'll take two of your teams with us. How big is the Thaxted police department?"

"Four officers. Two part-time."

"Christ!"

Thaxted Parish Church soared skyward from a hill overlooking the small town. It seemed out of place, its one-hundred-and-eighty-one-foot tower dwarfing the tiny village it served. The building, dating back to the fourteenth century, appeared ageless as it sat surrounded by a sea of gravestones, a cemetery documenting the history of Thaxted.

The three Americans walked inside the classic church, between the arched stone walls and the ancient wooden ceiling forty feet above them, with the current minister, vicar Williams.

The pastor thanked them once again, "Your donation was very generous."

"As it says in Matthew 22, verse 21, 'Render unto Caesar what is Caesar's'."

"You are well read, my son. Although my role here is hardly as imperial as the emperor's was." The vicar smiled in recognition at Alex's knowledge of the scriptures. "Some of our records you may be looking for are in the crypt but the majority of the BMD books are up here."

"BMD?" Eddie was not familiar with the term, "Is that a shorthand for texting, like OMG or YOLO?"

The vicar laughed, "No, my child. BMD is short for Births, Marriages and Deaths. They tend to be the most important records held at a Church. Our volumes from the late eighteen-hundreds are surprisingly complete."

"Why surprising?" asked Alex.

"Our vicar Donovan was a complex character. He spent far too much time with, let me say, ladies of loose morals. Plus, he liked his drink. It certainly made for..." he paused as he sought the correct words, "...an interesting combination. But he kept good records. Check these books. If you can't find what you're looking for here, then come and get me, and I'll open the crypt and you can go through the ones down there."

The vicar bowed and walked off, leaving them alone.

Eddie raised his eyebrows and looked to Alex for answers, "Vicar Donovan liked ladies with loose morals and drinking? I thought priests couldn't do that shit."

"It's Church of England. Vicars are allowed to drink in moderation and have girlfriends," explained Alex.

"My kind of religion," grinned Eddie.

"Boys," Cate brought them back to earth. "Time to get started." She picked up the first volume labeled *Births, Marriages and Deaths*.

It was forty minutes before Alex suddenly surfaced from one of the massive leather-bound books, "I have it right here! August 4th, 1888. Albert Christian Wettin and Mary Jane Kelly, both of London, were joined together, in holy matrimony, by vicar Donovan. We've found Mary's husband!"

The trio stood waiting patiently outside the carved wooden door leading to the rectory at the rear of the church. Vicar Williams reappeared lugging the big book with a sheet of paper balanced on top of it.

"It's not a great copy, but it's as good as my little machine can do. It hasn't been updated for at least a decade," he apologized.

Alex took the Xerox and glanced at it, "This is perfect. It's exactly what we need. Thank you."

"I'm happy you are pleased with it. When you're in the crypt, let me know if I can be of any help finding the records for you down there."

"We will." Alex led Cate and Eddie back down the long, narrow aisle and through the heavy wooden door to the ancient, well-worn curving stairs leading down into the church's crypt.

Had the stone walls not been so thick, and the crypt so deep, they might have heard the screech of tires as three para-military vehicles squealed to a halt on the gravel-covered driveway outside of the old church.

Colin and Simon, in black assault gear, were out of the armored cars almost before they came to a complete stop.

Simon was the first to spot the person they were looking for, "That must be him over there."

"You deal with him. You're MI5."

Simon shook his head at Colin's request, "No, you put this thing together. Plus, he heard it's a joint op and wants to talk with MI6. Says he's never met a spy before."

Colin saw a uniformed British Bobby pedaling toward them on a bicycle. The older police officer pulled up next to the two men, dismounted and took his time as he balanced his bike on its kickstand.

Colin couldn't wait any longer, "Constable Darby?"

"That's me, sir. I'm in charge while the sarge is on holiday in Benidorm. He'll be sad he missed a chance to work with MI6. It's quite something for us, having you here. Do you have a section card for our files?"

Annoyed, Colin reached inside his Kevlar vest and pulled out a card. Constable Darby studied it, and happy with what he saw, slipped it into his pocket.

"Are you're sure they're in there?" Colin's tone held nothing but haste.

"Hang on one second. Let me slip these off." Constable Darby bent down and carefully removed the bicycle clips from his pants' legs. "Better now. Have to wear them so my trousers don't get caught up with the pedals and gears. Makes an oily mess, and gives the wife some awful laundry to do."

"Right." Colin couldn't care less, he wanted his question answered, "So?"

"Sorry, sir, what was it you were asking again?"

It was all the MI6 officer could do not to scream, "Are they in there?"

"Yes, sir. I peeked inside and saw them myself after I got the call. And there's only two ways out. The front door and the vestibule. I've kept my eye on them ever since, and from where I was watching, they couldn't leave from either way without me seeing them."

"You're certain?"

"Yes, sir. This has been my church since I was a choirboy here forty-three years ago. I was a budding young soprano with a strong middle C," he said proudly.

Colin was done with him and his small-town pleasantries, and switched to Simon, "Seal both doors. Set a tight perimeter around the church. This time they are not getting away."

"Yes, sir," replied Constable Darby.

"I wasn't talking to you," Colin snapped. "You can stand down." He gestured to Simon, "His men from Five will handle it from here on out."

"Then what would you like the Thaxted constabulary to do?"

"You go...cycle over there and keep back the crowds." Colin pointed randomly into the distance across the cemetery. Anything to lose this fool.

"We don't have crowds in Thaxted. It's a small village, you know."

"Just do it."

"Yes, sir." Constable Darby bent down to replace his bicycle clips before pedaling off.

Colin ignored him as he conferred with Simon, "We don't have much daylight left; once the perimeter's set, I'm going in."

"How many do you want in your team?"

Colin pulled his Glock 17 and carried out a press check to confirm the chamber was loaded as he replied, "None. You maintain the perimeter. This time I go in alone."

Colin's reinforced boots sounded out of place as his footfalls echoed through the ancient church, dampened only by the seven-hundred-year-old stained glass, the intricate hanging wool tapestries, and the worn but beautifully carved wooden paneling running the length of the nave along the rafters. Hearing the unusual noise, the vicar left his rectory to find the source of the strange reverberations shaking his house of worship.

Despite the intruder's aggressive appearance, the minister greeted Colin with a welcoming smile, "We normally only see men in uniform for our veteran's day services."

"Every day is veteran's day for me, father. Three Americans are here, correct?" Colin was not wasting time.

"Yes, they are in the crypt."

"What are they doing there?"

"I think they're tracing their roots as many foreigners like to do. They were looking through our records. I gave them access to our books," he pointed to the five huge volumes he had not yet put away.

"Show me." Colin's tone indicated it was not a request.

"Certainly. Our church records are available to all." He pulled open one of the books and turned to the appropriate page, "This is the entry they were concerned with."

Colin read through it and stiffened in shock at what he saw, "Are you sure it was this?"

"Absolutely. I gave them a copy of it."

"They have a copy of this?"

"Yes, I made it myself on my little Xerox," explained the vicar helpfully.

The seething MI6 section chief struggled to keep calm, "Thank you, father, now please leave the church and wait outside. These are dangerous people."

"Strange to hear you say that. They have been very friendly and polite to me. Surely, they don't merit your concern? One is a man of letters."

"For your own safety, get out. That is an order." His voice was insistent.

The armed policeman's attitude stunned the vicar, "My son, you are standing in God's house. Only He can give orders in here."

Colin locked his eyes on the confused vicar, "At this moment, as far as you're concerned, I am God."

Vicar Williams bristled at his words, "Sir, I am sure your intentions are good, but what you are saying reeks of blasphemy."

"What I am saying reeks of the truth, vicar, and my will shall be done."

He grabbed the parish minister by his robes and dragged him down the aisle to the main door.

"This isn't right-"

Colin pushed the door open and shoved the vicar through it. "You'll thank me for this one day."

As the man of God stumbled across the gravel forecourt, Colin called to the waiting men outside, "Make sure he doesn't come back in. And no one else is to enter." Without a backward glance, he slammed shut the old wooden door and stormed between the pews towards the church's records.

Thirty feet below him, huddled in the underground chamber dating back to the church's original construction in 1340, Alex, Cate and Eddie gathered around a treasure trove of ancient books and parchments.

"These records are priceless!" For a man who loved the written word, Alex had found his Nirvana.

"But no mention anywhere about Mary's husband," said Cate, dashing the professor's excitement. "I've found nothing showing he ever lived here, or in any of the other surrounding villages."

"If neither of them were from here or had family close by, why did they travel so far to get married? Was it like a honeymoon thing?" asked Eddie.

"I doubt it. There was abject poverty throughout the working class of London back then, and few people would have been able to afford to do anything like that, and I certainly don't think a woman like Mary was in the position to take a honeymoon. But it is a good question. If this wasn't her fiancé's home, why all the inconvenience of coming here? There were more than fifty churches nearby them in London where they could have held their wedding."

Cate pulled on a cabinet door, "It's locked, and there may be more records inside showing birth and local residence. But I can't get it open."

Alex turned to Eddie, "Can you run up and ask the vicar if he has a key to this cabinet?"

"Will do, professor." Eddie was already bored with the research and book work, and happy to have the distraction. He grinned as he hurtled up the stairs, two at a time.

Eddie shoved open the heavy crypt door and emerged from the darkness into the last of the late afternoon sun flooding through the huge stained-glass gothic windows, lighting the church in a myriad of colors. As his eyes struggled to compensate to the change, he made out the silhouette of a dark figure halfway down the nave studying the books. He called out to him, "Vicar."

The hazy shape turned and as he did, Eddie realized it was not the vicar, it was Colin Brown, the agent hunting him, and he was reaching for a sidearm in his holster.

"Shit!" Eddie flung himself backward between the pews as the first two bullets ripped into the old, dried wood, showering him with shards and splinters.

Eddie stayed on his hands and knees and crawled as quickly as he could back to the crypt's entrance.

Three more rounds crashed into the pews, inches from Eddie, creating more matchwood. Even though Colin was firing blind, he was still too damn accurate with his shots and if it wasn't for the strength of the centuries-old carpentry, he knew the bullets would have found their mark.

The firing stopped and Eddie heard the MI6 operative start toward him, calling out as he approached, "No point in running, kid. You'll only die tired."

The boy launched himself headfirst through the open crypt entryway and whirled around, pushing the big door shut. He felt bullets slamming into the other side of the wood and prayed it was thick enough to withstand the high impacts. Perhaps it was because he was in a church, his prayers were answered, and the five inches of old English oak swallowed up the hollow-point ammunition made in Illinois.

He swung the hinged beam on the back of the door into place and locked it shut. That should slow Mr. Brown down, but what now, where would they go, how could they get out? Eddie sprinted down the stairs to tell his friends of the nightmare above waiting for them.

Colin stared at the closed door contemplating his next move when a warning yell behind had him turning in place.

"Armed police. We're coming in."

Colin stood and watched as Simon burst through the main entrance, heading an assault team, weapons ready, visors down.

Simon saw Colin standing there, and raised his hand to halt his men, "Are you all right? We heard shots."

"Get them out now!" Colin demanded, pointing back to the door in dismissal.

Seeing Colin was unhurt, Simon didn't hesitate instructing his men to leave the church, and carried on toward him, alone. As the director of MI5's operations approached, he could sense a bloodlust in Colin Brown. It was the feel he sometimes picked up when he was arresting an armed suspect after a prolonged chase, not something he was used to encountering when facing a fellow officer. Had any of his own men exhibited this kind of behavior he would have relieved them of their duties and arranged for them to have crisis counseling. But Colin Brown was not one of his team, he was a law unto himself. "What happened?" Simon asked.

"The kid pulled a gun on me. I fired to protect myself. But he made it through that door and locked himself in there." Colin gestured to the entryway to the crypt.

Simon stepped forward and pushed on the door. Nothing. No movement. "That's solid timber. It was built to take a battering ram. We'd have to blow it to get through."

"Exactly. And by the time demolitions got here, half the tabloid press in Britain would be on site wanting to find out who these three Americans are, why they're attracting all this attention and offering them a spot on next season's Celebrity Big Brother. If they talk to anyone now, this will all come down on our heads."

"It can't be that bad unless it has escalated way beyond what you said when you brought this case to me three days ago. I understand your concern, and the possible ramifications, but this was meant to be a simple locate and arrest op."

Colin gestured to the pile of books lying on a small table to the side of the aisles, "Let me show you something." He led the way to the stack and pointed to the writing in the open one, "They found this."

Simon read the entry in the centuries-old record book and was staggered by what he saw, "So what you said is true! They were married."

"Yes, one hundred percent legal, and in a Church of England ceremony. They came out here, away from London, because their secret would be safe. It worked for them and stayed that way for so many years."

"And with all our resources and more than a century of searching, we found nothing, but you bring in this American professor and he unravels it in a week? How did he do it? The man is a magician. What is your plan now?" Simon was lost.

"We do our job. The kid will use this information against us. You know full well who and what we are sworn to protect. You go out and stay with your men. I'll take care of things in here."

"This is a domestic threat. It's my duty to be present with you to bring it to an end."

"Damn it, you are present." Colin Brown's voice rose in anger, "But let me handle this and do what is necessary. It started overseas as an MI6 mission and I am simply following the pursuit to its conclusion. You would be better served outside with your men, and should the whole thing go tits up, you'll have plausible deniability. This is my job now."

Simon felt the threat in Brown's tone and saw the man's hand unconsciously tightening around his pistol grip, his knuckles turning white. His twenty years of field training kicked in and he found himself assessing the MI6 agent as a possible adversary. He took in the agent's strong build and powerful stance; he might be able to disarm him of his weapon, but then what?

He was all too aware of Colin Brown's reputation which had become legend throughout Britain's SIS – the Secret Intelligence Service. His operation in the Bahamas a few years before when he had located two stolen warheads, had saved the world from a nuclear catastrophe, and more recently, his almost single-handed destruction of the opium cartel in the East had virtually stemmed the flow of heroin into the United Kingdom. If it came to a hand-to-hand encounter, Simon held no false hopes, physical combat was Brown's specialty, and what could he do against a field agent with his kind of training and background? Better to cooperate and keep his eyes on him.

"Okay, I'll be outside with my teams, but don't do anything stupid in here."

Brown hissed his answer as Simon turned away, "I'll do whatever it takes."

The MI5 director walked towards the door, understanding for the first time the vast gulf existing between the two intelligence branches. The men and women of Five were usually brought into the Ministry with a background of being trained detectives or experienced police personnel, and remained committed to preventing acts of domestic terror and bringing potential perpetrators to justice.

The agents from MI6 were recruited under very different circumstances, often after proving their edge in bloody overseas actions with the SAS or UKSF. Their roles were intended primarily as assassins, sent to put an end to their targets by whatever means they deemed fit. That's why so few of the people they went after ever ended up in court or in prison. They simply ended up dead.

Colin remained a statue until Simon left the church, and then exploded into action. He selected a series of heavy wooden pews and dragged them one at a time across the stone floors to block the crypt's entrance. Within minutes, ten of the old benches were stacked against the oak door.

He turned back and saw dozens of prayer and hymn books had fallen from the narrow shelves of the pews as he'd lugged them into place, and realizing the purpose they could serve, he grabbed them from the floor, throwing them onto the pile.

As the stack grew, he raced back to the five massive books and picked them up. Surprised by their combined weight, he carried the more than two hundred years of irreplaceable records over to the waiting heap of wood and paper barricading the door.

He shrugged hard and tossed them onto the mound. He reached forward and found the incriminating page bearing Mary Kelly's marriage. The agent took a series of deep breaths to bring his fury under control, and muttered to himself, "How appropriate. You came looking for births, marriages, and deaths, and now you will have three of them."

With those words, he pulled a butane lighter from his pocket and lit the offending entry and watched with satisfaction as the old parchment curled and caught fire, eradicating the names of Mary Kelly and Albert Wettin. He pushed the burning book deep into the pile and in seconds it ignited the remaining four volumes, their flames rapidly spreading and turning the heap of hymn and prayer books into a blaze.

Colin stepped back as the pews began to catch and burn, and now the combination of ancient wood and dry paper turned into a raging sea of flames, licking hungrily at the wooden door, sealing the exit forever.

As the fire roared out of control, Colin reached inside his protective vest and pulled a snub-nosed .38 revolver, spinning the cylinder to check it was loaded. Satisfied, he shot three times in rapid succession at the vicar's pulpit, watching as the bullets buried themselves deep into the carved wood. Then he turned the small pistol around and fired it at his left arm, at point blank range, shooting himself, but only enough for the bullet to rip through his sleeve and tear open a nasty cut on the outside of his bicep, creating a jagged flesh wound.

He smiled at the blood running down his arm, dripping from his wrist onto the church's tiled floor. It should be convincing, but perhaps a little too convenient. There was still one more thing he needed to do to ensure he would be believed.

The MI6 agent measured his steps as he walked down the aisle toward the church's exit door. He went only a few yards before he stopped, but figured it should put him far enough away from the fire in case he blacked out for a minute or so. He couldn't imagine he would be unconscious any longer than that unless it came to a worse-case scenario.

Colin sat at one of the pews remaining in place and reached forward to the small shelf in front of him, removing a prayer book and a hymnal that waited there for the next service and a devout parishioner. He weighed them both in his hand; the book of hymns was thicker and heavier, so he let the volume of prayers drop to the floor. He slid the hymn book beneath the right side of his Kevlar vest. It was a tight fit getting it between the ballistic panels and his chest. Good, he thought, the four hundred plus pages and the heavy cover binding it should provide the extra padding, if needed.

For a second time, he twisted the Smith & Wesson revolver around and held it about twelve inches from his vest, far enough away so it would leave no gunshot residue on the protective fabric.

The agent pushed his back firmly against the wooden pew and tensed, ready to absorb the whiplash generated by the .38's round. Everything was in place, and with no time left to hesitate, he aimed the lethal handgun squarely at his chest, and pulled the trigger.

He barely heard the sound of the shot, as the impact of the 8.1-gram bullet smashed against the poly-paraphenylene fibers like a sledgehammer, forcing all the air from his lungs and jerking his body upwards on the pew, as his locked position against the bench avoided any violent backward, jarring movement.

Colin took a second to suck in a breath and assess his physical condition. He was alive, the bullet hadn't penetrated the Kevlar vest and had mushroomed slightly and wedged deep into the central protective panel, clearly visible for all to see, exactly the outcome he'd hoped for.

Colin pulled the hymn book, which had thankfully proven to be unnecessary, from beneath his vest and let it fall to the ground. He rose to his feet and flung the revolver across the church and into the conflagration behind him. He smiled as the little pistol disappeared into the flames, knowing its charred remains would be found there in the days to come.

Satisfied he had done all he could to cover his actions, and knowing it was now time to leave the burning church, he sprinted for the door, yelling as he ran, "I'm coming out. They've got guns!"

He burst headlong through the door and collapsed on the ground outside, clutching his bloody arm in full view of the MI5 response squads, before calling out to them, a desperate, pleading edge now ringing in his voice, "Get me a medic. I've been shot."

Deep in the crypt, Alex, Cate, and Eddie reacted in alarm as they heard the five muffled booms from the revolver.

"Jesus, he's firing again," called out Eddie.

"Who is he shooting at?" said Cate.

Alex sensed their growing panic, and felt it mounting within himself, but knew he had to act, "I'm going to go up and talk to him."

Eddie whipped around, "You can't. He's gone crazy. He didn't want to talk. He fired as soon as he saw me with no warning or anything. If you had been up there with me, he'd have tried to kill you too."

Alex paused and dropped his head. Eddie waited; hoping his words had gotten through to the professor. They had, but not in the way the teen planned.

Eddie's words triggered memories, memories of the terrible night in Prague when he had stayed in the hotel, lost in his own research, while his wife and child set out to explore the city and find a restaurant. Then, hours later, had come the knock on the door, and the two uniformed policemen standing there, telling him, in halting English, the news that altered his life forever.

He could still hear the first officer even now, as if Time itself had burned the voice into his consciousness, echoing through the years, "If you had been with them, you would have been killed too."

Maybe the policeman was right, and he would have been died in that senseless tragedy, but perhaps by being there he could have changed things, he could have saved them. He would never know and that question haunted him every waking minute.

Alex shrugged to bring himself back from the dark place he'd returned to, "I have to try."

Without waiting for an answer or his friends' approval, the professor ran to the long, curved stone stairs and raced up them to the door. He grabbed the blocking beam and readied to swing it upwards and unbar the entry.

He hesitated, and called a warning through it first, "Mr. Brown, if you can hear me, it's Professor Turner. I'm coming out to talk."

He pushed the heavy beam up, freeing the locking mechanism, grasped the raised handle and pulled the huge door open.

Alex leaped backward to save himself. He stared in shock at the out of control inferno only inches from him, as flames from the pews and books roared upwards, already igniting the hanging tapestries and oil paintings on the church's walls and flickering closer to the ancient wooden ceiling and rafters.

He desperately tried to close the door but burning sections of the blazing pews propped against the crypt's entryway tumbled through, breaking apart on the floor in a shower of sparks and charred splinters, blocking the swing of the door. The intense heat and rapidly spreading fire made them impossible to grab and move, and Alex was forced back into the crypt, his last glimpse of the interior of the treasured seven-hundred-year-old house of worship was as a huge wooden hanging candelabra, forty feet above the nave, erupted into flames.

He took the well-worn stairs three at a time, the heavy smoke from the blaze chasing him down into the vault.

Cate and Eddie saw his urgent return but before they could ask what had happened, Alex yelled his warning, "He's set fire to the church."

"How do we get out?" cried Cate.

Overhead, the string of small incandescent bulbs struggling to light the vast, dark crypt, flashed for a second then went out, plunging them into total darkness.

Eddie's voice cut through the wall of black, "We've lost our power!"

Colin sat on the low brick wall surrounding the cemetery. A medic made the two last turns with the bandage around Colin's arm before pinning it closed.

"You're lucky," said Simon. "If it hadn't been for the vest you wouldn't be sitting here now; and one inch further over on your arm and that bullet would have torn through your bicep."

"And four inches higher it would have given me a second Adam's apple," scoffed Colin. "Comes with the turf, right?"

A call from behind ended any chance of Simon replying, as Constable Darby ran up yelling, "She's on fire. My church is on fire."

Simon whirled around as a stained-glass window shattered from the heat, and flames roared out through the opening, ravenously searching for oxygen. The blaze, unseen until now, was obvious to all, as plumes of smoke billowed towards the heavens.

"She's going to burn down," Constable Darby was distraught and started toward the place of his youth.

Colin grabbed him with his good arm and pulled him back, "No one goes in. The Americans have guns. It's too dangerous for our men. We have to wait until they come out."

Simon turned to the distressed constable, "Darby, call the fire department right now."

As the policeman reached for his cell to do as ordered, Simon voiced his concern to the MI6 agent, "What if they don't come out? What if the three of them are trapped in there?"

"We watch both exits. The firefighters can hose the outside of the building but no one goes in until we know it's safe. We have to have the Americans in custody first."

"And if we don't get them?"

"Then we let the church burn. There's no other alternative. We can't lose any of our men needlessly." Colin stared at the flames now leaping from a second shattered window and held back the smile he felt building. This will be the perfect end to my hunt, he thought. In a few days, after the fire is out and the destruction is done, the forensic teams will search through the debris, find the bodies, the revolver, the expended rounds that would match the one lodged in his vest, and come to their inevitable conclusion. He knew it was a flawless plan; he wouldn't have to do anything except wait. There would be no awkward questions or chance of blame. And even better, no loose ends and no loose tongues. The boy, his companions, and all the damning paperwork, would be gone forever. And a century of fear and uncertainty would be finally over.

Smoke filled the crypt. The flashlights on two of the three cell phones lit the way as the trio moved deeper into the ancient chamber, away from fire and their only exit.

A blazing piece of wood, perhaps from a shattered pew or even the door's own heavy bracing beam, rolled down the stairs, thundering into a shelf full of books and manuscripts. In seconds, the dry paper erupted into a volcano of flame.

"The fire's in here now," screamed Eddie.

"We have to get to the far end of the crypt, away from the flames and the smoke," ordered Alex.

"That will take us away from the way out," Cate was panicked.

"We have no choice; the fire has sealed off the exit. We'll look for another door. Another stairway. Anything. For all their stone walls, these old churches are framed with wood and full of flammable paintings and tapestries. That means it'll go up in minutes, like Notre Dame did. We have to keep moving into the crypt."

"It would have helped if you had charged your phone, then we'd have three flashlights."

Alex shot an angry glance at Eddie for his comment, but it went unseen in the dark.

Their beams pierced the smoke, illuminating the back wall of the fourteenth-century crypt, along with a couple of wooden chairs and a gigantic fireplace carved into the stone.

"That's it. It ends here! We've got no place else to go," Cate almost sobbed as she swept her cell's flashlight side to side, revealing their plight.

Above them, the old church creaked and groaned, sounds that resonated even down into the foundations. Had there been enough light, Eddie and Cate would have seen the color drain from Alex's face. He understood what the aged building was telling him. He called to his friends in alarm, "We have to find shelter."

"Shelter? Where?" asked Eddie.

Alex swung around. There was only one place that could offer any protection. The deep, massive fireplace hewn out of the final wall. He pointed to it, hoping their lights would show his raised arm, "Quickly. In there. Now!"

A terrifying noise split the air, as above them the old stonework shifted, then with an enormous *BOOM*, the intense temperatures generated by the blaze cracked and forced apart the heavy supporting blocks.

"What is that?" screamed Cate.

"The church. It's coming down!" Alex ran for the carved fireplace, Eddie and Cate right on his heels.

Twelve firetrucks, summoned from every nearby town, surrounded the church, six of them already dousing the immense building with arching jets of water, the others searching for high-pressure hookups which were few and far between in this tiny village.

Four helicopters circled above, two streaming live footage to CNN and Sky News.

Because of the blaze and heat, and to avoid interfering with the firefighters as they took their positions, the MI5 perimeter Simon had set up was forced to withdraw an additional thirty yards from the church itself, but the attentive operatives kept their eyes locked on the two exits, even though flames now filled both doorways.

"Thank God this didn't happen in central London. There would be hell to pay," said Simon.

"There is no blame here. The Americans are the ones who started the blaze, probably hoping to cause a diversion and escape," covered Colin.

Simon's eyes showed he didn't fully believe him, "Are you sure?"

"Look at my arm. Those bastards shot me."

A thunderous sound drowned out any thought of further conversation as stone split apart and the almost two-hundred-foot-high spire wavered and in a nightmarish, inconceivable move, folded in on itself and then cracked, falling backward, its entire height and ten thousand tons of carved slabs, smashing down on the church's already stressed roof, crushing it and crashing through into the nave, causing the walls of the building to explode outward in a mass of shattered bricks and flame.

The MI5 assault teams and even the fire crews, used to being at the scene of intense blazes, dove desperately to the ground to avoid being struck by the blast of burning rubble and ash flung out from the impact zone as the collapsing gigantic tower drove the red-hot blocks through the ancient roof, flattening the church.

As the horrendous, scorching dust cloud parted, the men pulled themselves cautiously back to their feet. In the distance, screams and cries from the dismayed villagers, drawn to the conflagration by the sirens and lights, echoed through the air as they reacted in shock to the unimaginable destruction of their town's beloved heritage building.

Simon tried to take in the horrific scene in front of them, "They must be dead. All three of them."

Colin was not so certain, even as he gazed at the ruined church and the unrelenting blaze, "Let me have your radio."

Simon passed him the walkie-talkie set to the frequency monitored by the MI5 spooks surrounding the church, "All operatives, this is Signet. Did anyone get out? Report."

A dozen voices crackled back over the airwaves, one at a time. Their messages were identical, "No, sir. Nobody got out."

Colin handed the radio back to Simon, still not convinced, "It'll be days before forensics can get in there and be certain."

"Are you insane? No one could have survived that."

Colin would not let it go, "We have to be sure."

Simon moved closer to him and lowered his voice, "However this fire started is not important right now. One thing I do know is it ended your mission. No one got out and the records are all burned. It's taken a century, but your search finished here tonight. I can't keep my resources tied up unnecessarily. There will be too many questions if I do, questions I don't think you want asked or answered. It's over as far as Five is concerned."

"I understand what you're saying and why. Let's lower the alert level but leave some of your men here to maintain a perimeter in case somehow-"

He was cut off by the roar of a huge flame blasting upwards through the rubble as another section of wooden rafters from the crushed roof ignited.

It was enough for Simon, "They'll be no *somehow*. Go back to Six and get your arm treated. I'm pulling Five out now. Let the firefighters have full access to do their job. The local police from here and the surrounding towns can handle the rest." He gestured to Constable Darby who remained rooted in place, his mouth hanging open in shock.

The crypt was full of choking dust, smoke, ash, and rubble where parts of the ceiling had crumbled and fallen through. Across the length of the low roof above them, beams were already burning, and even though the three Americans had been partially protected by the thirty feet of dirt and rocks between them and the inferno above, they knew it was only minutes before flames consumed the entire crypt.

Cate was the first to speak, the fear present in her words, "What was that? It felt like an earthquake."

"The spire must have come down. If it did, it would have taken most of the church with it. Thank God for the way they built things back in the old days or we'd be gone as well."

Alex had barely finished his words as a blazing rafter separated from the ceiling and crashed to the floor, spreading the fire even closer to them.

"That doesn't help us, it's burning down here now and everything is going to go up in flames. This crypt is full of wood and paper and we can't get out!" Cate was so scared she could hardly talk.

There was a dark laugh from Eddie, "And we're going to burn to death in a fake fireplace. Look, it doesn't go anywhere. They put it in for show." He turned the light on his cell phone upwards, and as the beam cut through the dust and smoke it lit up a solid roof, covered with carvings, above the fireplace, not an open chimney flue.

Alex checked with his hands. It was unbroken stone. He spun around to Eddie and clasped his hands excitedly on the boy's shoulders "Of course! You're absolutely right!" He turned back to the inside of the fireplace and continued to feel the sculpted stonework.

Eddie was confused, "Why build it if you can't use it? Waste of time and money."

"I'll be sure to file a complaint with the vicar at his next Sunday service," quipped Cate, resigning herself to their desperate fate.

Another fiery joist smashed down, and now the flames were within a few feet of them. Alex continued to ignore the intense heat and everything happening outside of the fireplace and focused his attention on the intricate carvings inside. He grabbed Eddie's phone from him, "Let me have it. I need the light." The professor trained the flashlight on the wall and slowly moved the beam up and down.

"What's he doing?" Eddie turned to Cate for understanding, "Why is he looking at the artwork? We're about to burn to death, get crushed, or suffocated from the smoke, and he's checking out crummy antiques?"

Alex yelled to Eddie over his shoulder, "I'm finding a way out. There would be only one reason to build such an ornate fireplace, without a chimney, at the back of a crypt where it couldn't be used. And that's to hide a priest hole."

"What's a priest hole?"

"It's an escape tunnel. During the reformation, religious men were often hunted down and killed, many in their own churches, so the ministers and vicars put in priest holes to have a secret way out."

"Then where is it?" asked Cate, suddenly alert.

"Behind here somewhere, in the stonework. There must be a concealed door. We have to find a way to open it. Look for a slider or a hidden handle. Help me."

Those were the only words Alex needed to say, and now three sets of hands searched, pulled and pushed frantically as smoke filled the room and flames licked closer.

A section of the wall further into the crypt collapsed from the weight of the burning church above, spinning stone and dirt into the chamber and causing a flareup of the blaze. The heat became overwhelming, and even Alex doubted they would be able to find the secret door and get it opened in time.

Eddie coughed from the heavy smoke, breaking into a fit so strong he slipped backward from the inside of the fireplace, tumbling toward the flames. He shot his arm out, reaching to grab anything to steady his balance, and wrapped his hand around an inlaid crucifix. As he put his weight on it, the cross turned, and with it there was a loud, creaking sound and a stone door swung inwards, revealing a dark passageway.

"We found it! The priest hole!" yelled Alex. "Get into it now, while we still have time."

Cate, Eddie, then finally, Alex, dove headfirst into the low tunnel and crawled forward on their hands and knees as fast as they could, while behind them the crypt exploded with flames stretching upwards from the floor and curling across the ceiling.

With her phone in her teeth, its flashlight illuminating the narrow, damp shaft, Cate led the way, pushing through dense cobwebs and over mud puddles that had collected on the rough stone path scraping at her knees. Her backpack bumped and caught on the low, rock roof above, so she crouched down further to find room as she pushed on.

It seemed like forever the three of them crawled, until suddenly Cate stopped, pulling the phone from her mouth so she could call back, "The tunnel is changing. It's starting to go up."

She swept the cell's flashlight ahead of her and saw the passageway angling steeply upward and a few yards away it finished, an old, splintered wooden hatch marking the end.

Excited, she moved swiftly on her hands and knees up the slope to the flimsy barrier right above her, the two metal handles bolted into it showing it pulled open downwards. "I'm here," she told them. "There's some kind of overhead trapdoor. I'll see if I can get it open and climb up through it."

She wrapped her hands around the metal grips and tugged. There was no movement and the frail door remained closed, so she pulled again, this time locking her feet in place and putting all her weight behind her effort. There was a loud crack and the dry, broken wood splintered and fell apart in pieces on top of her, along with dirt, dust, and, horrifically, a shower of human bones tumbling down with it. As the ancient remains sought to smother her, Cate pushed them to the side, all the while stifling her impulse to scream, "I'm all right. I'm going up to take a look."

She climbed into a dark, tight space, the only faint light coming from the flickering flames that showed through a small crack in what seemed to be a solid covering penning her in. As she moved into the confined area, she felt more bones around her and realized, to her horror, their way out had led her into a raised concrete tomb.

There was a momentary urge to panic as all her childhood phobias flooded back – ghosts, vampires and zombies, being buried alive, trapped in a coffin with a dead body, claustrophobia, unable to move or escape – but Cate fought through them and reached up, forcing her fingers between the narrow gap and pushing hard.

The tomb's lid moved, and scraped to the side, allowing more light, cast by the flames from the burning ruin, to show her the way. She grabbed the edge of the marble vault and pulled herself cautiously out of the grave, her resurrection putting her inside a family mausoleum with an open iron gate facing the devastated church which smoldered a hundred yards away across the cemetery.

It was the first time she saw the extent of the horror they had been trapped beneath and found it hard to comprehend the scope of the nightmare she was witnessing.

The classic church was reduced to blazing rubble, with only two exterior walls remaining standing, the rest crushed by the massive spire's collapse.

Above the glowing ruin, an impossible vision unfolded as high intensity spotlights shining down from circling helicopters cut through twisting columns of smoke sucked upwards by their rotor blades, while below them a dozen glistening streams of water curved into the air, seeking to rain relief onto the burning embers, and framing the edge of the scene, sweeping blue and red beacons on top of the firetrucks pierced the night, adding to the surreal feel of the disaster.

Behind her, Alex and Eddie climbed from the tomb and in turn, stood in shock, trying to take in the magnitude of what had happened.

"This is crazy," was all Eddie could utter.

In the distance, past the security perimeter and firefighters, a series of TV trucks with raised antennas, transmitted live pictures of the tragedy to their news-hungry viewers around the globe.

"Can you see any police?" Alex whispered to Cate.

"Yes, a few. They are over with the firemen and reporters. They haven't seen me. They are mostly concerned with keeping the villagers back."

"Good. The tunnel has put us way outside of their cordon. We should get out of here while we can," said Alex.

He guardedly pushed apart the iron gate acting as the door to the ancient mausoleum and stepped through into the graveyard. Cate followed, and as Eddie brought up the rear, he slipped on a large bone. The boy paused, picked it up, realized what it was and gently placed it back into the open casket. He saw an aged, bronze plaque attached to the lid of the stone coffin with a name engraved into it, *Sir John Duncan 1421 – 1475.*

"Sorry, Sir John. I didn't mean to disturb your rest," he said respectfully, and joined the others.

Far outside the narrow police perimeter surrounding the entrance to what had been a treasured country church, three people were silhouetted against the flames as they hunched down and ran silently through the graveyard, moving further into the darkness and away from the catastrophic destruction.

CHAPTER TWELVE

Run

The narrow streets weaving through the center of the village of Thaxted were deserted. It seemed all two thousand eight hundred and forty-five people who called the former Saxon settlement home had congregated in the square in front of their cherished church, watching and sadly saying goodbye, as a major part of their town's history burned.

The only movement came as a dark figure emerged from the shadows and scurried toward a parked Ford Fiesta. He struggled for a moment, then opened the locked door, climbed in and vanished from view as he reached under the dashboard. Seconds later, the car roared to life and the figure popped back up and waved. Seeing his signal, two other people, a man and a woman, appeared and rushed to the car, getting quickly inside.

Eddie, smiling from ear to ear at his success, swiveled in the driver's seat, "Where to, boss?"

"As far from here as possible."

That was all Alex had to say, and Eddie slipped the Ford into gear, pulled away from the curb, and keeping the burning church in his rearview mirror, headed out into the night.

The sun was starting its rise as Eddie filled the car at the petrol station off of the A14. They had chosen this route north to Manchester as it avoided the M6 and the inevitable cameras waiting on the toll road there.

Cate strolled out of the busy snack shop, her arms full of sandwiches, drinks, junk food and two newspapers. She clambered into the back, and she and Alex waited for Eddie to finish with his gas duties.

As he jumped into the driver's seat, Alex gave his next directions, "Pull up about a hundred yards. There's a rest area by the big trucks. We can eat and drink and I can check the papers."

While the other two tucked into a world of fast food, Alex concentrated on the main front-page story in both publications, the bombing of Thaxted Parish Church. He read and re-read the articles before finally putting down the newspapers. Cate and Eddie stopped munching and waited to find out what the professor had discovered.

"The Express and the Daily Mail say we're dead." Alex stared at them, knowing they were tough words to hear.

"Dead? Whoa, that's weird," said Cate.

"You'll get used to it. It's the second time for me in one week," joked Eddie.

"The good thing about it is we have room to move, they won't be looking for us now. They think we were killed in the fire when the bombs we were planting went off."

"Why do they keep saying we are bombers?" wondered Eddie.

"To cover up the destruction at the church. As far as the readers know, we were terrorists trying to destroy a landmark and we made a mistake with the explosives. They tied it in with what happened at the British Museum."

"Yeah, but why that story? Why bombs?"

"To keep people frightened. There's so much fear in the world today," said Alex.

"Excuse me, Gandhi, but we're the ones with a reason to be scared. They're trying to fry our asses."

"And we still don't know why." Cate was confused.

"The answer may lie in finding out who Albert Wettin was," offered Alex.

"Do you think he was Jack the Ripper?" asked Eddie.

"Possibly. But even if he was, it wouldn't explain their interest in you."

"Interest? You call drugging me, flying me half-way around the world, trying to shoot me, then torching a church, interest? Haven't they got better things to spend their money on? Haven't they seen all the homeless everywhere?"

"You're right. Interest is an understatement. We have to make sense of this. If we find Mary's husband's roots, we may get an idea of what's driving them. We need a good library or bookstore where I can conduct some research. We can't go back to London, so we keep going north. Manchester is Britain's second biggest city; it should have what we're looking for."

Eddie reached under the dash and shorted two wires, starting the car back up. "The sooner we get there, the sooner we get this shit sorted out. You guys ready?"

Cate nodded.

"Let's go, Eddie. But stay within the limits. The last thing we need is to be stopped for speeding."

"Got it, teach." Eddie sedately backed out of the rest area and headed onto the A14 North.

Blackwell's Books featured an attached coffee shop with indoor and outdoor seating for both snacks and reading, which made it the perfect place for Alex to find the books he needed to reference and research while giving his companions a chance to relax, eat and drink.

He was pulling volumes from the shelves when Cate joined him, "I can't get on their Wi-Fi without a credit card, and that could be how they found us before-"

Alex cut her off with a smile, happy to be surrounded again by books, "Don't worry about it. Their ancestry collection is very comprehensive. They should have what we need here. If not, we'll find somewhere else you can go online."

Cate checked one of the shelves and took a step back in surprise, "You've got your own section! They have all your books. You're famous even here in England. You should sign a few of them for fun."

"Famous is the last thing I want to be about now. More importantly, I found these books on European names and lineage. You take this one, I'll go through these two, and let's see what we come up with." He led Cate towards a reading table. As they sat down, he noticed Eddie was missing, "Do you know where Eddie is?"

"He's fine. He's at the front of the store. That's where they have the graphic novels."

"Graphic novels?" Alex was not familiar with the term.

"Fancy way of saying comic books. Last time I saw him he was buried in a story called *Downing Street versus The Dead*. It's about Winston Churchill fighting Nazi zombies."

Alex was about to tell her he didn't remember that chapter of the Second World War but thought better of it and turned to his first research volume.

The top floor office at Vauxhall Cross was still filled with pictures of Eddie adorning one wall. Colin Brown sat at his desk staring at the river traffic cruising up and down the Thames, unable to shake the doubts lingering in his mind about the outcome of the previous night's operation. The plan had seemed so perfect, but until forensics could search through the debris and retrieve what remained of the bodies, he couldn't be one hundred percent certain. And with that much fire, devastation, and rubble to be cleared, they wouldn't be able to even start for days, which meant he might not get confirmation for weeks. Until he knew for sure, the boy's photographs would remain on his wall. Only after the results were in would he close the mission out. That was the way he had always worked in the past, and he was certainly not going to change now, not on such an important case.

The intercom buzzed and a voice informed him, "I have Simon Foster from MI5 for you."

Colin was instantly alert, "Put him through." He stared at his small phone bank waiting for it to light. The moment it did, he punched the button.

"What is it? Why are you calling me on an internal line and not my cell? The switchboard logs all incoming calls on this number."

"I am fully aware of that, but this is not ministry business, it's a courtesy call. That's why I'm using this line. Someone wants to talk with you."

Colin rolled his eyes, "More press? I've been putting out releases all morning with an explanation of how three Americans died trying to blow up British monuments. Not exactly the norm for a terrorist profile."

"We're doing the same at our end. One of the reporters I spoke to wanted to use the headline *The United States of Jihad.* I shut him down quickly. Our whole angle is pushing the theme it was a joint op, emphasizing domestic and international agencies coming together to protect the country. The tabloids love it when Five and Six are written about in the same story."

"Too true. Who wants to talk with me?"

"I'm sorry to bother you with this, Colin, but it's the cop from Thaxted. He insists on speaking with you, and I didn't want to give him your direct number."

"Thank you for that. Last thing I need right now is some Constable on the verge of retirement trying to get his kicks from a few spy stories."

"And that's about his speed. He's called me twice this morning already. I'll text you his number. If you can give him a ring, it should rid us of him."

"I will, and put an end to his annoyance." Colin clicked the phone off. Seconds later his cell buzzed as the text with the local policeman's number came through.

Colin stared at the display for a while, obviously irritated at the theft of his time, then steeled himself and dialed from his desk phone. The call was answered on the second ring.

"Constable Darby, here. How can I help you?"

"This is section chief, Colin Brown at Six. You wanted to speak to me?"

Constable Darby's voice picked right up at the sound of such a high-ranking person calling him, "Hello, sir, thank you for getting back to me. I need to get my report done before my sarge returns or I'll catch hell. He already heard what happened and called me from his holiday in Spain. I was hoping to attach a copy of your report to mine for confirmation. And if you have one with an MI6 letterhead, it would make a lovely souvenir."

"They're finishing the brief downstairs now. I'll instruct them to send it over to your station."

"Thanks. Never had nothing like that happen in Thaxted before. Plus, I was up 'till dawn on another call. Two unusual things in one night. You know what they say, if it's not one thing it's another."

Colin had no interest in colloquialisms, but this tweaked his suspicions, "Two things?"

"Yes. The other wasn't near as big of course, but what could be?"

"What was it?"

"Martin Pritchard's car got stolen."

"What is unusual about a stolen car?" After so many years of following leads and hunches, Colin felt the other shoe was about to drop.

"Well, to tell you the truth, we haven't had a car go missing in ten years. We're a small village so you'd notice if someone nicked your ride and was cruising around in it. I'm pretty sure it must have been outside folks who took it, 'cause Martin's car isn't anywhere in Thaxted anymore."

Colin jumped to his feet and yelled into the phone, his face inches from the speaker, "Constable Darby, I want everything on that car, and not only the make and license. I want to know if it has scratches, dents, bumper stickers, when the oil was changed last. And if the owner-"

"Martin Pritchard," Darby cut in, helpfully.

"Yes, whatever. If he has pictures of the vehicle, I want those too. This is your priority today, Constable Darby."

"But what about my sergeant needing the reports?"

Colin raised his voice, his tone one of command, "Goddamn it, Darby, I'm not going to say this again. Have this on my desk within the next two hours or your sergeant will be the least of your worries. I'll text you the number and email to send it to."

He slammed the receiver down, hanging up on the unfortunate constable, and furiously walked his room, considering his options.

Knowing he had no other alternative; he pulled his secure cell phone and dialed Simon Foster at MI5.

"Why did we leave so quickly? I hadn't finished the story. And this place sucks!"

Eddie was not wrong. The once lovely park outside of Manchester's booming business center had become a last resort for the poor and homeless of the city, displaced by the ongoing gentrification of the municipality. Litter blew across the barren dirt where carefully tended grass had grown years before, and a wasteland of tents, cardboard boxes, and torn mattresses mixed with the rocks, syringes, and broken bottles replacing the verdant shrubbery that had encircled the park in its long-gone glory days.

Over two hundred hopeless, derelict people gathered there in small groups, some sleeping, some smoking, others huddled close together to disguise what activity they were up to. It was a no-man's-land where lost souls disappeared. And that's why Alex had brought them there.

He paced back and forth in front of the graffitied bench, as Cate and Eddie stared at him. He ignored their looks and checked and rechecked the marked pages, hoping he had made a mistake with his research, but knowing he hadn't. His brow crinkled with deepening concern and he slammed the book closed and halted. He was silent as he locked eyes with his friends, his face a portrait of despair.

"We have to go."

"Good. Happy to leave this shithole," agreed Eddie.

Cate sensed there was something more, "Where are we going?"

"Anywhere." Alex's voice was flat empty, beaten, "But it has to be out of the country."

"Eddie can't leave. He hasn't got an ID."

"You're right." Alex put his hands to his face in desperation, "Fuck."

That single word shocked both Cate and Eddie. After all they had been through, they had never heard him swear or seen him close to this state. A man on the verge of giving up.

Eddie broke the dreadful silence, "There may be a way. We have Brown's passport. You can take a picture of me on my phone, and I can trick the photo out on Cate's laptop. Then if we find a good print shop, I should be able to finish the job and come up with a serviceable fake. I've done it with IDs before and it usually works if they don't check too closely."

"An ID is one thing, but getting into another country using an altered passport at their immigration, will be hard. It's not the same as changing the date on a driver's license to buy beer," warned Alex.

"Are there any countries that aren't as strict?"

Alex looked at Eddie, "I don't know, I really don't. I'm sorry."

"What's changed, Alex? What did you find? Wasn't it bad enough already?" asked Cate.

"I'll show you." He sat between them on the filthy bench and opened the book. "I bought this at the store because it has everything in it. Everything. And it's worse than any of us knew."

Cate and Eddie exchanged glances. Worse than attacking a legendary hotel, burning down a church, or innocent women being sliced apart by Jack the Ripper?

"We were wrong in thinking it was Mary's idea to travel to Thaxted and be married in secret because she didn't want to be recognized. It was, in fact, the wishes of her fiancé, Albert, to hold their wedding way out there."

"But why?" asked Cate. "Mary was the one with the scandalous reputation. What had Albert done?"

"Albert hadn't *done* anything. The reason he wanted to be married in a small town in Essex was because he was too well known throughout London, and any ceremony there involving him, within the city, would have caused a sensation," explained Alex.

"How come he was so famous? Was he a movie star or something?" wondered Eddie.

"This was long before movies were invented," said Cate.

"Eddie, your distant relative, Albert Wettin, was famous because he was the first-born grandson of Victoria Wettin. As such he was the rightful heir to his grandmother's empire, as would be the first-born male of his line."

"Empire?" Eddie wasn't expecting that word, at best he thought there might be an inheritance the long-forgotten in-laws were fighting over. "What kind of *empire* did this Wettin lady have? Was she like the Jeff Bezos of her time?"

"She was much more than that. Your great-great-great-grandfather died unexpectedly under suspicious circumstances. He was barely twenty-eight and they said he died childless. As a result, Victoria Wettin's line went to her second-born grandchild. Had they known Albert had a son with Mary Kelly, history would be very different."

"But she was a prostitute?" said Cate.

Eddie forced a laugh, "Watch your mouth. That's my whatever many times grandma you're talking about."

"It didn't matter what she did. Mary Kelly and Albert Wettin were legally married in Thaxted in a Church of England ceremony. Their offspring should have inherited everything from Victoria Wettin."

"Is that why they wanted Mary killed, so the other relatives would get the money?" It was beginning to make sense to Cate.

"If it was just money. But it's so much more. And to avoid the embarrassment of having a prostitute linked with her family, Victoria may have ordered not only her murder, but also the murder of Albert, her own first-born grandson, when he refused to obey her and went looking for his child."

"And I'm related to her, a woman who'd kill her own grandkid? Who was this Victoria? She sounds like a piece of work."

"She was." Alex focused on Eddie, "Your family, the Wettins, ruled with an iron fist over the largest empire the planet has ever known. Larger than that of the Romans, Mongols, or even the Persians. In 1917, when the world was at war, her family changed their name because it was too German sounding and they didn't want to upset their subjects."

"*Their subjects*? What does that mean?"

"It means they no longer used the name Wettin, and instead became The Windsors. The woman who began all this, your grandmother, five generations removed, is remembered as Queen Victoria."

Cate jumped up in shock as the implication became real, "You're saying Eddie's bloodline goes directly back to Albert, Queen Victoria's first-born grandson."

"Correct. And Albert's father became King Edward VII."

"Yeah, but what's that got to do with anything?" Eddie couldn't grasp the importance of such a far-off family tree.

"Eddie, the family who rule Great Britain and the Commonwealth are there because the line of succession passed to them when King Edward's son, Albert Wettin, died childless. But now we have proof he had a baby boy who should have been heir to the throne, and his blood runs in your veins. It was Prince Albert, the Duke of Clarence and Avondale, who they tested your DNA against. Hair and nail samples have always been saved from the Royal family. They must have found it matched and confirmed beyond any doubt you are the long-sought great-great-great grandson."

"And what does that mean to me?"

"Cate, do you want to tell him?"

Cate stood over Eddie and took a breath, "If you put aside counting all the great-greats and concentrate on following the bloodline, it leads straight to you and means the throne of the British Empire is yours by birthright."

It was Eddie's turn to be silent. He looked up at Cate, then turned to Alex, "Even if this DNA bloodline shit is true, it all went down so long ago, right?"

"Wrong," said Alex. "The Royal Family's bloodline is everything. The British crown traces its lineage back almost a thousand years to 1066. A century is nothing. The birthright is what counts."

"And that's why they've been after him – and because of what we know, after us as well? Correct?" asked Cate.

"Yes. Right now, the monarchy is in a very vulnerable position and if anyone found out about the existence of a true heir, it could bring it down - look what occurred after Diana's death with the uproar from the people against the Queen, and then the controversy with Harry giving up his Royal duties for Meghan. If Britain lost having the Crown to oversee Parliament, it could become politically unstable as has happened with Italy and France and Spain where socialism is on the upswing, and even fascism is appearing again. There are people on both sides of the Atlantic who wouldn't let that happen, after all, the United Kingdom is a major nuclear force, and is also the only power that always stands with America in times of conflict. Do you really think the United States government and the military-industrial complex would allow their multi-trillion-dollar resource to be lost?"

"But I wouldn't bring anything down." For the first time Eddie sounded like the young teen he was.

"Just your being alive could do that. That's why they want to kill you, to eliminate any potential threat to the throne and to the stability of America's number one ally."

"How come you didn't know this before? I thought you knew everything?"

"No one knows everything. European scandals and British Royals are not my field of expertise. Had it been American Presidents and a constitutional crisis, it would have been a different matter."

"I guess." Eddie's eyes were heavy, "Either way, we're screwed, right?"

"Yes. That's why we have to leave now," said Alex.

"Where can we go? Won't MI6 keep after us when they don't find our bodies in the church?"

Alex shook his head sadly as he replied to Eddie, "Yes. And the concern is not only with MI6 here in England." He took a long pause, knowing how hard the next words would be to hear, "The reason the British Secret Service were able to get to you inside a secure facility in California so quickly is because they must have had help internally there. And that means they are working with America's security agencies, probably the FBI, the NSA and the CIA too. Remember, there are military and big-money interests in both countries that do not want to be endangered. They will all be looking for you, and now, looking for us."

"Oh my God! Stop! I know what you're going to say. Don't even go there." Cate clenched her fists in angst.

"I'm sorry. We've opened Pandora's Box and unleashed a fury that is not going to end. With these forces in place we can never return home. They would find us there and we know too much. We have to disappear."

"I have family." She fought back the tears even as she knew Alex was right.

"Then do this to protect them and everyone you love. Right now, we finally understand why this is happening and we have a head start. In addition to all the cash we have, there is the two hundred thousand dollars Brown paid me to find Eddie-"

Eddie sat up in surprise, "How much?"

"Actually, in excess of twenty million. That's how much these organizations thought you were worth."

Eddie slumped back against the bench, speechless.

"We know how serious they are about getting their hands on you and what will happen if they do. But we can use their cash to run. This may be our only chance to get out. We leave England, see if I am able to transfer the rest of my money from the bank if it hasn't already been seized, then change our names, pick up new IDs, keep moving and try to disappear."

"Like Mary Kelly did over a century ago." It was hard for Cate to reconcile the irony.

"Yes. Even back then she knew they would never give up and was terrified about what they would do to her and her family. Mary was desperate not to be found, and that's why she moved so often, and changed their name twice."

"And now her offspring has to do the same. You're right, we have no choice, we have to run before they get to us and to our families. We should try to fix Eddie's ID, head to the airport and get a flight out," Cate knew now it was their only option.

"Where will we go?" asked Eddie.

"Somewhere within Europe. Internal flights are less regulated. We'll pick a smaller country, more off the map-"

"Not like Germany or Belgium?" said Cate.

"No. Northern European countries will be too restrictive and I'm sure have stringent passport controls. We'll choose a quieter, laid-back vacation destination. A little town used to getting summer tourists from all over, who rarely travel and might be using expired IDs, not major financial capitals dealing on a daily basis with businessmen and expecting their arrivals to have all the correct documents and visas in place. It'll be our best chance." He got to his feet, "We have to go."

Knowing they had no other choice, Eddie and Cate fell in line behind him, and the silent procession were lost in their thoughts, contemplating their uncertain future, as they left the run-down park, more dejected than the destitute and homeless remaining in the desolate grounds.

CHAPTER THIRTEEN

Typhoon Strike One

The badge on Colin's suit announced he was a visitor on someone else's turf, but the confidence and assurance in his stride showed he hardly felt uncomfortable or out of place as he marched with Simon Foster through the building housing MI5.

"How is your arm?" asked Simon as he led the way through the long, narrow corridors.

"My arm?" questioned Colin.

"Your wound. You know, where you were shot."

"Oh, that. It was only a scratch. Three stitches and a bandage. Nothing really."

"You were lucky. That was the best place you could have been hit." There was a hint of misgiving in Simon's voice.

"I guess sometimes the good guys luck out," smiled Colin.

"I guess." Simon pointed to the end of the hallway, "It's right ahead."

Blocking the corridor in front of them was a reinforced metal door, controlled by two armed policemen standing on either side.

"Going in, sir?" asked the first of the guards.

"That we are, sergeant," replied Simon.

The guard swiped his magnetic key card against the electronic reader panel, unlocking the heavy door which opened smoothly outwards on its hydraulic hinges.

"Thank you." Simon turned to Colin, "Follow me in. We'll see what they have for us."

The two top ranking spies entered the NCC - the National Communications Center, deep inside the headquarters of Britain's internal security service, in Thames House.

The air hummed, as a mass of electronics, fed by orbiting geosynchronous satellites linked to two super computers, went about their automated jobs of checking emails and phone calls made within the United Kingdom for key trigger words. Hundreds of monitors of all sizes filled three walls, and operatives jammed the room as they manned their stations overseeing Britain's six million surveillance cameras. The tension level was elevated as the techs switched rapidly from screen to screen, their speed and diligence making it obvious an urgent alert was in place. Even Colin Brown, used to the invasive drone technology MI6 developed for their global reconnaissance, was impressed at the attention and coverage Five was bringing to the forefront to spearhead this search.

A young female, scanning a desk loaded with three monitors, spun around, "I have footage on the car, sir, and a confirmed match on the plates. This is from a petrol station's security camera. Time stamp on it is from six hours ago."

She hit *enter* on her keyboard, and the video played back on the largest of her screens.

Colin and Simon locked their stare on the display and watched as Cate walked across the forecourt to the car, her arms full of groceries. Standing at the rear of the vehicle was Eddie York, pumping gas.

Simon pulled his gaze from the screen and looked at Colin, "You were right. They are alive."

Colin didn't reply to him, but his eyes burned with anger. Ignoring Simon, he spoke forcefully to the female operative, "Give me possible destinations."

"When they left the petrol station they were heading north on the A14. That's towards Wolverhampton, Birmingham, Manchester, even Scotland, if they keep going."

He fixed his glare on Simon, "I knew it. You have to make this priority one."

Simon felt Mr. Brown's ire, but this was not the place to address his counterpart's fury. Instead, he took control, "Now we have a location and a heading, I want all police cars north of Oxford on the lookout for the vehicle. Get boots on the ground in Birmingham and Manchester. Have every local agency throughout the entire Midlands check their CCTV from the last six hours. We're close people, I can feel it. Let's bring them in."

He looked back to Colin for his approval, but received none. Colin spun on his heels and marched out, too impatient to remain in a room that merely monitors action.

Late-season holidaymakers hoping to find the last of the summer sun packed Britain's busiest airport outside of London. Manchester International was the jumping off point for the Midlands and the North, and among the thousands passing through Terminal Three that day, were the trio waiting in the lounge for their non-stop flight on Northumbria Airlines to Portugal.

Alex nervously slapped the plane tickets up and down on his thigh as he waited to get onboard and leave the country.

Cate saw how anxious he was, "Want me to hang on to them for you? Or I can put them in my backpack with everything else. They'll be safe in there."

"No, I'll keep them. I'm getting used to it, unfortunately."

She looked at the reluctant traveler and sucked in a deep breath. There was something she had to say, "Your wife would be proud of you."

Alex flashed a surprised look at her, but it was clear he didn't agree with her compliment, "Thank you. But once again, what I've done is too little, too late."

"Not for us. You've kept Eddie and me alive."

The terminal's P.A. system cut off his reply, "This is the first boarding call for Flight 4052 to Faro. We'd like to invite our Premium Class passengers to board. Please have your tickets ready and your passports open to the photo page for inspection."

The crowd got to their feet, eager to start their holidays, and shuffled forward, even as the announcement repeated in Portuguese.

Eddie heard the strange language, "What is that?"

"Portuguese. It's what they speak where we're going."

"And I suppose you understand it?"

"Not a word, unfortunately," admitted Alex.

Cate cut in on their conversation and pointed to the two airline employees at the gate, "They're checking passports again and using scanners."

"I hope my fake one works. It's S.B.T.," said Eddie.

"What is S.B.T?"

"Sweaty Butt Time. When you're almost safe but not quite. Like if a cop pulls you over and you're not sure whether he's going to spot if the bike's stolen or not, you know."

Alex didn't know, and shook his head, as his attention returned to the gate agents inspecting the passports.

Cate interrupted his thoughts, "I have an idea." She slipped her backpack off and slid out her laptop, "Let me check something. The airport has free Wi-Fi with no login required. Thank you, Manchester!"

The Public Address system boomed out again, "We would like to begin general boarding. Passengers in rows twenty-eight to thirty-six may now line up ready for secondary inspection before boarding Northumbria Airlines Flight 4052 to Faro, Portugal."

"That's us," said Eddie, as he jumped eagerly to his feet.

Colin burst into the communications room of MI5 at Thames House and saw Simon hunched over the central console conferring with two operatives.

"What is it? What have you found?"

"Thanks for coming back. We're getting closer. We've located the stolen car," answered Simon.

"Where? Are they on the move?"

"We're not sure. The car is parked at Manchester airport." Simon put his hand on the tech's shoulders, "Can you pull up the footage?"

The center screen filled with the picture of the Ford Fiesta sitting there, one of a thousand vehicles in the huge, outdoor lot.

"Fuck. They're rabbiting." Colin swung from the image to Simon, "Tell me the airport is on lockdown."

"It is now. As soon as we picked up the car, I put it on a level three-"

"Now?" Colin was furious. "It should have been on level three from the moment we knew they were still alive and heading north."

"We called a level three for all ground transportation, and priority one reports on surveillance in cities and motorways."

"But not airports?"

"No. Everything they'd done before indicated they would be not using airports."

"For Christ's sake, Simon, they're fucking Yanks. They're trying to get home. Of course they'd hit the airports. Did you think they were going to swim back to America?"

"From what you told me," Simon looked at the men around him and guarded his words; this remained a classified op, "they weren't ready to leave the UK yet. They were still," he looked for the right word, "searching."

"Whatever they were doing, airports were an obvious target. Damn it, you know Six can't pull this coverage at home. Internal security is Five's department, not mine. Have your men bring up everything from the terminals. Notify the airport police to detain them as-"

"Sir, can I interrupt?" An agent stared nervously at the two high-level spooks arguing behind him.

"What is it?" asked Simon.

"I'm getting ticketing information with the suspect's names."

"Tell me."

"I heard you mention America, but they're not heading for the States. At least two of them aren't. I have passport confirmations on Alex Turner and Caitlin Shannon. They bought tickets for Faro, Portugal."

Even though the operative wasn't one of his men, Colin had to ask, "What about Eddie or Edward York?"

The operative checked the list on his screen again and looked back at them, "No. He's not on the passenger manifest."

Simon's face clouded, "They wouldn't leave without the kid. Not after all this. Can you check again?"

He returned to his display and scrolled down, then stopped. He rechecked the screen and turned back to his boss and the man with him, "I think you should look at this." He waved Colin, not Simon, forward, "I know who you are, sir, and your badge has your name on it. And the manifest says there is a Colin Brown traveling on the Northumbria Airlines flight to Faro, and his ticket was purchased with cash at the same time as the other two."

Colin's eyes exploded as he saw his name highlighted on the list, "Those bastards! They've used my passport for him."

The second seated operative, hearing this conversation, seized the initiative and whirled around, "Chief Foster, I have video from the gate of the passengers waiting for the flight. Would you be able to ID them from it?"

"I would. Play it," demanded Colin.

Security footage showed two hundred bored tourists impatiently waiting for their boarding call, kids running between their seated parents, teens texting, people munching on fast food and searching through their carry-ons for anything to pass the time.

Colin jabbed his finger at the screen, "There. Zoom in and clarify."

The tech increased the gain on the picture, and the three fugitives filled the display.

"That's them. No doubt."

"I'll run a facial recognition protocol-"

Colin cut him off, "No need. I can confirm a positive ID on all three."

Simon barked an order to his team, "Contact flight control. Have them hold the plane. No one gets on or off. Keep it away from any gate or jet bridge."

The tech was reluctant with his next words, "Sir, the footage you saw was two hours old. Flight 4052 took off on time, fifty-three minutes ago."

"That will put them in international airspace and out of Five's jurisdiction." Simon stared at Colin, "This is all you now. What assets does Six have in Portugal?"

"Portugal? No permanent assets. I have agents in Madrid and Barcelona, but they wouldn't get to Faro in time to meet the flight. Can Five order the plane back?"

Simon shook his head, "No, they are outside of British airspace now. The best we could do is request they divert to Paris, Marseilles or Biarritz."

"Shit! We can't let the damned French get their hands on this." Colin pounded his head with his fists in frustration then pulled himself together, "I don't have time to return to my office at Six. Can we use yours? Now?"

"Certainly. Follow me." Simon led the way out of the NCC, taking the painfully slow elevator up five floors to the Director's station at Thames House.

Unlike Colin's glass and marble office at MI6 headquarters at Vauxhall Cross, Simon Foster's was dated and damp, as MI5 was relegated to a stone and brick building completed in 1930 in Millbank, alongside the river. The windows were small and old, and the carpet worn. But Colin failed to notice the décor; he had other things to be concerned about.

"Is this room secure?"

"Of course. I'm the Director of Five. It's hardly an open-door policy here, you know."

"Are there any recording devices? If so, this is an official request that you disclose them to me, or if you fail to do so, any contents or recordings on those devices will be viewed as entrapment and cannot be used as evidence now or at any time in the future, in any court of law in the land."

Colin's formal tone and repetition of a legal warning puzzled Simon, "No, there are no recording devices. This is a secure room."

"Good. I'm calling the Minister of Defense on my cell. I want you here with me for authentication." Colin pulled out his mobile and slipped the mini-USB into the power connection at the bottom of the phone. Simon recognized it immediately as a high-level security device to scramble and avoid the interception and recording of calls.

Colin punched a number on his contact list and waited. The call was answered before the second ring, "M.O.D. here."

"Minister, it's Signet with Six. Raven is also here representing Five. You might have heard of the level three lockdown in effect. We now have confirmation of a Code Red strike in progress."

There was silence before the Minister of Defense replied, "I am required to ask, is this a drill?"

"Unfortunately not, Minister. We are confirmed Code Red."

"My God! Who? Do you have a target and time frame, and what measures are needed to stop them?"

"They are the same bombers who attacked the British Museum and destroyed the church in Thaxted."

"I was told they were dead?"

"We thought they were. But they have been seen boarding a plane bound for Faro, Portugal. All three of them. We have a positive ID."

"Faro? The Algarve? What is it, a terrorist holiday?"

"We wish it was, Minister. They intend to hijack the plane and fly it to Biarritz. There they will detonate it over the city. The death toll this time of year, with the town full of tourists from all across Europe, would be extremely high."

Hearing this, Simon took his eyes from the phone and stared incredulously at Colin.

The M.O.D. continued, "What could they possibly want with Biarritz?"

"We have been informed it's to make a political statement. They will send the French this information a few minutes before detonation. If we don't act to intervene, we will be blamed as complicit in the attack. The plane left a British airport carrying the three Americans. They will consider our inaction as a deliberate payback for not supporting us in the Middle East and for the growing tensions since Brexit and the closing of our borders to France during the Covid-19 pandemic. Who knows what their Socialist government will do, but we'll have thousands of dead and a political mess on our hands which the French could escalate to the entire EU and begin a crippling trade war."

"Damn it. With our economy in the shitter, this is the last thing we need right now. What does Six suggest?"

"We have been unable to turn the plane around, so we have to assume it is as good as lost already. We know from the destruction caused in Thaxted what these bombers are capable of. We must stop them from reaching French airspace and detonating above Biarritz. I need fighters to intercept and destroy the plane over the ocean."

"Did you say destroy it?" Britain's Minister of Defense was shocked, "We've done a hundred intercepts but never this. Certainly not with a passenger plane."

"Minister, we've never faced this before. These are armed terrorists who have already attacked British assets twice. And we know from 9/11 the devastation a commercial jet can cause to a town or city."

The line went quiet before the Minister of Defense spoke again, "Here's what I'm willing to do. I'll have the RAF put two Typhoons up to trail the plane. I'll hand control over to you only if the plane deviates from its set flight plan and heads for Biarritz."

"That's perfect, Minister. I'll stand by on this number for your call." Colin hung up.

"What the hell was that?" Simon demanded.

"Taking care of business."

"The MOD sounded as if he didn't know what this is really about and what the Americans are after. Have you even talked with him about this operation?"

"There was no reason to speak to him before. This has always been a need-to-know op."

"Wait." Simon was confused, "Who else have you left out? Does the Prime Minister, the Home Secretary, or even the Palace, know about any of this?"

Colin glared back at Simon, his silence answering the question.

"You're running this yourself, aren't you?" Simon continued. "You only brought me in because Six can't operate freely within England so you needed me and you needed Five's resources."

"I brought you in for a reason. You're the head of MI5, I don't have to tell you your motto."

"No, you don't." It was Simon's turn to get angry, "And it is very different from yours, from MI6's, Semper Occultus – *Always Secret*. Ours is not about concealment and self-interest, it is open and about service to our country, and I have lived with it and believed it, every word, for twenty-two years. Regnum Defende - *Defend The Realm*."

"And what is the realm if not the Crown? Why involve them unnecessarily? Would you have them fall?"

"I would never allow the Crown to fall. But the Americans must know? They gave you full cooperation when you were there."

"Yes, of course the Americans know. They don't have the same scruples as you. Their military is always their top priority. When they found out this situation, they were the ones who funded the operation. Do you think they would risk even a one-percent chance of losing their bases in the UK or any of our overseas territories? No, there's far too much money involved."

"But you are talking about killing people, innocent people."

"Don't try pulling that on me. I'm not deliberately targeting the passengers; they just happen to be in the way. If there was another solution, I'd take it. And what did you think we would do when we found the kid and the other two? Talk nasty to them?"

"There has to be a better way. There must be."

"No. While that boy is alive the freedom and safety of every person in Britain and America is at risk. If he took the throne and used that influence to rip apart our alliance, what would happen then? Without our support in Iraq and Afghanistan, the American losses would have been catastrophic, and without the US forces standing with us in Europe, the Russians would come through Germany and Poland so fast it would make World War II look like a Sunday picnic."

"But we don't know for sure the boy would cause those kinds of problems."

"My sources tell me otherwise. I already let you in on what his plans and leanings might be, and there are a lot of important people who aren't willing to take any chances. Like it or not, we're the guardians of the free world and neither country can do it alone. Isn't it worth sacrificing a few lives for the greater good of many?"

"Not if those lives include innocent passengers on that plane. You'd never get away with it," threatened Simon.

"How did someone so fucking naïve become the head of one of our security services?" Colin was disgusted, "Of course we'd get away with it. Write a few checks, pay a little compensation, send out some sympathetic letters and it will be forgotten in days. It was with TWA flight 800 when the US Navy blew it from the sky in ninety-six, and when the Russians took out Korean Air 007, it hardly made headlines, and we were so busy preparing for the Covid-19 outbreak in 2020 that when Iran, of all nations, fired their missiles and killed all one hundred and seventy-six people on the Ukrainian Airlines plane, nobody batted an eye. Who will give a shit when we say three terrorists who had already burned down a beloved church, died when they bombed a flight to Portugal?"

Simon stood silent in the face of Colin's twisted logic, but having dealt with so many in a position of power and wealth, he found it hard to dispute his claims.

"Do you have radio capabilities here in your office?" asked Colin.

"Absolutely. The entire building is linked with the center downstairs," replied Simon.

"Then have your people set up a direct line with the pilot of Flight 4052, then patch it through to me. I need to speak to him."

Praying it would bring about a peaceful conclusion, Simon grabbed the internal phone to have the communications put in place.

The sun was dropping toward the horizon as two Eurofighter Typhoons screamed skyward from RAF Coningsby. The pilots of Eleven squadron reached five thousand feet before banking their planes hard east to take them the forty miles across Lincolnshire and out over the ocean. There they could engage their afterburners, gain altitude and go supersonic in pursuit of their target, a lumbering 737 carrying two hundred and three passengers and seven crew.

The lead pilot checked his course; based on the relative speed and direction, they should be in range in thirty-one minutes. He glanced over his shoulder through the hardened Perspex canopy and smiled. That would still give them plenty of daylight to make a visual ID. He wasn't sure what this was all about, whether it was another exercise or one of the endless drills they were put through, but he did know that immediately prior to takeoff they had armed the four BVR Meteor advanced long-range missiles he carried beneath his swept-back wings. If this wasn't a training sortie, then someone was in for a very unpleasant evening.

"I have the pilot on the line. You're patched through," said Simon. He pointed to his phone.

Colin reached for it and hesitated, "Secure?"

"It's secure, and you can use the headset. But remember, it's a commercial flight; the plane will have their Black Box recording the call at their end."

Colin stiffened. He would have to deal with that eventuality later if the box wasn't destroyed in the blast or subsequent crash. He pulled on the headset and mic, "Flight 4052, come in. This is Colin Brown with MI6, London."

There was a momentary delay before a female voice came over the line, "MI6, this is flight 4052, pilot Angela Griffin. How can I help you?"

"Pilot Griffin, is your cockpit secure?"

"MI6, it is, and we have no problems or unusual activity onboard." A smile crept into her voice, "Apart from this. It's my first conversation with Britain's SIS."

"I'm sorry to have to make this call, and to inform you we have confirmed three armed fugitives are on your plane. For your safety and for the safety of the passengers, we need you to alter your course to Biarritz, and land there, where we will have a security team waiting."

"MI6, this is highly unusual. I need you to reconfirm this order."

"Pilot Griffin, it is indeed unusual. These persons have been pursued by the police and MI5 for several days and were responsible for the attack on the British Museum and the bombing of the Thaxted Parish Church."

"MI6, I am aware of both events. I saw them on the news. They're the ones on board?"

"I'm afraid so. They managed to get through the security in Manchester with arms and explosives. Please switch to radio frequency Alpha Bravo Seven, I repeat Alpha Bravo Seven, and lock all future transmissions to that bandwidth. That way, if anything happens before you reach Biarritz, we can monitor the cockpit radio broadcasts without them knowing we are listening in."

"MI6, will do. What should I tell the passengers about the course change?'

"You're the pilot, make something up. Weather or mechanical. Let them know it'll only be for a brief time. Once our people board the plane and remove them, you'll be on your way again."

"Got it, MI6. Anything further before we change transmission codes?"

"No, Pilot Griffin. Godspeed to you and your passengers."

"Thank you. Switching now."

The line went dead.

Simon glared at Colin, "If I'm not mistaken, Alpha Bravo Seven is a restricted MI6 frequency."

"Exactly. We'll be the only ones who can reach them."

"If you're wrong about this, hundreds of innocent people will die needlessly."

"I wasn't wrong yesterday. You were."

"What now?"

Colin tapped his secure cell phone, "I'll wait for the Minister of Defense to call me on the status of the fighters."

"You can stay here in my office. I'm going back down to Communications. I want to see if they've come across any new information that could help."

Colin nodded his approval, happy that Simon and his negative vibes were both leaving.

Simon rushed into the National Communications Center of MI5, desperate for anything to change the tragedy that lay inevitably ahead. "Give me an update, people," he demanded.

"We have firm radar fixes on Flight 4052 from our posts in Jersey and Plymouth. The plane is still on course for Faro," answered a tech monitoring her screen.

"I'm picking up two fighters in pursuit. Three hundred and ten kilometers behind and closing fast," called out another operative.

Simon paced over to the original technician who had found the names on the manifest, "Any changes to report?"

"Only this," replied the agent. "I pulled up these scans from passport control. All three check out. Alex Turner, Caitlin Shannon and Edward York traveling as Colin Brown, Positive IDs on their pictures. They went through security at Terminal Three in Manchester."

"Damn." Simon had been praying for a different answer.

"And I've contacted the airline for a copy of the final manifest after they land," added the tech.

Simon was taken aback by the comment, "Final manifest?"

"Yes, sir. It's something they complete on the plane when the doors are closed. It's not released until after they touch down."

"I thought we had the final manifest?"

"The gate has supplied the ticketed manifest," said the tech. "The final manifest takes into account any overbooking, stand-bys, and no-shows. It's standard airline procedure."

"Is there a chance they're not on the plane?"

"A very small chance. It wasn't a sold-out flight so they wouldn't have been bumped-"

"Is their car still in the lot?"

"Let me find out. I have the reference number for the camera. Give me a minute."

"Please hurry."

The tech could hear the desperation in his superior's voice, "Okay. This is a live picture right now."

Simon stared at the screen. Damn it, he thought to himself. The blue Ford Fiesta was sitting there. It hadn't moved.

The tech could feel his disappointment, "Sorry, sir, but if they split, they didn't leave in that car."

Simon swung his head away from the display to the technician, "What did you say?"

"That if they left, it wasn't in that car, sir. They would have had to have taken another."

"Oh my God! Get me airport parking control for Terminal Three on the phone right now."

The sky turned orange as a beautiful sunset drew in over the Atlantic. The two Typhoons adjusted their course and headed due south, their afterburners closing the miles between them and their target.

The lead pilot tweaked his heads-up display and the radar image of the passenger plane disappeared, and in the distance, he could pick out its vapor trail with his naked eyes.

He clicked on his radio, "M.O.D., this is Typhoon Strike One. We have a visual on the target."

The command center of the Ministry of Defense in Whitehall had switched to wartime mode. Military personnel crowded the room, barely giving enough space for the radio and video operators to man their displays. The Minister of Defense, in his full dress Admiral's uniform answered the call himself.

"Typhoon Strike One. Hang back and maintain distance. Do not lose visual contact, but you are not to engage unless ordered."

"M.O.D, this is Typhoon Strike One. Remaining fifty miles behind target. We will take no action unless instructed."

The Minister turned to his other officers, "So far, so good. The plane is still on course for Faro. If it stays that way the local police can handle things on the ground for Six and we can call off the hounds." He gazed at the radar screen mapping the relative positions and progress of the three planes, "But if not…" his voice trailed off at the possibility of giving the terrible order.

The Boeing 737, pursued by the two fighters, continued south across the Bay of Biscay.

"He's on the line, sir."

"About time!" Simon ceased his nervous pacing and grabbed the phone, "Who is this?"

The voice confirmed they had reached the right person, "It's Charles Perry, the supervisor for Terminal Three parking. What do you need?"

"My name is Simon Foster from MI5 and this-"

The voice interrupted him, "MI5? No shit. What's going on?"

"Mr. Perry, if you'll let me talk, I'll tell you. We have a high-level security threat we are handling and we need to know if you can access the cameras and registers of all the attendants on duty during the past ninety minutes?"

He took a long breath, "That's hard. We have eighteen cameras monitoring the lot. Actually seventeen, one's been sent out to be fixed. It was damaged in the last rains we had. And we have three exit booths, with two cameras at each, one for the license plate and the other covering the driver and the attendant. It would take a while to go through them all."

"I'm afraid we don't have *a while*. We have to have this now."

"Then help me out here. What are you looking for? A hit and run? Mugging? A smashed window? What?"

"We're looking for someone who left in the last sixty minutes, probably paid cash, and possibly had no exit ticket with them. And there would be three passengers in the car."

"What kind of car would it be?"

"We don't know."

"I thought MI5 knew everything. You're not giving me a lot to go on. Hang on. Let me call the cashiers and see what I can come up with."

"Thank you. And please hurry."

The passengers onboard Flight 4052 were drinking hard and buzzing with excitement as they prepared for their fun in the sun holiday on Portugal's famed Algarve coastline. Another hour and they would be there.

That was until the voice came over the plane's P.A. system, "Ladies and gentlemen, this is your pilot, Angela Griffin, and there is no cause for alarm but we have a warning light on one of our trim flaps. This doesn't affect the safety of our aircraft but it does mean we can't cruise at our optimum altitude. Because of this we are diverting to Biarritz in France to get the part replaced. I anticipate it will take less than two hours to have the problem resolved and then we'll be back on our way to Faro."

A groan arose from the passengers. Two hours of the vacation they had worked so hard for had just been stolen from them. A dozen lights went off simultaneously as the disgruntled travelers punched their call buttons to summon the flight attendants and get more drinks. As they waited to place their orders, the plane dipped its left wing and started into its new course.

Fifty miles behind Flight 4052, the two pursuit fighters watched the 737 bank into a long, sweeping easterly turn as it began its journey to the French coastline.

The pilot in the lead fighter clicked on his radio to report, "M.O.D., this is Typhoon Strike One. We have visual confirmation the target is changing course. Repeat target is changing course. Now heading east, southeast."

The reply crackled into the headphones built into the pilot's helmet, "Typhoon Strike One, this is M.O.D. Roger that. Maintain position and wait for further instructions."

The radio tech turned to the officers lined up behind her, "The Typhoons are waiting for your orders."

The Minister said nothing, overtaken by the dreadful weight of responsibility falling on him. A Brigadier General, standing with him felt the same anxiety but was forced to agree, "I don't see any alternative, Minister. This is going down exactly as Signet said it would."

"I am very aware of that," replied Britain's Minister of Defense, "but this is a last resort option. I'll be damned if I blow a civilian plane out of the sky without trying all other means." He barked at the radio operator who remained focused on him, "Patch me through to the pilot. I want to talk to them before I give the order to blast them all to hell."

"Will do, sir." She swiveled back to her monitor and set the frequency, "Northumbria Airlines Flight 4052, this is a priority one transmission from Whitehall. Do you copy?"

Silence answered her broadcast.

"Trying secondary frequencies now, sir." She repeated her call four more times as she went up and down the dial. Each time she was only rewarded with static.

Finally, she turned back to her superior, "I have tried all primary and secondary frequencies and received no response. Nothing on the emergency band either, sir. Unless they are on a channel I don't know about, then either the pilot's radio is dead-"

"Or the pilot is," The Minister completed her sentence. "Log those calls. I want it on record we made every possible attempt to reach the plane before…" he couldn't bring himself to finish his words.

"There's nothing else you can do, Minister," offered the Brigadier General.

"I know, but that doesn't make it any easier." In his forty-five years in the service, this elderly naval officer had seen combat in many hotspots around the world, from the Falklands to the Middle East, and was proud he had never intentionally harmed a civilian while in action. Now, nearing the end of his career, he was ordering the death of more than two hundred innocent souls. And virtually all of them British, his fellow countrymen and women. But he had no choice.

He felt himself slumping as the moment pulled him down, and forced himself upright, rigid, as if on parade. He had his duty to do, one he had sworn when he first enlisted all those years ago, to protect Queen and country. He spoke again to the radio operator, "Put me through to the fighters."

"Sir." She switched on her radio, selected the frequency and spoke swiftly into her microphone, "Typhoon Strike One, this is Whitehall. Come in please."

There was no lag as her call was answered, "Whitehall, this is Typhoon Strike One receiving you."

"Typhoon Strike One, stand by for the Minister of Defense, the Right Honorable Sir Michael Bennett." She gestured to the microphone, "Sir, they are waiting on your words."

Reluctantly, the old military man bent down and spoke slowly and clearly into the mic, "Typhoon Strike One, this is the M.O.D. You have a code 4-7-4 to proceed. Acknowledge."

"M.O.D., this is Typhoon Strike One. You are authorizing a code 4-7-4 launch. Confirm." There was obvious concern in the pilot's voice.

"Typhoon Strike One, M.O.D. confirms code 4-7-4. We are transferring operation control to Signet with MI6. He will confirm a secondary code and any action you are to carry out. Understood?"

"M.O.D., this is Typhoon Strike One. Understood. Standing by for Signet."

The Minister nodded to the radio operator, "Patch all calls through to this secure number. Signet will take over from here. Leave the channels open so we can hear as the operation takes place."

"Yes, sir."

Colin sat patiently at Simon's desk, his headset in place, the mini-USB on his phone blinking green. He knew if his plan was working it would be anytime now. The USB switched to red as the call came through.

"Yes?" Colin snapped into the headset.

"Signet, this is Whitehall. Transferring Typhoon Strike control to you. Patching you through now to Typhoon Strike One." There was a second of silence before she added the words, "Go ahead, Signet."

A slightly hollow tone sounded in Colin's headset as they linked him with the pilots high above France's Atlantic coast. Knowing everything was in place, he spoke quickly and firmly, "Typhoon Strike One, this is Signet. I have a secondary fire control designation code, Bravo, Kilo, Delta."

"Signet, Typhoon Strike One acknowledging Bravo, Kilo, Delta. My understanding is I am receiving an intercept and destroy code. Please reconfirm."

"Typhoon Strike One, this is Signet. Your code is correct, Bravo, Kilo, Delta. You are a go to intercept and destroy."

"Signet, Typhoon Strike One, we have confirmed your code. Acquiring target. Estimated engagement in three minutes."

The strike leader switched frequencies to inform the other plane, even though he knew the pilot had heard the entire conversation, "Typhoon Strike Two, this is Typhoon Strike One. We have a kill order. Ready all four BVR Meteors and follow me in. I'll lead, fire two birds and break west, maintaining altitude. You repeat the same action. If we fail to destroy the target on the first pass, we'll do a second go round with the remaining Meteors. Got it?"

"Typhoon Strike One, this is Typhoon Strike Two. Understood." There was a moment's hesitation, "This is for real, right, Stephen?"

His friend's voice rang back in his headset, "This is for real, mate."

The two Eurofighter Typhoons banked hard, engaged their afterburners and moved together in attack formation as they closed in on the 737.

At the Ministry of Defense headquarters in Whitehall, the Minister paced as waves of stress and guilt flowed through his body. He stopped behind a second radio operator, "Keep trying to reach the pilot. Use all frequencies to hail them. God help those poor souls."

Simon sat with the techs in the NCC at Thames house, his face in his hands, waiting for the word from the parking supervisor at Manchester Airport. Finally, a voice sounded from his speaker.

"We had a couple of things we caught on camera that might be of interest which happened over the last hour," Charles Perry was excited to share his news with the legendary MI5.

Simon paused, then realized Charles Perry was expecting a reply. "What?" Simon demanded.

"We had someone threaten one of our cashiers. Said they were being overcharged. Almost came to a punch up, but in the end everyone simmered down."

"How many were in the car?"

"One. A big guy by himself. Definitely not the kind of person you'd want to tangle with."

Simon grimaced in annoyance, this was obviously not who he was looking for, "What else do you have?"

"A lost ticket. Normally people make a bit of a fuss about it and all kinds of excuses, but this kid paid the full amount without question, one hundred and thirty-eight pounds. All cash, too. And didn't wait for a receipt or ask for a claim form in case they found the ticket later and could get their money back. That never happens."

"What kind of footage do you have on the car?"

"Pretty good," Charles answered. "Front and back plates, and you can see the driver. The other two passengers you can make out but not enough to recognize them in a pub. I've emailed you a couple of still shots from the video feed."

"Three people! Describe them," ordered Simon, as he pulled out his mobile to check his inbox.

"Like I said, it's not perfect, but the driver was a teenager, a boy, and he was the one who paid the money. You can see him real clear when he hands it to the cashier-"

"Yes, yes, yes," Simon was frantic, "and the other two?" The first picture came up on his phone's screen, as Charles Perry continued with his description.

"From what I could make out it was a man and a woman. The woman in her twenties, the man, early forties. Does that help? Hello? Hello?"

Simon was on his feet, clutching his phone, and racing through the Communications complex to the stairs.

The pilot could see the last of the sun glinting off the tail of the big Boeing ahead of them. This would be like shooting ducks in a barrel, he thought. He clicked on his air-to-air com, "Typhoon Strike Two, this is Typhoon Strike One. I have visual and radar lock. Cutting airspeed and falling back to sixteen nautical miles. Match my actions and prepare to engage and fire."

Simon knew every second counted and couldn't wait for the thirties-era elevator, so he took the old stone stairs inside Thames

House two at a time as he raced up towards his office, five floors above him. He had to make it.

The two fighters flew wingtip to wingtip as they reduced speed, allowing the passenger plane to increase the distance between them, a move known as lag pursuit, designed to not only give them room to maneuver but also so they would be able to break away after the launch and avoid the missile blast.

Satisfied with their positioning, the lead pilot returned to the radio, "Typhoon Strike Two, this is Typhoon Strike One. Ready to commence initial attack. I will lead; wait three seconds and follow me in. Launch BVR Meteors at the range of fourteen miles then take a hard ninety-degree westerly heading. We'll regroup and decide if a second go around is needed. Confirm."

The reply came through clearly, "Typhoon Strike One, this is Typhoon Strike Two. Roger that. Will follow your lead, three seconds behind. All four birds are armed and ready, and I have acquired target lock."

The pilot checked his armament panel. The computer reported the four missiles were hot. He opened the control cover and unlocked the red FIRE button, designating missiles one and three into armed and ready mode. He was set to engage. With that, the first Eurofighter blasted forward, seconds from missile launch.

Simon emerged on the fifth floor, his level. Damn it. If only his office wasn't at the end of the corridor. He had always dreamed of having the corner office, from his earliest days as a field agent, and when he had been awarded it, seven years ago, upon his appointment as Director of the United Kingdom's Internal Security Service, he had luxuriated in the spectacular view of the city and country he was entrusted to protect. But now he wished it was closer, right there, stuck between all the others and not a hard run down the long, narrow hallway. His legs were burning from the steep stairs, but he forced his feet to keep moving, he had no other alternative.

"Typhoon Strike One, firing missiles now."

The Minister of Defense shuddered as the words from the lead plane's pilot boomed over the speakers in the Whitehall command center.

Three seconds later another voice filled the air, "Typhoon Strike Two, firing missiles now." There was a moment's pause, "Missiles away, locked on target. Breaking west."

The old general sat down knowing he had authorized death. His two words were simple and said with a tone etched full of sadness, "It's done."

Simon burst through the door of his office and saw Colin, as expected, sitting at his desk, in communication with the attacking pilots.

"Call off the fighters," Simon could barely get the words out, he had no breath left in his body.

"Too late. They've fired their missiles."

Backing up his statement, the lead pilot's voice sounded over Colin's speaker, "Birds flying true. Impact in twenty-seven seconds."

"They're not on the plane. They stole another car and left Manchester airport ten minutes after the flight took off," panted Simon. "Look." He pushed his cell phone in front of Colin.

"There's nothing there."

Simon grabbed it back. The screen had gone into sleep mode during his frantic run. "Shit!" He punched in his five-letter code, *SPOOK*, to unlock it.

"Twenty seconds," came the pilot's voice on the speaker.

"A supervisor confirmed they left Terminal Three parking and has footage of them at the cashier's booth. We also have the car's plates. We can get them." The picture appeared again on Simon's phone, "For Christ's sake, it's them!"

"Ten seconds," the terrible countdown continued.

Colin stared at the image of Eddie leaning out of the car window, paying the parking cashier.

"Stop this, damn it! You can see them," screamed Simon.

Colin clicked his headset, "Typhoon Strike Force, abort attack. This is Signet, abort attack. Abort attack."

The soaring fighters were putting needed distance between their two planes and the target, and had steeply banked into a westerly course, towards the setting sun, prepared to turn back and use their remaining missiles should another pass be required.

The headset of the lead pilot crackled to life as the desperate message coming in from Thames House changed everything. With no time to respond or seek further confirmation, he immediately flicked open the security cover on his Fire Control panel, revealing a second large red button and punched it without hesitation.

It was after he had taken the action that he replied, "Destruct initiated, Signet."

Less than a hundred yards behind the airliner, the four BVR Meteor missiles detonated simultaneously, the high explosive blast-fragmentation warheads sending shock waves and shrapnel radiating outwards, rocking the Boeing and tearing off part of the top of the tail section.

The plane pitched wildly from the concussive blast and was flung into a plunging nosedive. The pilot grabbed her controls and fought hard to pull the 737 out of its unchecked descent. As she battled the massive, unexpected turbulence, she switched to 121.5 MHz, the international frequency for airline distress calls, "Mayday, mayday. This is Northumbria Airlines, Flight 4052. We have sustained unknown impact damage in our tail and rear flaps. Requesting immediate clearance to land, and have fire crews and ambulances standing by in Biarritz. We are coming in heavy."

The passenger jet began ditching all excess fuel over the Atlantic as Angela Griffin ran through the emergency landing training scenarios she had practiced so many times but hoped she would never have to use.

CHAPTER FOURTEEN

Ireland

A cold wind blew off the Irish Sea as the three fugitives stood at the back of the P & O ferry, staring at the lights of Liverpool fading below the horizon.

"I get switching cars at the airport so they couldn't follow us, but I still don't understand why we're going to Ireland?" asked Eddie.

"Because what Cate said was right, without us having a scanner, there was no way of knowing if the fake passport had a valid Covid-19 vaccination record listed, and even if it did and had worked to get us onboard the plane, and then gotten us through immigration into Faro, we would have been too easy to find in Portugal. We don't speak the language and would have been out of place. This ferry sails to Southern Ireland and they have a travel arrangement with England, so as long as you're carrying an ID, that's good enough for them, they rarely check it. When we went through, they didn't even open our passports. It's the same as if we were traveling between states back in America," explained Alex.

"And I have people we can stay with while we work out what to do next," said Cate.

"I thought we had to keep away from people we knew?" Eddie was still confused.

"They're not relatives or anything. I met this family when I was your age, hitch-hiking through Europe, then I went back four years ago on a whim. There's no way anyone could know about them. We'll be safe there for a few days."

Alex shivered from the chill, damp air and checked his watch, "It's nearly midnight. We should go below to our cabin and try to sleep. It's another seven hours until we get into Dublin."

No one disagreed with his logic and they followed Alex to the elevators to take them down three levels to their beds.

Colin was at his desk, hunched over paperwork in his office when his cell rang insistently. He tapped the screen, saw Simon's number and answered, "If you're calling about the plane, I already know. Landed safely, only a few bumps and bruises."

"If you call seventeen people hospitalized in France for broken limbs, concussion, and lacerations, bumps and bruises, then I guess you're correct," replied Simon.

"It could have been a lot worse."

"It *would* have been a lot worse." Simon kept his temper under control and refrained from getting into a drawn-out battle by holding back the condemnation he wanted to unleash.

"All right, I'll get you a medal. You were the white knight today."

"Thank you," said Simon. "And I received the internal memo that you have already launched an investigation into what happened with the Faro flight."

"That's correct. I thought it should be started right away," confirmed Colin.

"You certainly didn't waste any time. And it's very clever of you to get it going so quickly," said Simon. "The person who runs the enquiry tends to control the findings. You're covering your tracks."

"Now you're being cynical, Simon. I wanted to act before the wrong people looked into it and found things they shouldn't. Is this why you're calling me?"

"No," replied the director of MI5. "I'm still here at Thames House. We've had a fix come in on the Americans."

Colin sat bolt upright on the couch, "Why didn't you say so before? Where are they?"

"On a boat. The license plates we received from the airport cams were picked up multiple times on the M62 to Liverpool. About an hour ago they bought tickets and drove their car onto a ferry bound for Dublin. We have a positive match for their vehicle and confirmed facial recognition on all three from the boarding cameras at the dock. I even have their cabin number. P & O Lines have been very cooperative."

"This is great news. They have nowhere to run now."

"Exactly," agreed Simon. "This can be brought to a swift and peaceful end. I can arrange with my people at the AGS to take them at the dock in Dublin, or I can have the ferry held at sea before it enters Irish waters and send a cutter to arrest them."

"Wait," Colin was thinking this through. "I'm not sure either of those options would be our best bet."

"Not our best bet? They're trapped on a boat with no way off! This is the first time we know where they're going before they get there. We grab them and bring them in without anyone else getting hurt."

"It's not people getting hurt that bothers me," said Colin coldly, "it's where they are going. This whole nightmare started with a letter Mary Kelly sent from Ireland and that's where they are heading now. Do you think it's a coincidence? I don't. The professor may have discovered that something is there, a final clue to link the kid with the throne."

Colin's reaction shocked Simon. He was sure he would have wanted them seized immediately, "You told me you destroyed the records of their marriage. Without that, he has nothing now, nothing."

"This is not a normal criminal we're after. It was you who said the guy was a magician. Who knows what he can conjure up? I say we let them leave the ferry and follow them. They find us the last piece of the puzzle, then we take them. But I need your help on this."

"Why?"

"It's the damn Republic thing they claim in the south. MI6 are only welcome when they call us in for assistance to back them up on a problem they can't handle alone, like taking out a jihadi there who is stirring up trouble. MI5 is different. You said it yourself, you have people in their AGS, and I bet the SDU too, right?"

Simon's silence answered his question.

"Let's finish this as a joint op. Do you have any assets in place who can meet the ferry when it docks in Dublin?"

"Yes, that would not be hard to arrange."

"Good. I'll send you what I need done, and I'll organize the helicopters for transportation here at Six. You and your teams will travel with me from London. We'll take off for Dublin tonight and have boots on the ground in Ireland before the boat disembarks." Without waiting for Simon's OK, Colin clicked off the call and started making the arrangements.

Across the river, at Thames House, Simon contemplated MI5's next move, and buzzed on an internal line for Warren Bracker, his field command officer. It took several rings before the phone was picked up.

"Bracker here."

"Warren, it's Simon. I know you've been working late on this, we all have, but I just got off with Six and gave them the information on the ferry and its passengers." He paused, "They want to run one more joint op and I think we should comply."

Warren Bracker was the most experienced field officer MI5 had ever been fortunate enough to have, and had overseen operations from basic domestic security to hostage rescue, but his voice was puzzled as he replied, "I thought the word was you wanted Five off this case? Force the goons at Six to work with the local police departments from here on out and make Brown coordinate with the Dublin Gardai."

"You're right, I did. In a perfect world that would be the plan, but we both know Six's methods can be heavy-handed at best and cause as many problems as they solve. And with them running an operation in Ireland, so close to home, someone's got to watch Colin Brown, and I'm afraid that falls upon us."

"I understand, sir. I'll get the teams together. They'll be ready to roll in sixty minutes."

The line went dead as Warren Bracker started on his assignment of selecting Five's strike squads and the weaponry they might need.

The ferry docked on schedule at five thirty in the morning at Dublin's bustling port. In the enclosed car transport area below decks, four lanes of vehicles waited for the huge bow to raise and the ramp to deploy to allow them to drive off. The drivers and passengers stood patiently beside their cars, knowing it could be a few minutes before they were cleared to go.

Above them, an Irish voice bellowed from the ship's P.A. system, echoing along the metal decks, "Welcome to Dublin. If you are arriving here with a vehicle please go down to the transportation decks now and stay with your car. You will be instructed when it is safe to get in and when you can start your engines. You will disembark by lanes, so until your lane number is announced please leave your motors off and remain outside of your vehicles. Thank you."

A jovial sailor strolled between two of the car lanes, stopping to answer any of the passengers' questions. He approached Alex, Cate, and Eddie who stood alongside their Vauxhall Crossland SUV Eddie had appropriated at Manchester's airport, and greeted them with a rosy-cheeked smile and an endearing Irish lilt in his voice, "We'll be having the ramp down for you in a few minutes and you'll be off before you know it. I hope you had a fine crossing."

Cate couldn't help but be charmed by his Irish warmth, "We didn't hit any icebergs, so that's a plus."

He grinned and patted her on the shoulder, "You're a funny lass, and we are hardly the Titanic, even though that big boat was built right here in Ireland. Will this be your first time in our beautiful country?"

"No. It'll be my third. It's a great part of the world."

"Welcome back. We're certainly glad you're returning again to our green island. Have a wonderful holiday." He waved goodbye to the travelers and walked away towards the stern of the boat. He continued another fifty yards then stepped out of the line of parked cars and raised a concealed microphone to his mouth, "The tracker is in place and planted on the girl."

The cars and trucks slowly exited the massive ferry. The white Vauxhall SUV followed the line of vehicles down the ramp and to a checkpoint more interested in receiving the three Euro entry payment than examining IDs. The wooden arm raised, the green light flashed on, and Eddie rolled cautiously forward where he was greeted by a sign reading, *Welcome to the Republic of Ireland, Don't Forget To Drive On The Left.*

"Got it?" asked Cate.

"Got it," replied Eddie.

He kept a respectfully slow pace through the port and as they pulled onto Route 148, none of them noticed the innocuous stretched Ford Transit van parked there.

Had they been able to see through the Turbo Diesel's silver exterior, they would have been shocked at the amount of technology crammed inside, manned by four people in the relatively cramped, but efficiently laid out mobile command center of the SDU – Special Detective Unit – of the Republic of Ireland.

The first technician turned from his screen and spoke to the two partner agents from London, "We have a good signal lock. The targets are moving and leaving the Dublin docks now."

Colin nodded in approval, "How about ground assets?"

A second tech operator provided the answer, "We have two on them at all times, alternating between your MI5 teams and our local squads from the AGS. We've set up an invisible tail as requested, switching every ten minutes. We also have air cover, from our drones and your helicopter. As of now, they are heading west on R 148, possibly making for the M7."

"M7? Where does that go?" questioned Simon.

"If they get on the M7, it'll take them south west. It ends at Limerick."

Colin grabbed Simon's attention and lowered his voice, "Mary sent the letter from Limerick."

They had been driving for two hours, and the village of Castleconnell was three miles behind them when Cate recognized the surroundings and told Eddie to turn on an unpaved country lane, "It's down here. Another couple of minutes."

Eddie complied, and as he felt gravel and dirt replace the motorway's tarmac beneath his wheels and took in the verdant green pastures around them, he grinned, "I don't see anything but grass and cows."

"You will," she smiled.

Sure enough, after the next corner, a farmhouse came into view, its thatched roof and whitewashed walls glistening in the sun. Eddie pulled to a stop outside of it.

"This is ridiculous," he exclaimed. "It looks like a Disney movie. All we need now are the seven dwarfs."

"That would be seven leprechauns, here in Ireland!" Cate joked, pleased at his reaction.

Before Alex could join the upbeat conversation, the front door of the farmhouse opened and a buxom, smiling lady appeared and strolled up to the car, "Good day to you. Are you lost or will you be looking for bed-and-breakfast?"

Cate jumped out of the passenger seat of the SUV where she had been giving directions and ran to the woman with her arms outstretched, "That's exactly what we're looking for, Sally O'Grady. Particularly your breakfasts!"

Sally froze in happy shock, then gave Cate the welcoming bear hug of her life, "Oh bejesus, if it ain't our Caitlin back to visit. Let me look at you, with your new hair-do and so skinny. You could use some of my breakfasts, love. Don't they feed you in America?"

Cate laughed aloud, "You know I eat plenty, Sally. I left with a muffin top the last time I was here! These are my friends, Alex and Eddie."

Sally greeted each of them with a warm smile, "Lovely to meet you both. Now come on in, won't you? I'll put the kettle on for a spot of tea."

Alex and Eddie followed Cate and Sally, who were locked arm in arm and chatting nonstop, into the quaint farmhouse for a taste of Irish hospitality.

Less than a mile away, pulled over on the M7, the Transit van acting as the mobile command center, checked and rechecked the signal.

"They've definitely stopped, sir," said the tech. "Our maps show a farm where they are."

"Right," said Colin. "Pull back the teams. We'll wait here and watch. Put a drone up and get some aerial information."

"Will do, sir."

The weather that helped Ireland earn the deserved nickname of The Emerald Isle was, for once, cooperating. There was no rain, and the night was clear, forming a canopy of stars hanging overhead.

The farmhouse had become the center for entertainment in Castleconnell that evening. After a hurried conversation with her husband, Patrick, Sally decided the appropriate thing to do to welcome Caitlin back to County Limerick was to throw a party in her honor. It had only taken a couple of phone calls to spread the word, and almost half the village turned out to eat, drink, and celebrate the return of one of their favorite people.

A bonfire roared in the garden, three hand-pumped kegerators sat in large tubs of ice to ensure the beers flowed cold and non-stop, and two fiddle players battled each other to be the fastest musicians in the land. Their exciting musical duel was heating up, and dozens of enthusiastic villagers, unable to resist the wild tempo, danced to the traditional tunes in the fire's light.

Eddie stood watching the locals letting their hair down and enjoying the moment without any inhibitions, and felt himself relax for the first time in days, "These are my kind of people. They're having a blast and not worrying what others think of them."

Before Alex or Cate could respond, a pretty teenage local girl ran across the grass to Eddie and grabbed his hand, "Come on, you must have a dance," and pulled him out to join the partying crowd.

Cate turned to Alex, "It makes you wonder, doesn't it? Back home in Wisconsin, we struggle and work and rush all day, every day, trying to get ahead, but are we ever as happy as these people are, right here, right now?"

"That's a fair question, but we have little time for philosophy. We will have to go soon, tomorrow or the day after. We've got to keep moving until we can find somewhere safe to be, where we can stay for a while.”

“I know. But while we’re here can we at least enjoy it?”

“We can try.”

“Then dance with me.” Cate held out her hand.

Alex took a step back, “I don’t dance.”

A voice from behind contradicted him, “Nonsense. You’re in God’s country now. Everybody dances here. Saying you don’t dance is like saying you don’t breathe. Get yourself out there.”

Sally gave him a good-natured push and Cate completed the move by wrapping her hand around the professor’s wrist and pulling him onto the lawn.

In seconds, Cate and Alex were ringed by people singing the traditional Gaelic song and clapping to the beat. Cate picked up on the rhythm and urged Alex to follow her lead. She linked her arm through his and started into the twirling, high-stepping dance all the villagers seemed to know so well.

Reluctantly at first, he tried to keep up, then found himself dancing and spinning with the music as he attempted to match Cate’s energy. Even though his moves and footwork were far from perfect, he laughed as he realized he was having fun. For a few minutes at least, he let their problems disappear from his mind.

His mood would have changed had he known that three hundred yards away, on the ridge of a hilltop overlooking the farm and its rolling pastures, Colin Brown lay watching him through a set of night-vision binoculars. As the MI6 agent took in the enhanced low-light, green image of the professor circling the fire with his prodigy, Caitlin Shannon, he whispered to himself, “Dance while you can.”

CHAPTER FIFTEEN

The Riddle

Alex was surprised how late he'd slept in. Normally his internal clock had him awake before the dawn, but today, when he rolled over and saw how high the sun was in the sky, he knew it was long past that. He checked his watch and found it hard to believe it was a few minutes before eight. Feeling guilty, he sprung out of bed and hurried into the shower to prepare for the day.

When he walked into the sunny front room of the three-century-old farmhouse he was greeted by not only the smiles of his friends and the warmth of the O'Grady family already seated around the loaded dining table, but by the delicious aroma of a full Irish breakfast made with local eggs, rashers of bacon, home-grown tomatoes, beans, and toast, carved from freshly-baked bread.

"The learned man is up," laughed Patrick. "Take a seat. We'll get you a hot cup of tea. I just brewed one." He reached for the teapot and poured Alex a steaming mug, "That is unless you would want a coffee. I could go to the kitchen and put some on for you."

"Tea is perfect, thank you."

"We were asking young Caitlin what brings her back to our little piece of heaven, when you came in," explained Sally. "So, what is it, dear?"

At first, Cate was a little unsure of what to say and answered simply, "It was a letter."

"A letter?" Sally gave her a knowing wink, "From a local boy, no doubt. There's no denying it, Caitlin Shannon, the last time you were here you broke some hearts."

"No, it was not to me. It was written by a woman named Mary who sent it from Limerick over a century ago."

Sally wrinkled her weathered brow, "Now you are talking riddles, lass."

"I suppose in a way I am. The letter was kind of a riddle, but our professor solved it."

"Not all of it," said Alex.

"Then what was it that stumped you? I love riddles," said Patrick.

"Every Irishmen does," confirmed Sally.

"All right. One part of the letter was about Mary coming back to Ireland. She wrote her husband came here to see her and their son at Dara's. But we could never find out who Dara was."

"Well, that's where you went wrong," Patrick had no hesitation helping Alex with this, "Dara's not a person. Dara's a place."

"I don't want to be rude, but I did think of that," answered Alex. "I studied the maps of County Limerick and the entire district, and there is no Dara. I even went back and pulled maps from one hundred and fifty years ago, and then extended the search to take in all of Ireland, North and South, and Dara doesn't show up. Which means it had to have been someone's name."

Sally chuckled, "You wasted all that time when we could have given you the answer with one phone call."

"My wife's right. We'd have told you about Adare. The prettiest little village anywhere in Ireland, some say the entire world. We locals call it Dara, from its old Gaeilge name, Ath Dara, so unless you had a hand-drawn Gaeilge map, you'd never find that magical place. And it's less than twenty minutes from here. When the troubles were going on my....group used to meet there."

Patrick's words caught Eddie's attention, "You were in a group? Cool. What music did you play?"

Sally and Patrick exchanged a sly glance before Patrick answered, "It wasn't that kind of group, lad. A lot of the men you met last night at the party were in it with me, but it's mostly behind us now."

Sally cautioned him, "Mostly?"

"Aye, lass, mostly," Patrick shot his wife a guilty look.

Alex sensed they could gleam something more from their local knowledge and wanted to pursue this further, "Cate, can you show them the letter on your computer?" He turned to the husband and wife, "Was there a public bath in Ath Dara?"

"I never heard of one, why?"

Cate found a spot on the crowded table and swung her laptop so it was facing Alex, and he read out loud from the screen, "I ask, because there was something I could never quite understand. It says, *My Bertie came to Dara's to see his boy washed*, and we always thought she was referring to some kind of bathhouse."

"Now that's where you have it wrong again. It's not any kind of public bath, it's another local saying. Around these parts we call it washing, when the priest is putting the wee ones in water to be cleansed by God's Holy grace. Her husband, her *Bertie* as she calls him, came to Ath Dara to see his son baptized."

Alex was not expecting that answer, and his eyes opened wide in shock, locking on Sally, as he sat there silent, running through the huge implications of what she had said. Then he spoke, "Where would they have been baptized?"

"Were they God-fearing Catholics?"

"No, definitely not. They were protestant, Church of England."

"Well, the only place for that kind of baptism in Adare back then would have been the Augustinian Priory."

Alex's head was spinning and he leapt to his feet, excited and unsure of exactly what to do next.

Patrick couldn't understand why Alex had gotten up from the table so fast, "You don't like my wife's breakfast?"

"No. I mean, yes. It's wonderful. But...Cate, Eddie - I need to speak to you outside. Right away."

Without waiting for a reply, he hustled for the door and pushed through into the sunshine. Seconds later, Cate and Eddie joined him.

"What is it? Why did you leave the table like that?" asked Cate.

Alex was breathless as he answered, "There may be a way we can end this and go home."

She stared at Alex, "Go home? What? How?"

The excited professor swung his gaze to Eddie, "It's up to you. It would put you in an impossible position."

"After this past week that's going to be my new middle name, Eddie Impossible York. What are you thinking?"

"If we can locate the baptism record, it will not only prove the birth of a son to Albert and Mary, but it would also document their legal marriage status. We take that, along with the photocopy of the marriage certificate we were given at Thaxted church, and I'm sure the vicar will testify to its authenticity because he made it for us, and we go public with it. Then they can't touch us. Once the truth is out, it will be too late."

"And what do I have to do?" asked Eddie.

"Everything will come down on your head. You'll be in the middle of a legal nightmare which could continue for years. And you may remain a target during that time."

"Like they'll still try to kill me?"

"Yes, and they will make it look like an accident. A car wreck or a drowning, or something similar. Maybe even poison, like Queen Victoria is thought to have given her grandson, and then told everyone he died suddenly from influenza."

Eddie fell silent, before looking up at his two friends, "But you guys will be safe?"

"We will, if we can find the proof and give it to the press. You won't."

"And this baptism thing is that important?"

"Eddie, it would prove, beyond any shadow of doubt, that you are the rightful, legal monarch and ruler of Great Britain and all the Commonwealth territories."

"Shit!" The reality of this was hitting Eddie hard. Until now it had seemed so far-fetched, so distant, and their struggle to survive had blocked any consideration of this actually coming about, "If that happened and it all worked out, could I do things? Would I have any real powers?"

"Like flying?" joked Cate.

"No, stupid. I mean what can a...," he hesitated to say the word, "King do these days?"

"A lot." Alex spoke slowly so Eddie would understand, "Just like our President in the United States, The Crown is designated as the Commander-in-Chief of the armed forces. The King or Queen's army has bases all over the world. And the monarchy is part of the checks and balances of government; Britain's Prime Minister reports to the throne every week and can't proceed on bills or laws without first seeking formal Royal permission. Plus, the United Kingdom has the third largest nuclear arsenal on the planet with over 400 warheads and four ballistic missile submarines."

Eddie was stunned at the far-reaching implications, "This is a lot to take in. I'm going to have to read up on it to learn where I'm from. Could I borrow your books?"

It was Cate's turn to be surprised, "Don't books creep you out?"

"Newsflash. Compared with Jack the Ripper and the psycho MI6 dude, books are the last thing that are creepy. You know, I always felt sorry for myself. Parents dead, kicked out of school, locked up in Juvie Hall, but these last few days I've seen people so much more worse off than me, sleeping in parks and bus shelters and shit. And no one does anything about it; there's nobody to give them a chance at getting a job or finding them a place to live. You said all my family before me did things to help people, like they were firemen, policemen, and even my own dad was a soldier. He was a good guy, he died saving his friends. So maybe it's my turn. Maybe I can save my friends and even help change things a little if this goes down right. I say, let's do it. Let's go and find the proof."

Sally and Patrick gave Alex directions as he sat uneasily in the driver's seat of the Vauxhall parked in the long, unpaved driveway leading to the farmhouse.

"You don't seem comfortable," noted Patrick.

"I'm not. I'm only doing this because Cate's navigating. To be honest with you, it's been quite some time since I've been behind the wheel, and I've never driven on this side of the road before," answered Alex. "Eddie's been doing all the driving. He enjoys it."

"Then why isn't the lad doing it today?"

"*The lad* can hear you," laughed Eddie. "I have to miss out this morning because I'm stuck reading. I have a lot of studying to do to catch up with these two," he gestured to Cate and Alex.

Patrick's expression showed how strange he thought it was, a seventeen-year-old boy turning down the chance to drive a sporty SUV, and instead reluctantly coop himself up in the back seat with a bunch of books and notes. He tried to put it out of his mind and concentrate on helping Alex, "Most of the abbey's records are kept at the post office."

"Not the town hall?"

Sally grinned at Alex's question, "The post office is the town hall! It's also where we can get our passports, driving licenses, pay our electric bills, and lucky couples go there so they can file their wedding certificates. Adare is a tiny village, mostly hotels, pubs, and souvenir shops for the tourists."

Patrick was still concerned, "Are you sure you don't want me and my boys to come with you?"

"No, it's best you don't. But thank you for your hospitality and everything you've done for us."

"And you give me a kiss, young Caitlin. Promise you won't make it so long next time. I wish you would stay on. One night was not enough. You said it would be more."

"We hoped it would longer too. But we have to keep moving. Perhaps another time." She exchanged a grateful kiss through the rolled-down window with Sally, and as Alex pulled cautiously away, she waved sadly back at the O'Gradys who stood watching them leave.

The car disappeared from sight as it wound between the tall hedgerows, obscuring the view, and Patrick threw his arm around his beloved wife and they started back toward their farmhouse.

"Something wasn't right in Caitlin's voice when she said goodbye. She seemed sad, not excited to be back here on holiday," said Sally.

"I picked up on that as well," agreed Patrick. "And I didn't like the way she said they had to keep moving."

"And I overheard the professor last night telling little Caitlin the same kind of thing, that they couldn't stop until they found somewhere safe to be. As if it was dangerous just being here."

As they reached their door, the sound of a helicopter echoed off the old stone walls and they turned to see a black chopper moving slowly southbound, about a mile away from them.

"Now that is strange," said Patrick. "Unless there's an accident on the motorway, what is one of them whirlybirds doing up around here this time of day?"

Sally shook her head in puzzlement.

"I'm going to make some calls." Patrick pushed inside, heading straight for the phone.

The fugitives' SUV headed south on the M7 at a painfully slow pace as Alex attempted to get used to driving on the *wrong side*. Neither the driver nor the two passengers noticed the helicopter following behind, matching their speed.

Adare lived up to the description Sally had given it, and it was easy to understand why it was known as the prettiest village in all of Ireland. It was as if a child's fantasy had exploded around them as thatched roofs, whitewashed walls, brightly painted, undersized doors and colorful wooden window shutters were everywhere.

Eddie glanced up from his books, "Are we still in Ireland or did we just arrive in the land of the Hobbits?"

"That's what I was thinking. I can't believe I've been to County Limerick twice before but never been here," said Cate. "It's beautiful."

"Hopefully we can sightsee when all this is behind us." Alex focused them firmly back on reality, "But first we have to find out where the post office is and try to locate those records."

He cautiously pulled over to the cobbled sidewalk and quickly received directions from a helpful villager.

"He said we can't miss it. Straight down this street on the left. Look for the little building with the bright green door next to the Pat Collins pub with the tables out front."

Cate smiled at Alex and started to speak, but he shut her down, "No, we don't have time for a drink. We have to do what we came here for first. This could be it." Alex tried to contain his excitement, but it was readily apparent in his voice.

In less than a minute they were stopped outside the little post office. All three fell speechless at the sight in front of them.

Eddie broke the silence with a laugh, "They weren't kidding it's green. Green door, green windows, green sign. And what would you call that green? I've never seen anything like it."

"Ummm," Cate had to think, "It's like something out of the Wizard of Oz. Maybe lime green?"

"On steroids."

"They call it shamrock green." Alex brought the guessing game to a close, "A very appropriate name for Ireland. And I have to admit, it's an incredibly vibrant shade."

"I'm coming in with you," said Eddie. "I've gone through my crazy family tree twice, and just about got it memorized. I'll finish the rest of my reading later. I want to see if this place is as green on the inside, too."

They climbed out of their car, so distracted by the unique coloring that they failed to notice the familiar stretched silver Ford Transit, parking across the street, sixty feet behind them on Blackabbey Road.

Concealed within the van, Colin made his first demand of the technicians, "I need audio from those three, now."

"Sir, I can get it for you as long as they remain outside on the street, but once they're inside a building, we'll lose it entirely. Without a bug planted, the old stone walls around here are too thick."

"Damn it. We know they're not going in there to buy stamps for a postcard. Can we get someone inside with a listening device?"

"It's a tiny shop, sir. We have a tracker on the girl, but trying to put a microphone and transmitter in such a small space in full sight of the targets already there, is risky at best. It could blow our invisible tail."

"Figures. Ask you to do something a little more difficult and you can't pull it off."

Colin sensed Simon's condemning gaze at the way he was talking down to his men and tried to put his frustrations to the side, "Okay, what can you do?"

"Let me get agents in place at a table at the pub next to the post office. They'll have a device on them. Between their mic and our listening capabilities in the van, we'll hear everything they say outside. And we'll put a second tracker on the car and make it impossible to lose them."

"Do it. And let's hope they talk when they come back out."

The post office was one half of a converted house, and the postmaster saved himself any commuting worries by living upstairs. He greeted his visitors with the big smile which seemed standard in this part of the world, "Good afternoon. What can I do for the three of you?"

"We're looking for records from the abbey. I understand you have them here?"

"Indeed we do, or at least, most of them," said the postmaster. "The Black Abbey, as we call it round here, is a little too damp to store their important papers. When they built it in 1316 for the Friars, they weren't concerned about keeping out the mold like we are these days. What exactly are you looking for?"

"Baptism records. Ideally from 1891 or very early 1892. The parents would have been Mary Kelly and Albert Wettin."

"That shouldn't be too hard to find. I'll go back and look right now." He caught Cate's eyes, "Be a love. It's quiet today, but if anyone comes in can you ring this for me?" He pointed to the little bell on the counter, "If I hear it, I'll hurry back out."

"Will do," agreed Cate. With that, the postmaster disappeared into one of the storage rooms behind him.

He was gone less than ten minutes and reappeared carrying four small books. "Here we go, and to save me doing anymore searching around, I brought you all these. They cover every Church of England baptism in Adare from 1890 to 1893. There's not many, because most of the folks around here are good Catholics, like me, so Christian and Anglican baptisms are a lot rarer. But take a look and see what you can find." He laid the books on the counter and turned back to sorting through today's mail and slipping the envelopes into the PO Boxes on the wall.

Cate took the records for 1890, and Alex began with 1891. As he flipped through the pages, he saw the postmaster had been correct, there were only fourteen Anglican baptisms for the entire year, and almost immediately found the one he was looking for.

"I have it!" He didn't mean to yell, but his excitement was hard to conceal. In seconds, both Cate and Eddie were staring over his shoulder at the records transporting them back to the fading years of the nineteenth century.

"It's right here. Mary's name, Albert's name, the baby's name, the priest's name. Their signatures. The date. Their marriage status. Even the Holy Seal of the abbey. It's everything we needed."

Alex's excitement was so contagious, the postmaster leaned over the counter to see the entry in the open book, "I'll be buggered," he said out loud. He switched his gaze to Cate and apologized, "Sorry, miss, for the language, but this got the better of me. Are you three Royal scholars?"

"He is, sort of," she pointed at Alex.

"Well, you have quite the find here. It's signed with the father's full name, Prince Albert Victor Christian Edward Wettin, Duke of Clarence. That's a first, English royalty in Adare. He must have come here unannounced or I would have known about it. I've studied the history of our little town. We had a famous politician visit once, from your country. Ted Kennedy, back in the sixties, but never any British Royals. Do you want me to copy this for you?"

"Absolutely. And we need to get it legally certified. Do you know where that can be done?"

"Right here." He grinned at Alex, "I'll do it for ten euros. I'm the postmaster, notary, and until the next election, mayor."

"And I bet you mix a mean margarita," said Cate.

"I don't know about that, but I do pour a good pint of Guinness next door at Pat Collins' pub on a Friday night." He laughed as he took the book, "My copier is right here. I'll make two copies for you, no extra charge."

His old Xerox sprung to life, and Alex waited anxiously as the machine scanned then printed the pages.

The postmaster held up the prints to the light, checking their quality, "Looks good to me. I'll need someone in the back to witness my notarizing these copies. If you want to come around the counter…"

Both Alex and Cate stepped forward. Eddie waved them on, "You guys go ahead. I'll wait here. I should check out my great-great-great-grandparents' signatures in the book." He hoisted the small, leather-bound volume.

The postmaster overheard his comment and stopped, "Did he say-"

Alex cut him off, "He was joking. You know what we Americans are like."

"Yes. You Yanks are always joshing. Like that Will Ferrell. Every Christmas my wife and I put on a marathon of his movies starting with Elf. It doesn't hurt his name is Irish. Come on." He vanished into his little office with Alex and Cate on his heels.

Eddie opened the book and stared at the three signatures and thought over his strange destiny that had begun so many years before.

Six minutes passed as the postmaster notarized and dutifully logged the two copies, and as Eddie saw his friends re-emerge from the back room, he could sense a change in Alex, as if a weight had been lifted from him. He started to speak, but Alex raised his hand to silence him, and turned instead to the postmaster.

"Thank you for this. It's going to make a tremendous difference to us."

"You're very welcome." The postmaster patted the three books laying on his counter, "I'll put these little gems back into safe keeping, in a few minutes. Now you run and enjoy your holiday in our lovely country."

The trio walked silently out of the store and approached their parked car. It was there Alex paused, "I didn't want to talk in there, certainly not after the comment about it being your distant family."

"Sorry about that," said Eddie.

"No, it was fine. He still thinks it was a joke." Alex held up the copies, "But these definitely prove otherwise. This was the last piece of evidence existing out there, and we have it! With these notarized baptism records from an Anglican abbey, no one can refute what we have found. You are about to change history, Eddie."

"What do we do now?"

"I've spent a lot of time thinking about our next steps, and we have to take these to the press first. I mean, right away, today. The word must get out before we go to any government agency or embassy, or even the police. Once it's in print, we'll be safe. The records will be copied and protected. We would have nothing if these were taken from us."

"You think?" laughed Cate.

"You can help. We need the nearest big town which might have a newspaper."

"I'm pretty sure that would be Limerick. It's only thirteen miles away. We can be there in less than half an hour. I saw Patrick reading the Limerick Leader at breakfast this morning. That's a newspaper."

"Perfect. Even the smallest papers these days have an arrangement with other news groups. They probably deal with the major British publications and even have some reciprocal affiliations with the American press, perhaps USA Today or the New York Times. They would be able to get this out, worldwide, in minutes. You drive, Eddie. I need to get my thoughts together and decide exactly how we break this story to the reporters."

Inside the Ford Transit command center, Colin pulled off his headphones, his face as white as a sheet. Simon was quiet as well, knowing the significance of what they had heard.

"Here's what we do. You pull AGS and all the local police off this case right now. I don't want some republican down here getting a whiff of this; you know what they think of the Crown in Southern Ireland. Have them stand down immediately. Your two remaining teams from Five will be enough to stop the car and grab those three. I'm going into the post office to have a conversation with the postmaster and remove the originals. That will take care of the last of the paper trail forever. I'll have the chopper come and get me when I'm done and join you wherever you have them pulled over. Don't wait, make the calls."

Simon hoisted his radio microphone to thank the Irish Security Agency for their help and dismiss them as they were no longer needed.

Colin stared through the dark-tinted glass of the communications vehicle at the parked SUV and could see the three people he had chased so far struggling with a big map as they searched for the best roads to take them to Limerick.

Simon was on a second call to his own men when the watched Vauxhall started up and pulled away from the curb. The head of MI5 saw them leaving and talked quickly into his headset, "Pursuit vehicles, be aware the target is on the move. Stop them as soon as you can. Do not let them get to Limerick."

Colin nodded approvingly to Simon, jumped out of the surveillance van and hurried across to the post office.

CHAPTER SIXTEEN

Birthright

"If only our cheap phones had Google maps," moaned Cate as she wrestled with the overly-large paper one she held. "I think if we follow the main street out of town and keep going straight, it should take us to the M20 and then right into Limerick, or we can hang a left in about two miles and go through the back roads."

"I vote for the motorway. I can put my foot down and see what this baby does, and I'm the driver so I count for two votes," laughed Eddie.

Alex rolled his eyes, "Now is not the time to get pulled over for speeding. If you-"

BANG!

A black Land Rover sideswiped their car, sending it spinning across the road.

"What the fuck?" yelled Eddie, as he fought for control of the SUV.

CRASH!

A second black Land Rover rammed the back of the Vauxhall, jolting the passengers and slamming the lighter SUV forward.

"Go!" screamed Cate.

Eddie didn't need the encouragement. He dropped the car into second gear and floored the accelerator, racing away from the two vehicles.

There was no hesitation from the trained drivers behind them, and the Land Rovers sped up and gave chase, hurtling through the little village, forcing pedestrians to dive for cover as the three big cars powered down the narrow street built centuries before to accommodate horses and wagons..

Eddie saw fields approaching and a small traffic circle ahead marking the end of Adare. He entered it on the wrong side and swung the wheel hard to the left, and tires squealing, burned rubber into a tiny lane.

"Where are you going? The motorway is less than a mile from here," yelled Alex.

"We'd never outrun a Land Rover on a straight road. Those things haul ass. This is our best chance."

"He's right," agreed Cate, instinctively ducking as the hedgerows smacked against the side of the thundering car.

In seconds, the two Land Rovers reappeared on their tail and Eddie forced the SUV faster and faster as they flashed past farmhouses, fields, and streams, scattering sheep and cows as they slowed for nothing.

Eddie's years spent stealing and joy-riding in hot cars had seen him taking part in pursuits several times before, and for all his youth, he remained cool behind the wheel even as the huge black cars stayed right on his rear fender, ramming it every chance they had.

Cate crouched in the back, clinging onto her seat belt for dear life while Alex clutched the notarized copies to his chest as if they would protect him in a crash.

Overhead, a black helicopter appeared and joined the chase, keeping pace with the manic racers as they tore through the dense countryside below.

Eddie saw the lane ahead narrowing even more, and with mud from recent rains having been washed down onto what was already becoming a rough cattle track, it gave him hope. "It's getting tight in front of us. Their cars are bigger than ours. They could get stuck."

Cate risked a glance over her shoulder and saw what Eddie had said was true. The lead Land Rover was already becoming hemmed in, scraping and snapping off branches from the encroaching hedgerows on both sides, while its wheels flung heavy mud back onto its sister car behind.

"You might be right," Cate called to him, "I think they're slowi-"

"HOLD ON!" yelled Eddie.

Just feet from them, a fence marked the end of the lane.

With no way to stop, Eddie's only choice was to accelerate into the fence, so he jammed his foot down and used their speed to crash through the barrier, scattering it in pieces on either side of them as they demolished the wood and barbed wire, plunging into the tree-lined field beyond.

The car bounced violently as it powered over roots and rocks, flinging Alex and Cate around in their seats. Eddie braced himself with the steering wheel and kept going, always forward, with no other choice, as the Land Rovers were through the destroyed fence now and gaining on them.

"A few more seconds," called Eddie. "There's a clearing ahead."

The car flew out of the trees, a small raised bank lifting the wheels from the ground, sending them airborne, and as they made contact again, Eddie screamed one more warning in the form of a single word, "Shit!"

He flung the wheel hard to the right while slamming his foot on the brakes, locking the pedal to the floor. The SUV skidded sideways, ripping moss from the damp earth before spinning to a dead stop on the banks of the River Maigue, its engine stalling and shutting down from the stress.

Eddie reached down to the pair of dangling exposed wires to restart the car, but even as he did, the two Land Rovers appeared and came to an immediate halt behind, boxing them in.

"What do we do?" Eddie asked. Alex struggled to think of the appropriate response, and before he could, the question was answered by the four men leaping out of the lead Land Rover, weapons drawn, and aimed squarely at them.

Simon ran with his team to the SUV and stopped just yards from it. He called to the occupants, "Armed police. Step out of the car with your hands raised. No harm will come to you."

Alex's expression spoke for him even before he uttered the words, "We have to."

The three of them climbed slowly out, and as they did, they heard a thundering above, and a black helicopter descended into the wide clearing they had sped through.

The cornered fugitives stayed silent and watched as the ominous chopper touched down, its landing skids barely having made contact with the ground before Colin jumped out, clutching an assault rifle.

At his appearance, Alex expelled a deep sigh, reflecting his feeling of hopelessness.

Colin strode up to the trapped trio and stood there, gloating, allowing himself a moment to take in the dejected look on the captured Americans' faces, and the successful conclusion to his six-thousand-mile chase.

Eddie was having none of it and fearlessly locked eyes with the famed MI6 agent and quipped, "Hey, *Uncle*, where's your Beemer?"

Colin refused to be riled. The game was over and he had won. That was satisfaction enough, "How appropriate it ends here. So close to your great-great-great grandmother's birthplace."

"And who were your grandparents? Jack the Ripper?" mocked Eddie.

"Jack has been misunderstood all these years. The truth is, the good doctor was only trying to help his country."

Cate would not let him get away with this and chimed in, "Yeah, Jack the Ripper, you and Bin Laden, three great patriots, right?"

Alex stepped forward, standing beside Cate and Eddie, demonstrating his unity with them, "You're too late, Mr. Brown. We're not the only ones with the proof now."

"Oh, I'm sorry," smirked Colin Brown. "Did I not show you this?" He slung his semi-automatic rifle over his shoulder, and reached into his jacket, pulling out three small books, "The postmaster in Adare told me what you found is in here. I must congratulate you, Professor, you're even better than I thought you were. You accomplished what a thousand scholars and a hundred detectives, on both sides of the Atlantic, searching for more than a century, were unable to do. Quite an achievement. A shame no one will ever know of it. Now please, give me the notarized copies."

Alex raised his hands, "I don't have any copies."

Colin pulled his sidearm, pointing it at Cate's forehead. "I'm not a fool and if you treat me like one, I will shoot the girl. She has zero value to me. The postmaster told me everything. The copies now or the girl dies and I get the copies a minute later. It's your choice."

"Please, whatever you do, don't shoot her. It's not necessary," Alex knew it wasn't a bluff and reached into his jacket. He reluctantly retrieved the papers and held them out as Colin ripped them from his grasp.

The MI6 operative checked them over; both of the copies and the attached certification pages were there. He smiled as he slipped them inside one of the books and knelt down, his gun not wavering from Cate's head. With his free hand he pulled out a lighter, flicked it on and put it against the protruding notarized copies. The paper burned quickly and in a few seconds the flames spread and the books caught fire, forming a small blaze on the ground in front of Colin, consuming the abbey's precious records.

He stood back up and stomped on the charred ashes, eminently satisfied at what he had achieved.

Eddie saw his expression, "You like starting fires, don't you?"

"You might think you're funny, boy, but I'm sure your professor doesn't." He turned his nasty glare to Alex, "It must make you want to cry, to see history gone forever. And now, I'm afraid, the same fate for the three of you."

He tensed, deciding whether he would dismiss Simon's men and rid himself of any witnesses before pulling the trigger.

It was then a voice from behind gave him reason to pause, "I wouldn't do that. Not before we find out what a bunch of little men with big guns are doing in our peaceful country."

Colin, Simon, and the two MI5 strike teams spun around to see ten men in civilian clothes, standing there with twelve-gauge shotguns and semi-automatic weapons trained on them.

Patrick stepped forward slowly, so as not to trigger the fire-fight, "I thought something wasn't right when you were leaving, Caitlin, so I called up my friends, and we followed you. Looks like it's a good job we did."

"What are you yokels going to do, shoot us?" Colin's tone was dismissive.

Patrick didn't take the bait. Instead, his measured reply had an ominous but truthful sound, "It wouldn't be the first time I've shot an Englishman in a uniform."

Colin looked him up and down, "What are you? A bunch of left-over IRA, longing for your glory days? That will make this even easier for us to explain."

He gave a nod to his men who raised their weapons. Simon, who had stayed out of this so far, dropped his hand to his holstered Glock.

"I'd be very careful if I were you with your next moves," warned Patrick. "This is our land you stand upon and our friends you threaten. We have all fought and bled for this country before. None of us will walk away from you in fear."

"Fear or not, you're right about one thing, none of you will walk away from here," snapped Colin.

A silence fell over them as the tension from the standoff reached a fever pitch. It was about to become very bloody when a single figure moved between the two sides and their guns. A teenager with his hands raised. Eddie swung to each of them, addressing both groups, "This is about me. It always has been. There's no need for anyone else to get hurt. I'm the one you want."

The MI5 teams and the ex-IRA members hesitated at this unexpected offer of sacrifice.

Eddie sensed he had their attention and spoke, "I don't know what he has told you, but my name is Edward Albert York. I didn't know much about myself, or about anything, until recently. Then those two found me and I learned about my background and my past. I didn't want any part of it at first, but who gets to choose where they come from?"

"This is nonsense," screamed Colin.

"Let him speak," ordered Simon.

"Thank you," said Eddie. A change seemed to come over him. His slouch disappeared and he stood tall and straight as he continued, "The reason I have been hunted by this man," he pointed to Colin, "is because I am the legitimate first-born descendent of Queen Victoria, Prince Albert and King Edward VII. I am the legal heir to the Houses of Saxe-Coburg and Gotha, Hanover and Wettin. The throne of the Empire and Commonwealth is mine by Royal birthright. If you are loyal to Britain and the monarchy, then I order you to arrest him for treason against the Crown." He gestured again to Colin.

Hearing this, Warren Bracker raised his hand to have his MI5 strike teams hold, then spoke up, his comment addressed to both Colin and Simon, "We were told we were after terrorists and bombers, nothing about this. Nothing about the monarchy."

Simon stayed silent, but Colin yelled back, "They are terrorists. He's lying. Follow your orders. It's just empty words. He can't prove anything. Not now, not ever."

Eddie kept his voice controlled, "That's where you are wrong. I can show you."

He looked at Warren Bracker, sensing his command over the armed squad, and held out his right hand, palm up, seeking permission to move.

Bracker nodded, adding, "Let him. But be slow, boy"

Eddie took his hand and moved carefully with it, so as not to alarm the men with their trigger fingers on their guns, and slipped it inside his jacket, pulling out a small book. "This is what you were after, Mr. Brown. There were four books back in Adare we looked through, not three. I forgot to tell the Postmaster I borrowed one. I guess it's a bad habit of mine. You burned the books from the wrong years. This is the one with the Royal record."

He opened it to a page he had marked and lifted it high to show the MI5 teams. "I am holding the baptism record of the first-born male descendant of Queen Victoria's grandson. My great-great-great-grandfather, Prince Albert. It shows a direct bloodline leading to the throne of Great Britain, the throne you are sworn to protect. Kill me if you will, I can't stop you, but when you pull the trigger, know you are killing your king."

He reached out and offered the irreplaceable volume to Walter Bracker who took the book from him and read over the baptism entry. After a few seconds he looked up at his men, "The names are all there. What he's saying may be right. We should have it checked by higher authorities before something happens here that can't be taken back."

The Field Supervisor tried to pass the book to Simon, who put his hand up to refuse it, "I already know what is written in the book. The boy is speaking the truth." His words fell like a hammer on the ears of the loyal men of MI5.

Simon locked his eyes on Colin, "You told me he was a radical and his actions were deliberate. That he came to Britain to cause anarchy. You risked so many innocent lives for your own distorted ideals and strange visions of power. This boy is not here to destroy our traditions and overthrow the Crown and the government. He was unaware of all of this. It's only now he's learning about himself. You were the one who knew everything and yet concealed it. Our people deserve to hear his story and give the past a chance to come to light and see how it plays out."

Colin spun to him, stunned, "You are a fool. What do you think you're doing here?"

"Something I should have done long ago. Something we all promised to do. Every one of us at Five, all of these men, took the same oath, Regnum Defende. Today we are defending the realm."

"You have no jurisdiction here," snapped Brown. "MI5's charter is only within Great Britain. Outside of those boundaries MI6 takes over. This is the Republic of Ireland. These men can no longer follow your orders." He turned to them, "Under the Security Services Act of '89, I am assuming command of this mission. You will only take my orders from here on out."

Simon addressed his teams, "This agent has gone rogue. He has twisted facts and lied to me and to his superiors. He is running an illegal operation using his own authority without the knowledge or sanction of MI6, The Crown, or the Government. We owe it to our country to find out if these claims of Royal birthright are true." He turned back to a seething Colin Brown, "You'll have to shoot all of us before we let you shoot the boy."

Walter Bracken's words rang across the clearing, "You heard the chief. Lower your weapon, sir." He swung his SIG Sauer 516 semi-automatic at the furious MI6 agent, his eyes leaving no doubt at the seriousness of his intentions.

Brown said nothing, but knowing he was out-gunned, turned his pistol sideways and bent forward, placing it on the ground.

"And your rifle, sir. Don't forget that."

Colin reached for his carbine's sling and slowly removed it from his shoulder and laid it down next to the pistol.

"That's very good, sir. Now if you would, take two steps back, away from the guns."

Again, Brown complied, remaining silent.

Walter Bracken marched forward, his aim not wavering from his target, and picked up the two surrendered guns.

Simon nodded in approval to his senior field officer, and turned to his men, "I think we can all stand down now."

On his words, the MI5 teams lowered their weapons and holstered their sidearms.

Walter turned his attention to Patrick and his group of armed Irishmen, "Now if you good gentlemen could do us all a favor, and put your weapons down too? Guns make me nervous," he smiled.

"We'd be happy to do so," grinned Patrick. He hoisted his gleaming AR-18, "Been sometime since I fired this beauty in anger."

Patrick clicked the safety on, grabbed the strap running from the barrel to the stock and slung the Armalite across his back. His nine friends quickly followed suit.

The tension gone; his men cheered. Hearing the locals' pleasure, even the hardened MI5 field squad broke into a relieved series of smiles. There would be no blood spilled here today.

Patrick grinned at Eddie, "You must know we're not much for Kings and Queens down here, but should I start calling you, *Your Majesty?*"

The boy smiled, "That might take some getting used to. I think we stick with Eddie."

As they continued their jovial exchange, with everyone's attention focused on this strange, and possibly royal, history-making teen; unnoticed by the others, Colin reached behind his back, pulled a concealed pistol and swung it at Eddie.

Only one person saw the hidden gun appear, Alex.

The professor had no hesitation and leapt in front of Eddie as Colin fired twice. The hollow-point bullets from the 9mm tore into the academic and spun him around in midair, knocking him backward into the boy, sending them both sprawling.

Colin adjusted his aim, and a third shot rang out. The MI6 agent stood there, his pistol locked on Eddie's head, then faltered and fell forward, dead before he hit the ground.

Simon lowered his smoking handgun and raced to Eddie and Alex. He pulled the heir to the British throne from beneath the unmoving body and saw he was covered with blood.

"Are you all right?" asked Simon.

"It's not my blood, it's his."

Alex lay motionless, face down, his two bullet wounds staining the heather red.

Simon barked an order to his men, "Get him in the helicopter now. Evac him out of here." He turned to Eddie, "You too." He apologized to Cate, "No room for you, miss. My men will take you back."

"No, we'll look after our little Caitlin. She can come with us," interrupted Patrick.

"How about him?" asked Warren, pointing to Colin's body.

"Put him in the back of one of the Land Rovers and clean up this whole area before you leave, blood, shell casings, everything. None of this happened here today, understood?" instructed Simon.

"Understood, sir."

"We've forgotten already," said Patrick, as he and his men escorted Cate back to their cars parked behind the trees.

Before they had reached their vehicles, the black helicopter clawed its way into the sky making its rushed seven-minute flight to St. John's Hospital in Limerick, carrying with it the future King of England, and the victim of a tragic hunting accident.

Four Weeks Later

Cate exploded into the room, a ball of energy and excitement, "Did I make it? The traffic is crazy! All of London is shut down. I had to jump out of my Uber and run the last three blocks. Sorry if I'm sweaty."

Alex looked up from his hospital bed, "You're here just in time. It's starting in five minutes."

"Great. I wanted to be with you to see this."

"I thought you received an invitation to be there in person? I did, but obviously I can't go like this, not yet."

"Yes, I did too," confirmed Cate. "But I wasn't going without you, no way. How's the rehab?"

"Painful. My shoulder is beginning to get back some movement. They replaced my glenohumeral joint and they say it'll last longer than I will. The good news is the surgeons were finally able to remove the remaining bullet fragments from my spleen and my spine, and now I'll be allowed to get up and start walking again. Apparently, after ten days of physiotherapy they'll let me out of here. I can't wait. It's been four hospitals in as many weeks."

"That's because you're special. Nothing but the best for you."

"Tell that to whoever makes the hospital meals."

"Not as good as my pizza and Starbucks?" laughed Cate.

"Not quite," agreed Alex. "What have you been doing to keep yourself busy in London? I haven't seen you for a week."

"Research. I figured with all the resources here-"

Alex cut her off, "Sorry, Cate, it's beginning." He painfully raised his arm, pointing to the TV set on the wall, and turned the volume up with the control by his hospital bed.

The picture on the screen showed Buckingham Palace and the hundreds of thousands of people surrounding the Victoria Memorial and spilling down the Mall. The excitement could be heard in the normally restrained voice of the BBC announcer, "…it seems as though all of London and the most of the population of the adjacent counties are present today to see history made. Early estimates have put the crowd gathered here as the largest since VE day in 1945."

The TV cameras panned across the unending sea of faces stretching far into the distance.

The announcer continued, "In just a moment we are expecting the Royal Family to appear on the balcony of the Palace to greet the crowd. And with them will be not only the Prime Minister and the Chancellor of the Exchequer, but also the President of the United States and the American Secretary of State, along with the President of the Republic of Ireland. This is all to celebrate an event which will bring these three great nations closer together than they have ever been. The rea.." The announcer paused as the first of the Royal Family appeared, "And here they come now, making their way onto the balcony, and you can hear from the cheers how excited everyone is. With the Royals in place, the elected officials are joining them, and if we could have a shot of the crowd, you'll notice it's become a sea of flags as Union Jacks, Stars and Stripes and the Irish tricolor are all being waved frantically."

The announcer stopped speaking to allow the spectacle of the flags' colors to dominate the screen, "And here he comes, the reason for all of this celebration. The person whose bloodline joins together the Royal houses of Saxe-Coburg and Gotha directly with the Windsors, and for the first time, links that heritage to both the Republic of Ireland and the United States of America, making him truly an international Royal who knows no boundaries. Edward Albert York, who has now been graced with two titles created specifically for him, the Duke of Wessex and Prince Regent of the Commonwealth. And as the world knows, a third title awaits him at some point in the future, and that is King Edward the Ninth."

"It's so good to see Eddie up there, with the crowd cheering for him, but I'm going to have to turn this off. I still don't have my strength back and I get tired very easily," apologized Alex.

"I understand," sympathized Cate. She hesitated before continuing, "I want to leave this for you to read when you wake up and feel more focused." She pulled out a thick file and placed it on the table by Alex's bed.

"What is it?"

"Ummm…" She looked down, hoping he wouldn't be angry, "It's something I thought should be done. I know why you were in Prague. You were searching for your own family line, like many adopted people do later in life, and I know your research was interrupted by what happened that awful night, and you never went back to it, so I decided to finish it for you."

This was totally unexpected, and Alex looked at her with surprise, and thought before he spoke, "Did you have any success?"

"You could call it that. I was able to trace your entire lineage and," she hesitated, "while I was doing it, I came across something else…" her voice trailed off.

"What? What else?"

Cate got to her feet and bent over, giving Alex a brief kiss on the forehead. "I'll go now and leave you to sleep. You don't want to read this while you're tired. Call me when you finish it. You have my new cell number. We're going to need to talk about what I found, because as soon as you're back on your feet I think we have some more adventures ahead of us." She headed for the door.

Alex called after her, "Adventures? What do you mean? What kind of adventures?"

She shot a glance back at him over her shoulder, "Sleep well. And don't worry about your passport; I'm holding on to it, because after everything I discovered, you're definitely going to need it again very soon."

THE END

ABOUT THE AUTHOR

Richard Blade is the best-selling author of *World In My Eyes*, his autobiography, published November, 2017 and *SPQR*, published December, 2019. He is one of the most popular and best-known DJs in America, and hosts a daily radio show on both SiriusXM 1st Wave Ch. 33 and on KCBS.

Richard was born in England, educated at Oxford, and came to the United States in 1976. In the 1980s he was the top-rated morning drive DJ on KROQ, Los Angeles, and hosted and directed numerous TV shows and series including *Video One*, *MV3* and *VideoBeat*.

He has won numerous awards including the Golden Microphone, California's Best DJ, and the American DJ Association's Lifetime Achievement Award. Richard has also appeared in many Network TV series and starred or co-starred in a number of feature films including *Girls Just Want To Have Fun*, *Spellcaster,* and *Long Lost Son*, which he also wrote.

Richard lives in L.A. with his wife, Krista, and their two dogs, and travels extensively as he continues to DJ live, and is in high demand as a speaker and host at events around the world.

www.ingramcontent.com/pod-product-compliance
Lightning Source LLC
Chambersburg PA
CBHW061436150726
47987CB00001B/237